History Makers

...in their own words

To John,

DAVID K. WEINER

With Best Wishes,
David K. Wei___

PublishAmerica
Baltimore

First printing

ISBN: 1-4137-7137-8 (softcover)
ISBN: 978-1-4489-0350-4 (hardcover)
PUBLISHED BY PUBLISHAMERICA, LLLP
www.publishamerica.com
Baltimore

Printed in the United States of America

DEDICATION

To the many writers of history who have come before me and have brought to the world the astonishing legacy that is our past, this book is respectfully dedicated.

ACKNOWLEDGMENT

Every writer of history is indebted to some of the writers who proceeded him, and I am no exception. To the authors and publishers listed in the Appendices of this book, I acknowledge your help in providing my characters with a life of exploits and adventure.

I value highly the editing done by Janet Sadler, and the illustrative work of Yvonne (Winnie) Godek. I also appreciate the friendship, challenges, inspiration, encouragement and support of Sylvia Rosen and her Creative Writing class members who meet at the nearby Jewish Community Center. And to the Masonic Grand Lodge of Massachusetts, I offer my thanks for providing me with the text of the speech that Paul Revere made when he concluded his service as their Grand Master.

And, of course, I thank my wife, June, for her ability to survive while I spent untold happy hours in my study fleshing out the many characters that populate this book.

CONTENTS

INTRODUCTION

History, like moonshine, means different things to different people. History to the student is usually a jumble of dates tied to certain events that may or may not be interesting to the young reader. History to the adult is usually a compilation of events that interests the reader in direct proportion to his or her recall of the events or curiosity regarding the subject matter.

It is a well-known fact that to truly inspire interest in a significant event occurring in the past, the writer of the history has to directly involve the reader in the event. *History Makers...in their own words* was written with the intention of bringing the reader face to face with the characters highlighted in the story. The first person approach used by the author of these fictional autobiographies engages the reader in ways that other accounts of factual history do not. It allows the reader to stand with each historical figure written about as the character encounters the events, enjoyable or perilous, known to have occurred and described by many other biographical or historical writers.

Whether the newly-employed cooper, John Alden, is fearfully watching the water gushing down from the ruptured deck of the *Mayflower* into the passenger hold, putting the damaged ship in danger of flooding when only half way to America; or the character, Philip, is encountering a full lunar eclipse in the company of his bewildered and frightened Indian friends; or the rebel, Paul Revere, is evading the Redcoat sentries as he sneaks back from Cambridge to his home in Boston to visit his loving wife, the reader is witnessing actions that really happened as if being a party to them. These first person accounts, so seldom used in other historical writing, are a means to involve the reader at a level that fosters interest in the events and provides personal memories of the fateful actions taken in times past.

The readers of this book are asked to share the adventures of the three heroes written about as they brave the fortunes, good and bad, that destiny has laid in their path—events characterized in most other books as simply history.

JOHN ALDEN

Mayflower Man

THE PILGRIM STORY

Shunned believers, steeped in faith,
Left their home and ways,
Searching for a freer place
Where they could spend their days.

Gathering in Southampton,
They waited for a ship
To carry them to parts unknown,
A fearful, risky trip.

Plymouth was their starting point.
Landed there, because,
Problems with a sister ship,
Had forced a nine-day pause.

Soaking rain and tow'ring waves
Faced throughout the trip,
Made the ride uncomfortable
For all aboard the ship.

Mayflower was a sturdy craft.
Run by able crew.
Carried safe her manifest
Of souls, five score and two.

Land first seen was old Cape Cod.
Dropped anchor in the Bay.
Spent many weeks exploring sites,
Deciding where to stay.

Finally found a special place,
Good for settling down.
Living seemed quite tol'rable.
They called it Plymouth town.

Many died before their time,
Due to colds and flu.
Indians became their friends;
They helped to pull them through.

Pilgrims all, they kept the faith,
Building home and farm.
Putting God above all else,
He kept them from great harm.

Words cannot describe their feat,
Each of us now sharing
Freedom, and a nation strong,
All based upon their daring.

—David K. Weiner—

JOHN ALDEN

MAYFLOWER MAN

Prologue

O n Wednesday, September 6, 1620, the crowded vessel *Mayflower*
departed England a third time for its voyage to America. The first
time, about a month earlier, with 90 passengers, it had sailed from
Southampton with a smaller sister ship *Speedwell* hard astern. Five days after
the two ships left that port, *Mayflower* received flag signals from *Speedwell*
stating that she was leaking and wished to put into Dartmouth, the nearest
port. *Mayflower* accompanied the leaking ship in, for the leaders were
determined to travel together to their destination, a parcel of land across the
Atlantic Ocean in the patent[1] of Virginia called Hudson's River. The two
vessels dropped anchor in Dartmouth Harbor and waited for repairs to be
made on the troubled ship. On August 23rd, they both weighed anchor and set
sail a second time for Virginia. Three days later, about 100 leagues[2] from
Land's End, *Mayflower* again received frantic signals from *Speedwell* that
she was leaking dangerously. After hours of communication using signal
flags, the anxious masters of both ships concluded that they should return
together once more to the English mainland. This time, they anchored at
Plymouth.

The next day, August 28th, at a contentious meeting, the masters agreed
that *Speedwell* could not survive a stormy voyage in her present state of

repair. They decided to send the stricken ship back to London, together with the 18 passengers who had changed their minds about making the trip. *Mayflower*'s master, Christopher Jones, was questioned about the remaining passengers. After consultation with the shipboard Elders who were financing the voyage, he agreed to include the 15 *Speedwell* passengers who wished to continue on to America, to his own ship's complement. Over the next three days the additional passengers, their belongings, and other supplies from *Speedwell* were hurriedly transferred to the larger ship. Master Jones knew that each day lost meant additional stormy weather to be faced, and more peril to his ship. Finally, the overcrowded *Mayflower*, rated at 160 tons burden and now carrying 102 passengers and a crew of 34, left Plymouth by itself, heading for New England, some 2700 nautical miles from old England.

CHAPTER ONE

My name is John Alden. I was born twenty-two years ago in the small town of Harwich, in county Essex, some 20 leagues northeast of London, on the Strait of Dover. My father, John, is a gentleman farmer there. When I was thirteen, believing that I should learn a trade, he sent me to Southampton to serve as an apprentice to James Barker, an accomplished cooper with whom he had done some business. Mr. Barker provided me with a room and proper victuals as well as great knowledge about barrel-making and other mechanics. Both he and his wife taught me about the arts as well as worldly affairs.

One sunny day in August, I traveled by wagon down Saint Mary's Street, past the crumbling old ramparts of the once-walled town to the center of Southampton. There I was to pick up some iron rings for my employer. About noon, with the supplies lashed securely to my wagon, I sought out a place to eat before returning home. I had visited The Crowing Cock before, and since the pub was on my way I stopped for some stew and a glass of ale. As I was preparing to leave the crowded establishment after I had finished eating, I heard a familiar voice calling to me over the conversations of the boisterous customers.

"Hail and good day, bonnie John, 'tis a pleasure meeting you here!"

It was a distant relative, Christopher Jones, master of the *Mayflower*, a merchant ship that was berthed in the port of Harwich near where I lived. Master Jones was a heavy man, with a tanned, deeply creased face that barely showed beneath his full white beard. He always reminded me of Saint Nick, the friendly saint my mother told me stories about during the Christmas season. The old seaman had visited us on a number of occasions at our home, between his sailings to northern and Mediterranean ports.

"What brings you to Southampton at this time of day?" he asked when he was next to me.

I told him the reason for my trip and added a few words about the good health of my parents. Master Jones sat, then called loudly for another pint of ale. I sat across from him, and we spoke of common experiences for a few minutes. He then asked me if I had ever thought of the benefits of traveling to faraway lands.

"I have dreamt about it often," I said. "I even saw on my trip here today many postings on the trees along the way, seeking passengers for ships preparing to sail to places across the sea. Methinks I would truly enjoy such an adventure."

"I am sailing soon to northern Virginia, my lad," he replied. "I will be carrying passengers for the first time. Would you care to join me on such a voyage?"

I was surprised at his suggestion, but not unpleased. I told him of my isolation at the Barker farm, and my increasing desire to travel.

"Why don't you come with me to my ship to see Master Bradford?" he asked. "He is the Elder in charge of all aspects of our voyage. He can tell you about the journey on which we are about to embark."

"I would like to talk to him very much, sir, although I fail to see why he would want me to join his party." Master Jones coaxed me a bit more and I finally agreed to accompany him to the harbor. When we arrived I saw that Master Bradford was busy making arrangements for the voyage. After my relative explained my interest in seeking passage with his party, the Elder approached me directly.

William Bradford had a commanding presence, much more so than either my employer or Master Jones. He was nearly as tall as I and had steely eyes and a deep voice, but his demeanor was gentle and respectful.

"It was good of you to come, young man," he said. "And what makes you think that you can be of benefit to our company?"

I told him of my training as a cooper and a mechanic and my wish to travel. I assured him that the hardships and perils of the journey would not diminish my fervor for a chance to visit foreign lands. I affirmed that I had completed my apprenticeship and that my parents would certainly approve of my decision.

"I know the boy," my uncle added, "and I will gladly keep my eye on him."

Master Bradford looked directly at me with his piercing eyes. I felt the color drain from my face.

"There is one thing I must know before we talk more," he said with great solemnity. "What is your religious persuasion, my boy?"

"I am a believer in Christ, sir, but beyond that I can speak no further."

The Elder continued. "Our company consists of many who are very firm in their religious conviction, son. I, too, adhere to their Separatist views. Do you know how you shall tolerate, throughout the long voyage, the strict faith that so many of the passengers possess?"

Without hesitation I replied that my soul would no doubt find such dedication to the teachings of Christ to be helpful in my ongoing search for divine truth. When I had finished speaking, I saw the muscles in Elder Bradford's face relax. The slight trace of a smile appeared.

"We shall gladly employ you as ship's cooper, then, if you desire," he said with renewed vigor. "The law of the land requires that we carry such a craftsman; one who can assure the integrity of our barrels and casks. The food, drink, ammunition, and other goods that they hold must remain tightly sealed against leakage throughout the voyage. It would be your duty to provide this inspection and repair service."

I breathed a sigh of relief and glanced at my uncle. Behind his heavy beard, I could see a grin.

"We shall pay you seamen's wages and transport you as part of the crew," Elder Bradford continued. "When we arrive at our destination you may stay there, or return to England. Is such an arrangement satisfactory, Mr. Alden?"

I looked directly into the Elder's eyes and without hesitation I answered, "Very much, sir."

"We plan to set sail in five days." he said. "If you can arrange your affairs and be back by then, ready to embark, we shall add you to our complement."

His face turned reflective. "Hmmm. A hopeful young man such as you can certainly benefit our company. Indeed, you remind me of my own son, John, who is back in Holland. He is a bit older than you, but he shares your high spirit."

I thanked Master Bradford for his consideration and returned in good disposition with Master Jones to my wagon. With a look of satisfaction on his bronzed face, my uncle shook my hand and expressed his pleasure with my decision. He bade me good fortune and headed back to his ship. I rode to the Barker farm at great speed for I had many things to do.

When I told my employer of the commitment I had just made to join my relative on the voyage, Mr. Barker gave me his blessing. He also presented me with a newly printed Bible.

"This book, which I give to thee with pleasure," he said solemnly, "was presented to me a fortnight ago by my brother, Robert. He is a printer in London, and, in that capacity, faithfully serves our King. See, there is his name and the date it was printed. It is but small repayment for the many kindnesses that you have so liberally bestowed on my family. May it serve to lift your spirits on your long voyage to America, Master Alden. I, and my family, sincerely wish you Godspeed."

It surprised me greatly when the usually frugal Mr. Barker also offered to pay for my coach rides to and from my home in Harwich. His good wife, meanwhile, made no effort to hold back her tears. By the time of my departure, however, she had apologized for her show of weakness. She graciously presented me with a small basket of fruits and sweets as I boarded the coach that was to take me to my parents' farm.

My trip home was uneventful and boring. I was alone on the bumpy ride. The driver, sitting outside on a seat above me, kept yelling at the horses and whipping them unmercifully. As I neared my parents' house I began to feel some trepidation about the venture that I was about to undertake. By the time I arrived though I was thinking more about the taste of my mother's cooking than about the perils of the journey.

My visit, as usual, was pleasant and rewarding. I shall always remember the firm handshake and encouraging words from my father when I took my leave. Nor will I ever forget how my mother, with watering eyes, admonished me to remember the many good things she had taught me. I pulled from her embrace with great reluctance. As I re-entered the coach that was to bring me back to the coast I acknowledged the fact to myself that it could possibly be the last time I would see my parents. My trip back to the docks was consumed with trying to put that unsettling idea out of my mind.

CHAPTER TWO

The bustle on the docks at Southampton gave me little time to concern myself with thoughts of kinship. I brought my trunk and loose belongings to the crew's quarters on the *Mayflower* amid the commotion and foul language of the deck hands, who were busy loading provisions onto the ship. After settling in, I went aft to the 'tween deck where most of the passengers were housed. I was surprised at its congestion and small size. Grownups and children were busy positioning their food and belongings in the many compartments. Makeshift bunks were crowded together, separated by hanging canvas hung from wooden beams. The room had only a five-foot ceiling, which prevented me from standing erect. I was told earlier by a fellow crewman that the space had been a gun deck when *Mayflower* was sailing as a merchant ship. I saw a few cannon, still in position, pointing out to sea through open ports. *Precious little protection now from pirate ships*, I thought.

By word of mouth I learned that there were restrictions on any fires started by passengers, and that I was to go to the galley in the forecastle to get my meals. Many passengers invited me to attend church services. These were led by Elder Brewster on the main deck when weather permitted. They were held at six bells each day, and twice on Sunday.

The day after my arrival, under pleasant skies, but with strong winds, we hoisted anchor, unfurled a first sail, and put to sea. The swashing of the ocean was, for a short time, drowned out by the sounds of the many prayers being offered up throughout the ship. Most of the passengers and some of the crew knelt with hands clasped and eyes to God beseeching Him for His protection throughout the trip.

Our first departure, as well as the next, was aborted due to the desire of the Elders to travel together with the ill-fated *Speedwell*. Our third attempt, this time without the unseaworthy *Speedwell*, but with some of her passengers, met with success.

Throughout our first two days, with sails full despite a steady gale, we made good progress. More than half of the passengers suffered seasickness. Many, with churning innards, hung over the rail of the upper deck, happy to offer food to the fish. Others, below, filled buckets with their last meal. The rest of the company attended to assigned duties with little apparent distress. In the early afternoon of the next day, Friday, deckside passengers shouted that the last view of England could be seen. This created a rush topside. When I arrived on deck with the others, I saw the hills of the Scilly Isles sink into the horizon. With the final disappearance of land, some passengers showed relief, others showed sadness, but I am sure we all felt the inner fear of uncertainty. And more than the usual number of passengers attended that afternoon's prayer service. When the devotions ended and the final "Amen" was spoken, I saw the ship's master moving slowly through the dispersing crowd toward me.

"Would you care to join me in my cabin, lad?" he asked when he arrived at my side.

"It would be my pleasure, sir," I replied, and I followed him aft to the officer's quarters in the Great Cabin, which was positioned high on the sterncastle. When we were inside the large room, I looked about. I was surprised to find that we were alone. There were many built-in bunks along the sides. Sleeping rugs covered much of the floor. The large side windows were composed of many diamond-shaped panes of glass. Through them shafts of sunlight brightened the room.

"How are you faring so far?" the master enquired when he saw me stop surveying the surroundings.

"It is much like I thought it would be," I said. "The ship seems a bit overcrowded, but she appears to be sturdily built."

"We, indeed, are carrying more than I originally contracted for. We picked up passengers from *Speedwell* in Plymouth, you know. But *Mayflower* is a strong ship and she should cause us no displeasure. I gave up my own quarters so some women and children could be more properly housed. I bunk with my officers. Would you have an interest in who the passengers we are carrying might be?"

"Certainly, sir," I answered. "I've been really curious, but was, well, afraid to ask."

"Our present passenger complement is 102," Master Jones explained, "made up of 49 men, 22 boys, 20 women, and 11 girls. Of these, 15 are Separatists from Leyden, Holland, who came to us at Plymouth from *Speedwell*. The rest of the company, those who boarded from England, is made up both of Separatists, and some who do not share their religious views."

With thinly repressed scorn and a dismissive wave of his hand, he continued.

"These godless people, some call them strangers, were recruited by Weston & Company, the venturists who financed our voyage. The backers felt that not enough Separatists had volunteered to form a viable colony, and others were necessary to make the venture profitable."

The old master's face relaxed and his voice became more congenial.

"You, of course, were one of the last to sign on," he said. "Your hiring as a cooper for the ship places you in the category of crew." I nodded agreement, and asked a question that had been bothering me.

"What prompted the Separatists to leave both Holland... and England?"

"That, my boy, you shall have to find out from one of their leaders," he answered. "Perhaps you could enquire of Elder Bradford or Elder Brewster. Both of them were instrumental in organizing the Separatists, and encouraging them to take this voyage."

As I pondered the old seaman's suggestion, he asked, "Now, young Alden, would you care to join me for dinner?"

"I would consider it an honor, sir," I said quickly, looking forward to more of a variety of foods than the ship's biscuit, pickled beef and pork, and peas, that, aboard ship, I had so far been privy to. Master Jones summoned a sailor and told him to bring food for the two of us. When the young seaman left, my uncle asked if I would like to share some spirits. I gladly nodded agreement. My relative went to the rear of the room and brought back a silver flask of wine, a carryover, no doubt, from his many years as master of the *Mayflower* when she transported wines from France. While we waited for our meal from the galley, we made many toasts and he told me about the events that had brought him to his present position.

He was brought up in Harwich, as I was. His father, also named Christopher, was a ship owner and mariner. The poor soul died when his son was eight years old. He left the boy an interest in his ship, *Marie Fortune*, to be turned over when young Christopher attained the age of eighteen. When he did come of age, my uncle sold his interest. Much later, he became master of the ship, *Josian*, named after his second wife, the widow of a man named Richard Grey. Soon after, he joined three other men—Christopher Nichols, Richard Child, and Thomas—and together they purchased the *Mayflower*. He became master and commanded her for twelve years, transporting tar, lumber, and fish while traveling to Baltic ports, primarily Norway, and then wine and spices from Mediterranean ports, chiefly in France.

In early 1620, Thomas Weston, John Carver, and Robert Cushman, representatives of the Separatists, had approached the owners of the *Mayflower*. The three agents arranged for the hire of the ship and its crew. They planned to use the *Mayflower* to transport a group of settlers to Northern Virginia, where they proposed to plant a colony.

The plan was to leave England during April or May. The spring departure would allow the settlers ample time to plant a crop for autumn harvest in New England. As a result of the delays in converting *Mayflower* from a trading vessel to a passenger ship, which required cabins, bunks, hammocks, and other necessaries, and the additional waiting attributed to the troubled ship *Speedwell*, final departure was not possible until September. Master Jones acknowledged that such a late sailing would certainly involve greater exposure to severe weather, but he extended every effort to ready his ship. He related to me how Weston & Company, known as the London Adventurers, were the financiers, and how they had grudgingly advanced only part of the money that they had promised. They did nothing to assist in the fitting out of the ship. They did, however, greatly interfere with preparations, he told me.

Before he could continue his story, we heard a sharp knock on the door. It was the seaman bringing the evening meal that my uncle had ordered. After clearing a small table of charts and navigating instruments, the two of us sat and enjoyed the food that had been brought. To my great delight there was warm bread from the oven, cheese, salted pork, and boiled beans. For drink we had cider. The meal was completed with a serving of raisins and a slice of lemon from the master's private stores. He apologized for the lack of butter, but explained that several thousand pounds of it had to be traded to get clear of the ship chandlers at Plymouth to whom money was owed, mostly for repairs on *Speedwell*. He commented that by overcharging for most goods, the greedy merchants were rightly called "land sharks."

After sharing the delightful meal, my uncle excused himself "to attend to ship's matters." I, full and contented, headed for the hold to once again perform my own duties with the barrels and kegs. It was dark outside as I walked along the upper deck, but the moon and candles in the hanging lanterns provided plenty of light for me to see my way to the bulkhead leading to the decks below. The pleasant murmur from the few people that I passed mixed with the gentle slapping of the waves against the hull were comforting, and they assured me that my decision to travel to America was one I would never regret.

CHAPTER THREE

For the next week and a half we were blessed with warm weather and favorable winds. The occasional light gales were not severe enough to cause us to reduce our "full sail" condition. Along with many others I spent a good deal of time on the upper deck inhaling the fresh salt air and letting the cool spray freshen my face. During the day children played there, attempting to climb the rigging when their mothers weren't looking. Many of the youngsters pleaded with the crew to be brought to the rudder room to see the mechanism that steered the ship.

In the evening harvest moons brought solace to me and, I am sure, comfort to those sharing the deck with me. Some nights before a storm, however, were not so idyllic. Strange lights often appeared among the sails. They were a ghostly blue-white, and appeared to dance around wherever sharp points existed in the rigging. I asked a sailor what caused the eerie spectacle, and he told me it was called Saint Elmo's Fire. He said it was always a good luck sign to all at sea. Many of the passengers on deck, though, didn't look upon the flashes as desirable. They were sure that the lights were omens of disaster. Some panicky souls knelt to pray when they appeared.

Meanwhile, the conditions below were getting increasingly unpleasant. The foul odors, although somewhat ameliorated by the sweet smell of the wines that saturated the deck planks when the *Mayflower* had been a merchant ship, were sickening. To make matters worse, the canvas sheets covering the gratings on the main deck were not completely water tight, and seawater often found its way down onto the lower deck, wetting clothes and bedding. With the weather, however, we were well favored. The usually severe autumn storms were delayed so that we were able to press on for weeks at acceptable speeds. Our good fortune, though, did not last.

On September 23rd, a seaman who had been ill for many days died in his bunk in the forecastle cabin where the crew slept. He was buried at sea, with proper ceremony. As if his death were indeed an omen, the next day saw a sharp change in the weather. Westerly gales of great intensity began to buffet the ship unmercifully. To protect our masts, all sails were furled. This allowed our ship to be thrown about like a piece of driftwood. The pitching and bobbing were frightening. Our master attempted, with only minor success, to hold her port side to the weather to minimize the dangers to the ship. Most everybody was seasick, yet nobody dared to climb to the upper deck for fear of being washed overboard. Moaning, crying and praying could be heard constantly. To add to their discomfort, one foulmouthed sailor taunted the passengers persistently and in the most obnoxious terms threatened to rob them and to throw overboard anyone who got in his way. There seemed no way to lessen his obscenities and threats of violence. Even the master appeared to be powerless.

During the fourth night of severe weather, I was in my bunk trying desperately to sleep, when I heard screams of terror from amidships. Since I, like all others, wore the same clothes both day and night, it took me no time to arrive at the scene of the commotion. There in the 'tween deck, men were trying to comfort women as water poured down around them from the deck above. I looked up to where the water was entering and saw a cracked and bent ceiling beam. This allowed the upper deck to sag, creating both a separation between deck planks and a "vee" channel for water to arrive at the opening. I looked anxiously for the master and saw him in an animated discussion with the ship's mates, some Elders and a number of sailors. I hurried over to the cabin wall to join the group. They were arguing about the severity of the situation and whether we should return to England or continue on into the storm. The sailors wanted to go on because they would get no wages if they returned to home port. Others argued that by turning back we would be favored by lighter winds and this would mean less stress on the framework of the ship. I interrupted the disagreement and suggested that we should attempt to repair the damaged timber right away, for if we didn't, both options would bring us to disaster. This thought seemed to quiet the arguing parties, and reason prevailed.

John Parker, one of the mates, was first to speak. There was noticeable urgency in his voice.

"What we gotta have is a strong timber to wedge up against the broken beam to return it to its old position. That would force the deck back into place."

Another mate spoke with equal anxiety.

"We could cut our spare mast down to size," he said. "But that would leave us with no replacement if one of our standing masts should bust in a storm. We sure as bloody hell don't want to be forced to sail mid-ocean without our main sheets."

"There may be a means to save us," Elder Brewster said calmly. "When we left Leyden, we took along a large iron screw. For what purpose, I do not know. It just seemed to be too important an item to leave behind. It's down in the hold with our supplies."

"I'll go get it," declared the carpenter, and he took two seamen below to retrieve the piece. When they returned with the long screw, the three men placed it upright, wedging it between the broken beam above us and the deck on which we were standing. With great energy they pushed on the bottom portion of the screw sliding it along the deck and bringing it to a more upright position. This action forced the top end of the shaft to lift the beam, along with the distorted decking, back toward their original positions. As the opening in the upper deck closed, the stream of water slowly lessened until only a slow drip was remaining. The sobbing and moaning stopped along with the water, and the relieved passengers let go of each other and applauded loudly. All of the small openings were then caulked and the repair was considered complete. The distraught passengers who had temporarily traded their seasickness for terror returned to their pails.

"We might have to hold back somewhat on our sails," said the master later, "but it looks like we can continue on to our destination in safety with the beam braced up as it is. That is what we shall do—if the weather ever eases enough for us to put up some sail."

CHAPTER FOUR

A s I prepared to go back to the crew's quarters, I felt a tap on the shoulder. I turned and saw a well dressed man of about fifty, with gray hair and a neatly trimmed, pointed beard, looking up at me. The lines on his face and his sad eyes attested to much adversity. I had seen him many times preaching to the congregation. He introduced himself as William Brewster, an Elder of the Leyden Church.

"I would like to thank you for your suggestion that we find a solution to our dilemma rather than continuing the dispute about our course," he said, looking directly at me. "It brought us back to consider ways to correct our problem, rather than spend time discussing which direction we should take. You are a perceptive young man, and it is our good fortune to have you on board. If there is any way we can show our appreciation, please let me know."

"There is one thing, sir, that would amply repay me for what I consider an insignificant contribution," I said.

"And what would that be?" he answered. "Something within my power, I pray."

I asked him if he could explain to me why his band of Separatists has undertaken such a dangerous voyage. He hesitated for a moment, then asked me to accompany him to the chartroom where it was quieter and where, he said, he would be happy to answer my question. I followed him aft as he requested, frequently bracing myself on the crossbeams to counter the violent rocking of the ship. I was eager to hear his story.

As we sat facing each other over a small table in the empty room, he enquired whether I was familiar with the Parliamentary Act of 1593. I shook my head. He told me that infamous law required all persons over sixteen who refused to attend services at the established Church without good cause, be committed to prison. He further stated that belonging to the Church of England meant conforming to a doctrine with which many people disagreed. Not the Christian ideals part of it, he assured me, for his people were in agreement with them, but how the Church was organized, and how the congregation had to worship.

"We Separatists want no bishops or deans, no sacraments, except Baptism and Holy Communion, no set prayer book, no ritual, altars, candles, organs, or incense," he said, shaking his finger as he spoke.

"I, at an early age, became one of the dissenters," he continued. "I began to attend private meetings with a group of like-minded people at a manor house near Scrooby. This, of course, was a dangerous thing to do, as the authorities regarded such behavior as treason. By 1607, the situation was intolerable. We were hounded and sought out, and many of us were sent to prison for our anti-establishment views. After much discussion among our congregation, we voted to emigrate to Holland, where we knew that there would be no trouble from the authorities, and where work, although menial, was available."

The Elder paused to be sure that I was comprehending what he was saying. He then continued.

"After a year's stay in Amsterdam—where immorality proved to be rife—we moved to Leyden, about twenty miles to the south. Leyden is a fair town made famous by its university. At that institution Elder Bradford and I were even allowed to take part in debates about theology. The people accepted us and work was readily obtainable. We resided peaceably there for ten years.

"Why did you leave, sir," I asked. "if it was such a satisfactory place?"

"It was indeed a splendid location, but there was no future for us," he said. "We were getting older and newcomers had little incentive to join us. Our children were becoming little Dutchmen, growing up among corrupting influences, without the means to obtain a satisfactory education. And the opportunity to advance the Gospel, which is our great duty and desire, was passing us by."

He paused for a short time and appeared to be reflecting on the past, then went on.

"In the summer of 1617, after great discussion among our congregation, it was decided that we should leave Holland. But where to go was the question we asked ourselves—we couldn't return to England, for persecution still awaited us there. We considered Spanish America, but the Spaniards have a reputation for being as savage as the Indians of North America. We finally decided we should go to Virginia, where some English colonies had already been established."

He hesitated again and then continued, speaking in a lower tone.

"To accomplish our mission, John Carver and Robert Cushman were sent secretly to England with an application to open negotiations with the London Virginia Company, a group that was granting large tracts of land to Englishmen who would emigrate at their own expense. Their directors, however, were not pleased to associate with us, as you might expect. They insisted that we have approval of our application from the King. I contacted an old friend, Sir Edwin Sandys, and asked him to intervene on our behalf. Sir Edwin was head of the Council for Virginia, a knighted Member of Parliament, son of the one-time Bishop of York, and he had the ear of the King. I knew him through the old Scrooby House where our secret meetings were first held in 1602. The good gentleman recommended acceptance of our application to the Kings Council, and they indicated that they would indeed approve it."

Elder Brewster seemed to brighten as he spoke of Sir Edwin and I felt my own spirits rise as I pictured the two old friends working together with a common goal. I was anxious to hear more of the story and I told the Elder so. He smiled and continued.

"The King appeared to be satisfied with our proposal, but he had second thoughts and referred it to the Archbishop of Canterbury for review. The Church immediately rejected it. Sir Edwin again used his powerful influence on our behalf. The matter was passed on to the Privy Council, and they created a confusion that lasted for months. The King finally became tired of the constant petitioning and he announced that he would not stand in our way. He refused, however, to put his seal on his ruling. We took his vague consent to be sufficient for our purpose, and we immediately made plans for a hasty pilgrimage to Virginia."

"Is that when you hired the *Mayflower?*" I interrupted.

"No," he replied. "There was much more to be done before we could make the trip." He continued speaking with a renewed enthusiasm.

"Robert Cushman and I then traveled to England to reopen negotiations with the London Virginia Company in order to obtain the patent that would allow us to make the venture. On the ninth of June past, after many delays, we were granted a patent. It was secured in the name of Mr. John Wincob, a gentleman who, at the time, intended to go with us. He was a member of the household of the Countess of Lincoln, and seemed a good candidate to make the application for us since he was known for conformity, unlike ourselves. Alas, he never did join us." As my companion silently contemplated the reason that Wincob did not join the others, I looked around. The bright rays of the sun were gone and the room was darkening. *Oh great. Evening or another storm is coming*, I thought. I considered ending our conversation, but my curiosity was too great.

"Where did you get the finances for the trip," I asked, "since the Virginia Company said that they would not assist you in that regard?"

"I told you that you were perceptive, son, and the question you ask is an insightful one. When our intentions became public knowledge, the New Netherlands Company approached us in Leyden. They asked us to settle in New Amsterdam, where one of their trading stations had already been established. They said that they wanted to expand their presence in that area and were prepared to finance our voyage. Mr. Bradford, whom you've met, deemed the offer a good one, but a Mr. Thomas Weston, an ironmonger from London, intervened. He warned us against becoming too deeply involved with the Dutch. He proposed that he and some of his business associates be allowed to finance the venture. He assured us that there would be no shortage of money to charter ships and provision them. He suggested further that we draft Articles of Agreement that he could take back to England for approval by those who were to finance the enterprise. We considered his proposal and looked favorably on it."

I asked if the proposal was to be just a financial arrangement or one that set out codes of conduct. Elder Bradford said that it was to be primarily financial because that seemed to be all that Weston was concerned with. The Elder acknowledged my question with a slight smile and continued.

"We then prepared a fairly short agreement, delineating terms favorable to both parties. Mr. Weston returned to England with it, but when he arrived there he unilaterally altered some of the terms, to our great detriment. After weeks of feuding between Weston and our people, we agreed to the new terms. There were many delays in getting money from Weston & Company, but by summer we finally had enough to procure two ships for transport to Northern Virginia. One was to carry the Separatists from Leyden—those who wanted to leave—and the other, to transport those who boarded in England."

"And the first ship was *Speedwell*, which finally remained in England," I offered.

"That is correct," Elder Brewster stated, "and we are now being tossed about on ship number two, which I pray holds together until we reach our destination."

"As do I, sir," I said, but I refrained from continuing, for four people had come through the chartroom door and were making their way directly to us.

As they approached, I perceived them as a family. The father, about 40 years old, had dark hair and was clean-shaven. His shiny boots reflected the candlelight in the room. His countenance was troubled, and he appeared anxious to engage Elder Brewster in conversation. The mother, probably a few years younger, was thin and had an attractive face framed with long dark tresses under a bright white cap. She firmly held the hand of a young boy. The fourth member of the family was a daughter, whose degree of beauty I have rarely encountered. Like her mother, she had dark tresses under a white cap. She was well-dressed, and looked to be about eighteen. Her appearance and graceful movement captured first my notice, then my heart. Her bright brown eyes looked away as soon they met mine. I was transfixed. I felt agreeably favored by fortune, and I silently vowed that I would see more of her in the future. Her father was the first to speak.

"Elder Brewster, my name is William Mullins, and this is my wife, Alice. We come to you with our children, Priscilla and Joseph, as representatives of the many aboard this stout vessel who share our views. We are regularly harassed and imperiled by a seaman who threatens to throw overboard any of us with whom he comes into contact. His foul speech is such that we must keep our children and our own ears unfairly restricted. I implore you to provide us with some relief from this scoundrel, who is making this arduous journey evermore difficult."

"I, myself, have been offended by this creature," Elder Brewster replied. "I have pleaded with Master Jones to confine him, or at least restrict his movements, but to no avail. The master is firm in his conviction that he will not interfere with any passenger issue as long as we do not attempt to involve ourselves in shipboard matters. I wish that there was something I could do, but it seems that we shall have to endure the rogue until we reach land. Perhaps prayer is our best course for the present." The group, dejected one and all, turned and left us alone again in the chartroom. I thanked Elder Brewster for his story and his time and returned to my quarters aft. Visions of the lovely Priscilla continued to fill my mind, and I did little to discourage their manifestation.

CHAPTER FIVE

Fierce storms continued to assault the ship without mercy. Another week passed, and there was still no letup in the weather. The ship continued to pitch violently from side to side, bruising passengers and crew and causing tempers to flare. The passengers, wet and miserable, were torn between staying below decks in the foul atmosphere or risking the hazards of the open deck. In one heavy squall, John Howland, a manservant in the employ of John Carver, volunteered to go above to check if any fittings were working loose. He climbed up on the deck, but he was caught off-balance and was pitched into the sea. After he hit the water he seized a topsail halyard that was trailing overboard and held on to it even as he kept being dragged under. His screams were heard on deck, despite the loud sounds of the sea, and half a dozen men came to his aid, pulling on the hawser, then bringing him alongside with a boat hook. When the roll of the ship brought him within reach, their outstretched hands grabbed his hair and clothing, and they pulled him back on board. It was truly a show of heroism by a crew heedless of their own danger.

The violent weather persisted without relief, but not all was misery. One stormy night, Elizabeth, wife of Stephen Hopkins, a gentleman from London, gave birth to a son. The boy was healthy, and the parents named him Oceanus, no doubt because of where he was born. His frequent crying appeared to bother neither passengers nor sailors.

A common prayer was answered when the ugly-tempered seaman who was harassing the entire company was suddenly taken ill. His sickness was extremely painful and he suffered a long time, then died. His body was thrown overboard without ceremony. According to the Elders sailing with us,

God had intervened to put a stop to the persecution and to punish the persecutor.

Toward the end of October, over a month and a half into the voyage, the skies finally cleared. With winds favorable again, Master Jones felt that he could have most of the sails hoisted. The seasick passengers appeared to regain their composure, and everyone made a great effort to clean their things. Passengers washed their clothing and bedding and spread everything out on the deck to dry. The ship truly resembled a sailing bed-clothing store.

Sadly, on November 6th, William Butten, the young servant of Dr. Samuel Fuller, died unexpectedly. He, too, was buried at sea, but with proper ceremony. His death was the first among the passengers. That fact was remarkable, since, for long periods, the passengers had been confined below decks in a dangerous, foul atmosphere and had been thrown about so that they had little strength left with which to brace themselves. They also had been malnourished because of the lack of opportunity to cook their food and had often been too seasick to even look at the cold food that was offered to them. They appeared to be in a mood that approached the ultimate depths of melancholy. My disposition was not much different.

Later that evening, as I walked along the crowded upper deck for my daily constitutional, I saw the two Mullins children standing by the rail watching a blazing sun sink into the white-capped sea. I approached them with trepidation. As I got near, Miss Priscilla turned and saw me. Our eyes met for an instant, then she quickly looked down at the deck, a movement which I interpreted as meaningful. I felt obliged to speak.

"Good evening, Master Joseph and Miss Priscilla. It is quite a beautiful sunset, don't you agree?"

Young Joseph answered, "Indeed it is, sir."

His sister continued to look intently at the deck. I addressed her directly.

"Have you ever seen such beautiful color, Miss Priscilla?"

She slowly looked up at me. I saw sadness in her eyes. She spoke thoughtfully.

"There is no brighter color than that in England, sir. If I could be standing on the seashore even at Cornwall, I would be there this very minute." Her response surprised me.

"Is it the tedious journey that has brought on your melancholy?" I asked, "Or have you something back in England that you value more than the freedom that is hopefully in your future?"

"My heart is not there, nor is it here, sir. It remains in Holland with a gentleman named Jacques de la Noye whom I shall never see again."

Her look of sadness turned to a look of longing.

I asked, "Pray, tell me why you are not there beside him if he is indeed your true love?"

"My father would not give him leave to court me, sir, for he is not of our kind—he is a Huguenot."

"'Tis a pity, miss, that you are separated from your beloved," I said, "but I am sure you will find many a gentleman in Virginia who will be proud to call you wife. I, myself, find your beauty beyond compare, and your demeanor all I could, in my fancy, wish or desire. And I say this with all due respect for your present distress."

Despite the darkness of the evening, I saw a faint blush on her fair cheeks.

"I thank you for your interest, sir, but we must go below at once. Our parents are no doubt seeking us out at this very minute."

Turning to her brother, she said, "Come, Joseph, it is time for us to leave."

"But it isn't even dark yet," Joseph objected. "We've only been up here a short time."

"Do come, Joseph," Priscilla said sternly. "We must go below at once."

Taking Joseph by the hand, she turned and walked purposefully toward the forward companionway. As I watched them disappear into the crowd, I thought that there is, indeed, a good reason for me to stay in Virginia.

CHAPTER SIX

I awoke the next day, November 7th, and decided to take a stroll on the top deck before eating breakfast. The air was clear and extremely cold when I arrived there, forcing me to pull my jacket tightly around me. The sun was slowly pushing its way out of the ocean and the clouds reflected its color, turning the sky red, then pink. On the surface of the water I could see bunches of yellow seaweed float by. In the distance, flying fishes popped into view and porpoises arched their backs playfully on the waves. The water was still cobalt blue, not murky as it was for the first two weeks out from Plymouth. I stood in awe of the spectacle for a very long time, not bothered by the influx of others that joined me to see the dawn. I hoped for the appearance of the Mullins children, or should I say, Miss Priscilla, but I had no such good fortune. When the pangs for food finally increased to the point of pain, I headed for the galley in the forecastle. Before I arrived, however, I heard increasingly loud discourse among the passengers on deck with me. One of them announced that he had seen gulls in the distance, and word of his sighting was being passed through the crowd. I looked in vain for a sight of the birds, a sure sign of imminent landfall, but I saw no trace of any on the forward horizon. *The imaginings of someone bereft of patience*, I thought, and I resumed my quest for food. When I got below, many of the company were discussing the reported sighting. Prayers seemed to be emanating from all directions. *But I didn't see anything*, I wanted to shout. Then I realized that the sighting rumor was probably a blessing—a form of catharsis for a group penned up in an overcrowded ship for far too long. Soon the excited company quieted down and the rest of the day passed without incident. New hope was restored to the passengers the next morning when gulls were unmistakably detected by a number of early risers. There was little doubt then that landfall was near. Gaiety and prayers were prevalent throughout the ship. Children danced about and many of the bedridden were brought up from the lower deck to see the flying harbingers of land. I, myself, felt a sweeping sense of relief, knowing that fresh water, hot food, firm ground and personal safety soon would supplant our dismal shipboard existence.

We continued sailing westward at a good speed, for winds were favorable and the weather remained clear. There were more gull sightings and an occasional observation of debris in the water, but no triumphant call of "Land ho!" By noon the upper deck was packed with passengers and seamen, all wishing to be the first to see the coast. The afternoon passed but not a single person could lay claim to have spotted even the suggestion of land. As darkness arrived, most of the observers went back below deck. The determined few who did remain appeared to be hoping that some light from the shore would penetrate the ever-increasing darkness ahead. At midnight, with an even smaller contingent on deck still staring into the blackness, I went back to my quarters to seek the sleep that had been elusive for so many of the past nights. The next morning, November 10th, I was awakened at daybreak by the call that everyone onboard was waiting for. Above the usual din below deck, I heard many of the passengers shouting, "Land ho!" I rushed with many others to the upper deck to observe the landfall. In the far distance I could see the thin line resting on the horizon that was soon to be our home. Our crossing had taken over two months, somewhat longer than usual, but unlike lots of others, it had been a successful one. Throughout the voyage, I had witnessed much misery and suffering. We had lost three souls and gained one. I joined the other people who fell to their knees to thank Divine Providence for our deliverance. The next months, however, were to prove much more threatening, more hazardous than any one of us could imagine.

CHAPTER SEVEN

A s we neared land, Master Jones told me that we were approaching what he called Cape Cod. He said that he had a copy of a map prepared by Captain Gosnold, who on his ship *Expedition* had visited the area in 1602 looking for fishing grounds. He also said that the venturous master was so overwhelmed by the abundance of codfish at the site that he labeled the adjacent land with the fish's name. As we closed in on the Cape, Master Jones called for a meeting with the elders. I joined them in the Great Cabin. At the meeting the leaders made a determination to change direction and head south toward Hudson's River, our planned destination. This we did, but shortly after noon the wind died completely, and we began to drift helplessly toward shore. Without steerage, we headed for roaring breakers and dangerous shoals. These hazards, Master Jones said, were also encountered by Captain Gosnold, who labeled the breaking surf *Tucker's Terror* and the shoals *Point Care*. Master Jones feared harm would come to his ship from the treacherous waters he was heading for, so he took advantage of the first puff of wind and ordered the crew to tack around and head back to the open sea. Before nightfall we were out of the troubled waters. The master then decided on his own to return to Cape Cod instead of sailing south, and he had sails set for that location. As we moved away from the dangerous conditions, I felt the exultation of the passengers as they began to comprehend the salvation that had been afforded to them.

The next day, however, elation turned to dissent. Disputes arose between those who wanted to disembark immediately and those who wanted to wait a few days for weather to improve so that the ship could sail back toward Hudson's River. As arguments intensified, someone suggested to the group that they re-read the *Large Letter* given to them by Pastor John Robinson, the minister they had back in Leyden. Tempers abated when the letter was found. In it Pastor Robinson wrote that he foresaw the rebellion and advocated the establishment of a pact with which to govern the new settlement. He recommended that the settlers draw up an agreement of association to facilitate working together, along with laws of governance and the plans for the election of officers to ensure proper adherence to the laws. With this as incentive, and knowing that we were now sailing toward land where we had no charter rights or authority of any kind, the Elders determined that preparation of such a document should become the first item of business. William Brewster confirmed that Cape Cod was north of all territory then covered by patents, and it was necessary to establish some kind of written statement by which we could govern ourselves. The Elder believed, as did Pastor Robinson, that without an agreement, avarice and selfishness would reign.

In the fading light in the Great Cabin, an agreement, based on the common law in England but with parts reflecting the desires of the settlers, was quickly drawn up. Later, in the main cabin Elder Brewster read the conditions aloud to the anxious passengers. All eligible males, except two hired seamen and those too ill to participate, came forward to sign the document. I was one of the first ones to do so. Once the signing was complete, Master Carver, the appointed governor of the ship for the voyage, was elected as governor of the colony for the next year.

We continued sailing to the northeast and soon rounded the tip of Cape Cod, where we enjoyed the safety of the Cape harbor. Master Jones brought the ship as close to land as he could without risk, then dropped anchor. The shore lay about three-quarters of a mile away. From on deck I could see a variety of trees, various waterfowl, and miles of desolate, sandy beach. Our new governor told us that the next order of business would be to seek a suitable place for habitation. Master Jones ordered the longboat to be lowered, and 15 men put out to seek firewood and drinkable water. When the boat returned, the men told us the following story of their daylong adventure.

Halfway to the beach, the boat ran aground, and everyone had to wade though the ice-cold November water to reach the shore. Once on land the explorers found ash, birch, walnut, and juniper trees, all laced with holly vines. They saw fowl, but no animals nor signs of human habitation. Fearful of Indians, they stayed just close enough to shore to locate drinkable water. When one seaman found fresh water, all parties partook greedily while filling the casks that they had brought with them. Carrying the filled containers and many juniper branches, they waded to the longboat and then rowed back to the *Mayflower*.

This was the first time anyone from the ship had set foot on land since leaving our home in England. The same group, in the afternoon, made a second excursion to shore seeking signs of habitation, but, again, nothing of significance was found.

The next day was a Sabbath and there was no exploration. I could sense all day, from the passengers' demeanor, that a heavy burden had been lifted from them. I attended the shipboard service with the others. It was punctuated by hymns sung with uncommonly cheerful voices.

On Monday, parts of the shallop[3] were brought together on deck. This 40-foot boat, owned by the settlers, had been disassembled and used for tables, walls, and wherever stout lumber was required. Some even made beds, using suitable timbers from the dismantled ship. All of the pieces were then transported by the longboat to shore where they were to be re-assembled by the carpenter into a craft capable of use for fishing and exploration. That day also saw many women go ashore to clean themselves and their family's clothes, which had not seen fresh water since leaving England. The next day the carpenter went ashore to begin work on the shallop. Most men stayed aboard making their weapons ready for upcoming explorations.

On Wednesday morning, November 15th, the master and the boat's crew went ashore in the ship's longboat to look around. In the afternoon an armed party of 16 men, under the command of Captain Miles Standish, left for a two-day exploration. Masters William Bradford, Stephen Hopkins, and Edward Tilley were with them to act as advisors. They took provisions to last a week, along with hatchets and cooking equipment. The weather was mild, and the ground, I was told later, was not yet frozen. The master and his crew returned at nightfall, but no word was heard from the exploring party on that day or the next.

Early Friday morning I was awakened by shouts on the main deck. I hurried to the source of the commotion and found that a fire had been seen on the other side of the bay. The master advised us that it was a prearranged signal fire built by the exploring party. He, Governor Carver, and a goodly number of others went ashore in the afternoon to meet the returning explorers. Hours later, we heard gunfire, a signal that the two groups had met and were soon to arrive at the nearby shore. John Clarke, First Officer, was in charge when Master Jones was not onboard, and he sent the longboat to fetch the combined company. When all were back on the *Mayflower*, the adventurers gave us a chilling report about their experiences. Master Bradford began:

"On the first day after progressing barely a mile," he said, "we saw five or six Indians and a dog approaching us. When the savages heard our shouts, they fled into the woods. Captain Standish here called for us to follow them, but they quickly disappeared."

Captain Standish, a short man, drew up to his full height and interrupted.

"We followed the savage's tracks for about ten miles," he stated, "then approached a steep hillside. We were fearful of an ambush in the waning light of evening, so we abandoned the chase for the night. We lit a large bonfire, and kept it burning brightly until dawn. The next day, after little sleep, we continued our pursuit along the beach. Soon we reached the head of a long creek. Tracks there led into the woods. We followed them easily for about two hours. The ground then began to be less sandy and the tracks were harder to follow. When the footprints disappeared completely, I had the men fan out to probe a larger area, but they found no sign of Indians. We stopped to rest and ate the Holland cheese and hard biscuits that we had brought along."

Standish shook his head when he spoke about the food, then continued.

"With no water in sight, we shared the only liquid refreshment available, a small bottle of brandy. About ten o'clock we continued with our search. We spotted a deer, and farther along a spring of fresh water. We rested there, replenished our water supply, then headed back to the beach. Once we arrived we lit a large bonfire as a signal to the ship."

This must have been the fire that we had seen earlier, I thought. The passengers on deck and I listened with increased interest as Standish went on.

"As soon as we were satisfied that our fire had been spotted," he continued, "we moved forward. After a short time, we found a large, freshwater pond and an area of land that appeared to be planted at one time by Indians. Close by was a well-trodden path. We followed it for a mile or two, then came upon what appeared to be an Indian burial ground. There were heaps of sand everywhere. One of them was covered by an old mat. We dug down a little and found a bow and arrows, all of which were rotten. We were going to dig more but Master Bradford stopped us from further exploration. He exhorted us to leave the area because he felt it would be sinful to desecrate the ground more than we had already done. Continuing on, we encountered a field with stubbles of corn, walnut trees, and strawberry vines. Close by was another field with the remains of an old shack. Next to it were four or five planks laid together and a large, rusty ship's kettle. We concluded that the cauldron was taken from some

English ship long ago. One seaman probed a mound of earth nearby and discovered buried baskets of corn. Other mounds held additional corn. We discussed our finds and determined to take the kettle and some corn and return them, or things of equal value, to the Indians when we met them to parley. We put as much of the corn as we could in the kettle to bring it back to the ship so that we could have seed corn in the spring. Many of the men filled their pockets with it, too. We cut a stout pole and hooked it under the handle of the kettle. I had two men carry the heavy load. We retraced our steps to the freshwater pond and set up camp there for the second night."

The captain paused and looked around to see how well we were paying attention. Assuring himself that we were all interested in his relation, he resumed telling his story with great relish.

"It started to rain shortly after dark," he said, "and the downpour continued throughout the night. Everyone got soaked to the skin. The next day, we arose early, that is, those who were able to sleep, and wrung the water from our clothes. The men who had filled their pockets with corn were furious. The rain had turned their prize into a sticky mess. After a small breakfast, we sank the kettle into a pond at a spot where it could be found later, then continued our exploration. Forging through the dense, clinging, wet underbrush, we discovered a young tree that had been drawn tautly across the narrow path. Believing it to be a trap for deer set up by the Indians, we attempted to avoid it. Master Bradford, bringing up the rear, failed to hear our warnings, or to see the loop of woven rope that lay on the ground. He sprung the trap and his leg was caught by the loop. The tree whipped upwards and he was snapped upside down above us. As we cut him down I admonished the party not to show signs of mirth. Thankfully, he was unhurt. We brought the crude trap back for you to see. It's still in the longboat."

Master Bradford laughed at his folly, then he spoke, slowly. I detected a new relief in his voice.

"We continued on and soon found our way out of the woods. We saw three deer and three partridges along the way. Our wet powder prevented us from shooting any of that game, or the wild geese and ducks we encountered along the shore. Before long, Governor Carver and his party met us and with the dry powder they provided, we fired a salvo to alert those aboard ship that we were ready to be retrieved."

The listeners mumbled approval when the narration ended. *It was indeed an exciting adventure*, I thought as the crowd dispersed. But it would take another much more hazardous exploration before a suitable site for settlement was found.

CHAPTER EIGHT

The next day the carpenter on shore continued working on the shallop. He reported that reassembling her was going to take much more time and labor than originally thought. Most of the settlers spent the day aboard ship, gathering and sharpening their tools. A small group did venture to go ashore for wood and water. I tended to my duties in the hold. I saw that food supplies were becoming scarcer. I conveyed my fear of an imminent lack of provisions to the ship's master, but he assured me that there was plenty of game and fish on shore, and soon it would be available to us in quantity.

"With the settlement about to be established," he proclaimed to the Elders, "one of the first priorities of the colonists must be to stock food and fresh water. I would like that to happen very soon for I want to return to England as quickly as I can." I was hopeful that his statements would prove to be true, but I feared that the expected winter weather would delay their achievement.

On the following day, a Sabbath, services were again held aboard ship. Many of the crew ignored the call to worship and went ashore. As they went over the side to get into the longboat, I saw that they were bundled up in heavier clothes than usual, for the weather which had been mild during the previous few days, had turned much colder.

On Monday, several men went ashore to help the carpenter finish work on the shallop. Most of the others worked aboard on their tools, and on articles needed for turning the wilderness into a suitable living space.

The next few days were extremely cold. The low temperature combined with high winds, limited access to shore. Some hardy souls did face the elements, however, to bring us more wood and water. Despite the foul weather, the carpenter and his helpers remained on shore to complete work on the shallop. When I had occasion to go below deck, I could tell that the coughs and colds of the passengers and crew were increasing in severity. The ship's doctor, Giles Heale, warned everybody about the dangers of scurvy. *It was, I thought, indeed a sick ship.* The biting cold above and the forced confinement below deck did little to alleviate the misery.

By Saturday, work on the shallop was near completion. The Elders made plans for a group to go ashore on Monday despite the bad weather. They wanted an extended exploration of the territory using the reconstructed craft.

On Sunday, Master Jones was advised of the plans, and he stated firmly that the planters had better find a permanent location very soon. He noted that the first of December was only five days away and he was anxious to unload everything and return to England.

The next day he was invited to join an expedition and act as leader, which he agreed to do. He offered nine of his crew and the use of his longboat—offers that were readily accepted. By mid-morning, the exploring party of 34, packed into both the shallop and the longboat, made for shore amid gusting winds. Those of us on deck could see that the wind was too strong for the shallop to hoist sail. We could see both boats being slowly rowed to shore. It appeared that neither boat could make it all the way in, forcing the men to wade in above their knees again to get to dry land.

Soon the snow that everyone dreaded began to fall, creating frozen patches on the deck. I went below with most of the others to avoid the cold and the slippery planks. As I neared the crew's quarters, I heard excitement amidships and went back to see the cause of the commotion. Pressing my way toward a small cabin, which seemed to be the center of attention, I was stopped by Edward Thompson, a servant of Master William White. His apprehensive eyes met mine.

"My mistress has just birthed a son," he said. "Calling him Peregrine, I guess. Does all his screaming mean he's of good health?"

"I'm certain it does, lad," I answered. "And the name they chose is a fine one. It means pilgrim, which is just what each one of us is." I told the boy that the birth was a happy event, then I pushed my way back through the gathering, thinking about the many prayers that were answered by the bringing forth of one screaming, healthy child.

That evening, as I made for the hold to perform my duties with the casks and hogsheads of drink, I purposely walked through the 'tween deck to see how the planters and their families were faring. I was surprised at the number of people who were in bed, shivering and coughing. By the dim light of the hanging lanterns, I saw that many had their covers over their heads to preserve body heat. Others were in bed together sharing each other's warmth. The atmosphere was cold and dank, not at all the conditions the travelers expected in their new world. Near the gangway to the hold, I encountered Mr. Mullins. He was speaking to Dr. Samuel Fuller, who had come on the voyage to minister to the passengers. I stopped and listened to their discussion.

"There are many here who should be in a hospital," the doctor pleaded. "We have neither the medicine nor the facilities to properly tend to their discomforture."

"We shall have to endure our miseries until we can get rightful accommodations," Mr. Mullins said. "God willing, it shall be soon. We can only pray that the weather clears quickly so that we can find an area for settlement."

"How serious is the situation?" I interrupted.

"If we do not find a place within the next fortnight or two. where we can free ourselves from these miserable surroundings and build fires to warm our bodies, I fear that many of us shall not live to see the spring," the doctor answered.

"Then we must impress upon the Elders our perilous condition, if they do not already know, so that greater haste can be made in finding us a suitable landing spot," Mr. Mullins concluded.

"Indeed, we must," said Dr. Fuller, turning to go aft.

After the doctor left, Mr. Mullins tapped me on the arm, and asked me to stay.

"I fear for my family, Mr. Alden," he said. His voice seemed unusually somber. "You appear to be young and healthy, praise God. If something happens to me, I shall consider it an honor if you will look after them until they are in the care of some family much like my own."

"Sir," I said, "if you would be kind enough to inform your fine family of your desires, I shall deem it a honor to stand in your stead. But, by the grace of God, I pray that I shall never be called upon to act as you now request."

"You are an admirable gentleman," he responded. "I, too, pray that you shall never have to act as my surrogate."

I said my farewell and walked toward the companionway that was my original destination. I felt a great elation as I, with a copper lantern in my left hand, climbed down the ladder into the dark and smelly hold. I skipped every other rung.

CHAPTER NINE

Two days after leaving with the exploring party, Master Jones returned to his ship with part of his company. He had left some on land to continue the search for a suitable location for a settlement. Many of us crowded around him as he related his experiences. He appeared to enjoy his celebrity as he spoke.

"When we left the *Mayflower* on Monday," he said, "we planned to form two parties, one to travel on land, leaving the longboat docked on shore, the second party to sail a parallel course in the shallop following the others. Both were to look for the mouth of a river I had previously seen from the rigging on the *Mayflower*."

John Howland, one of the shore party, interrupted.

"The weather was blustery," he said, "and the going was difficult because of the loose sand on the beach, but we made our way for six or seven miles before making camp for the night. Heavy rain started to come down about midnight, and it soon turned to snow. We were all cold and our clothes became stiff. None of us got any sleep. The next morning it was still snowing, and we were exhausted. We called to the men in the shallop and they brought us back on board."

Master Jones was obviously unhappy with the interruption. He continued his story.

"As we traveled along the coast," he said, "we found the river that I had seen. We took soundings, but deemed it too shallow for a large boat. In the afternoon, the skies cleared, and I took a small party ashore to march along the beach, with the shallop following. The snow on the sand made progress almost impossible, so I had the party move inland. After covering a mere five miles, we were compelled to make camp because night was not far off. Luckily, the men had shot three fat geese and six ducks. We roasted them for our supper. The next morning, I wanted to explore upriver, but I was fearful of climbing the slippery slopes ahead of us. We headed for the creek where the previous expedition had found the Indian burial ground, the ruined shack, and the cached corn. On our way we found a recently used Indian canoe. We used the canoe to ferry ourselves to the other bank of the river."

A young sailor added, "We could only bring eight at a time, 'cuz the canoe was so small."

Master Jones smiled at the boy, who took on a sheepish look, then went on with his story.

"When we were all safely on shore, we searched for, and found, the undisturbed hoard of corn. We also found a bottle of oil, a bag of beans, and a store of wheat ears. These were good finds, and we should have continued on, but I started to feel uneasy about being away from my ship. I feared that the weather might turn bad again, and believed that I should return to the *Mayflower* just in case. The others agreed and suggested that I should take the corn back with me. Sixteen of the men, all of whom were concerned about their families or felt too ill to continue, asked to return with me. Of course I agreed and promised the ones that stayed that I would be back the next day with tools that would allow deeper digging in the frozen soil, hopefully to find additional grain. When I sailed away on the shallop in the evening, I could see the remaining men setting up camp on the snow-covered ground.

"Now, thankfully, I am back here among you. The exploration was fruitful, but tiring."

When Master Jones concluded his story, everyone was quiet. The only sounds were from the wind and the waves lapping gently against our sturdy hull. The master then left for the solitude and warmth of his cabin. I joined the others on deck. We thanked the Lord for the corn and asked His protection for the stalwart men still on shore.

The next morning, as promised, Master Jones sent men in the shallop, with pick-axes and spades, to the party on shore. Each member carried a musket and sword for protection.

The shallop returned with the remaining explorers just before nightfall. They brought back many Indian trinkets, as well as baskets, pottery and wickerware, all items that they had found on the ground after the master left. Below deck, many of us gathered around the weary men, anxious to hear their story. Though tired, the leader of the land party, Samuel Sharpe, a portly, lightly-bearded man with a pockmarked face, happily related what had happened to the company after Master Jones left them alone a few hours before sunset. He spoke in a monotone, but that didn't dampen our interest.

"We ate what was left of the roasted ducks that we had killed earlier," he said, "then we made camp for the night. We took advantage of the tall, leafless, but protective, walnut trees all around us. We kept a bonfire going all night. We drew lots, and the losers took turns acting as sentries. In the morning we ventured along a track that led into deeper woods, hoping to find an Indian village. When the path widened to two feet, we came to a halt. Some men feared an ambush so we loaded and primed our muskets. We then moved forward, cautiously. After five or six miles, the track petered out. The men decided that it was a drive that deer used when hunting together, so we turned back and followed a different track. When we came out of the woods, we found a mound grave, much bigger than the previous ones we had encountered. Two men shoveled the snow aside, and discovered wooden planks covering a large hole. They pried them up, then dug deeper until they found a mat, then a bow in usable condition, then another mat. They removed the second mat and found a carved and painted board, over two feet in length, with three prongs cut into one end, suggesting a crown. They removed another mat and discovered trays, bowls, dishes, and an assortment of trinkets. The men continued digging. They found yet another mat, the largest, and under it, two bundles. We opened the bigger bundle, and in it were the remains of an Indian with yellow-dyed hair. Completely covering his body was a fine, red, sweet-smelling powder. Next to it was a sailor's blouse and a pair of cloth breeches wrapped around a knife, a packing needle, and some strange-looking pieces of iron. We carefully opened the smaller bundle and it contained the body of a child, also protected by the red powder. The small, partially decomposed body was decorated with strings and bracelets made of beads. We found a small bow about two feet in length beside it. We believed that we had unearthed an Indian king and his prince. We replaced both bodies, with the greatest of reverence, and returned the site to its original condition. The few articles we took away with us were items that, we thought, would prompt discussion back here at the ship. We found additional smaller mounds nearby, but none of them contained anything of value or interest so we continued our exploration. We finally met the sailors that were sent out from the *Mayflower* to find us."

One of the two sailors sent to find the exploring party interrupted Samuel Sharpe's narration.

"These good gentlemen didn't know it," he said, "but when the two of us were put ashore to find them and bring them back to the ship, we searched along a likely path and discovered two strange dwellings. Someone must have been in them just a short time before we arrived, for we found burning embers on the floor. We must have frightened the savages away when they heard us coming. We loaded our muskets and prepared to fight if we had to, but no one appeared. The two of us grabbed up a few things, then continued our search for the land party. We didn't have far to go before we found them. We were in a large field when they came out of the woods. They scared the daylights out of us when they showed up. We nearly shot them dead. Luckily, we recognized their pantaloons, and we held our fire."

Master Sharpe appeared irritated by the seaman's interruption and continued speaking as if he had never been stopped.

"When we met up with the two sailors, they told us about their discovery," he continued, "and we followed them back to the dwellings. We examined the buildings closely and found that they were constructed of long, pliant saplings bent around in half-hoops so that both ends could be set in the ground. The structures were covered with mats, and the occupants used a longer mat for a door. When we entered one of the huts, we found that we could stand upright. Thinner, well-decorated mats were hung inside to form an inner skin. On the floor were forked sticks with cooking pots hanging, and around their fireplace, which was in the center of the room, were other mats that must have been beds. Also on the floor were different pots, wooden bowls, dishes, and trays. There were baskets, too, made from the shells of crabs laced tightly together. We saw tobacco and different seeds in other pots, and a bucket without a handle that surely must have come from Europe. The walls were covered with deer's feet and antlers, and eagles' claws. The occupants must have left in a hurry, for there was a fresh deer's head, and some pieces of fish near the fireplace. When we went outside, we saw a pile of bulrushes, likely for making mats, and a piece of venison that must have been food for a dog. We took only a few souvenirs, for we didn't want to be known as scavengers. Soon after we left the area, the sailors who had come for us became uneasy and urged us to hurry so that we could get to the shallop before the tide went out. We did, and here we are. You can take a look at the things we brought back. They're out on the main deck."

The storyteller pointed the way with one of his thick, calloused fingers. I joined the other passengers who hurried topside to survey the relics by the light of the large copper lantern that was swinging from the mainmast. Before I retired for the night, I marked the date in my book. It was November 30, 1620.

50

CHAPTER TEN

Over the next two days the leaders discussed again and again the findings of the explorers and possible places for settlement. On the second day I became aware of considerable excitement on the main deck. I hurried topside. Whales were playing about the ship. Two colonists, eager to prove how simple it was to catch one, fired musket shots at the closest whale. One of the muskets exploded when fired, sending pieces of stock and barrel flying. Everyone on deck praised God when they found that no one was hurt.

The next day was a Sabbath. The weather varied between sleet, snow, rain and clearing, but remained cold. It seemed that everyone on board, both passengers and crew, had bad coughs. Many of the passengers were confined to bed and could not attend services. Illnesses, some severe, were in every quarter. I saw grave concern on the faces of all of the leaders. The seriousness of our physical condition must have weighed heavily on their minds.

On Monday, settlement plans continued to be discussed by all in charge. They were interrupted, before noon, when news that Edward Thompson, a servant of Master William White, had died in his bed. After a solemn service by Elder Brewster, a burying party for the young man was chosen. I offered myself, and was included. That afternoon, we wrapped his body in canvas and two men carried it, supported by a pole hoisted at each end, toward the longboat, which was nestled beside the ship. The two carriers had great difficulty climbing down the rope ladder with their precious load. At one point, the canvas wrap became tilted, and the body slid forward, nearly falling into the angry waters below. I elected to carry three spades for digging the grave. A fair distance from the shore, the longboat ran aground, and all of us had to wade through the shallow but icy surf to reach dry land. We labored across loose sand and snow-covered soil until we reached a high, flat spot inland, hidden by trees. There we dug a shallow grave, said parting prayers, and gently lowered the canvas-covered bundle into the stark, rectangular opening that we had chopped in the frozen ground. After filling the hole with dirt, and leveling the top so that the grave couldn't be detected by Indians, we headed back. Along the way I viewed, for the first time, the unforgiving, snow-covered landscape that had been selected by others among us as our new home. For a fleeting second, I wished we were all back in good old England.

The next day, the weather turned even colder, and the sky grew darker. The change in the weather appeared to be an omen, for on that day we almost lost our ship. Francis Billington, son of John Billington, himself an ill-mannered man not of the Separatist company, shot off his father's fowling piece in a cabin between decks. The flints and small pieces of iron the youth had loaded into the gun, scarred the makeshift cabin. Many people were nearby, but, of more consequence, a small barrel of gunpowder stood open in the cabin. Some of the gunpowder that was scattered on the floor did catch fire, but the flame was quickly extinguished by two nervous passengers. By God's grace nobody was hurt, and the powder keg did not ignite. If it had, there would surely be no one left to tell the story.

In the afternoon, after returning from the hold where I examined barrels that contained a dwindling supply of beer, I became conscious of the sounds of a loud discussion coming from the Great Cabin. I hurried there to investigate. Inside, many passengers were still arguing about the place for settlement.

"We just can't wait any longer," one said, hoarsely. "If we stay nearby we'll have plenty of fresh water and some of the ground is already cleared for us to begin planting early."

Another added, "And the fishing here looks good. Even the mouth of the river appears to be able to accommodate small boats."

A third in the group that favored settling close by offered a warning.

"Look," he said, "the weather is only going to get worse. We will be risking everything by waiting. Additional expeditions will take time, and that is something we don't have."

"But if we go farther into the bay area," one of the opposing group stated, "the weather would be less severe. And the soil would be better for farming. Even the fishing would be better, and that's a big plus."

"We'd also have a deeper harbor for bigger ships," another enjoined.

"The freshwater ponds around here aren't that big," a third member said. "They'd probably dry up in the summer when we need them most."

Another counseled, "We must consider the fact that if the place around here turns out to be unsatisfactory, we'd all have to pack up once again and move inland. I, for one, don't like to look forward to that alternative."

Governor Carver held up his hands. "Friends," he said calmly, "We have been thrashing this around for too long already. I have listened to your arguments and concluded that we should make one more try at finding our final settlement location. We indeed have a limited time to spend looking, so I suggest that we stay within the limits of Cape Cod Bay. There must be a place that meets all of our requirements, and I am sure that we will find it very soon. Master Jones has often told us that when the ship's supplies get down to the amount he requires for a trip back to England, he's going to leave us here to our own devices. That time is rapidly approaching. Let's work together and push to find our Eden."

There was absolute quiet for a short time as both groups pondered the governor's decision. Robert Coppin was the first to speak. He was the pilot on *Speedwell*, but transferred to our ship when the leaky ship was sent back to London.

"I know of a headland no more than 24 miles west of here," he said. "I was with Captain John Smith when he visited it six years ago. He mapped the area then and gave it the name Plymouth. Master Jones has a copy of the map that he made. There appears to be a fine harbor there, good fishing, and fertile land. It could be the spot you are looking for."

The governor's face showed a look of satisfaction that I had never seen before. There was new lightness in his voice.

"Then the matter is settled," he said. "We shall send the shallop out tomorrow to investigate Pilot Coppin's claim. Let us pray this evening that the location proves to be everything he says it is."

CHAPTER ELEVEN

The next day, December 6th, I rose early. The weather was cold and foreboding. On my way to breakfast I was told that Jasper More, a lad bound to Governor Carver, had died during the night. He had been ill for many days. A group was again selected to bring the young man's body ashore for burial. Weary, I disdained from the duty on this occasion. After a short service led by Elder Brewster, the burial party boarded the longboat for its solemn task. *Another hidden grave*, I thought.

The exploring party was then assembled on deck. It was made up of eighteen men. It included: Governor Carver, William Bradford, Edward Winslow, Miles Standish, John and Edward Tilley, Richard Warren, Stephen Hopkins, John Howland, Edward Dotey, and two of the colonist's seamen, John Allerton and Thomas English. With them, of the ship's company, were two mates, John Clarke and Robert Coppin, the master-gunner and three sailors. Governor Carver was in command. He continually urged the sailors, who were fetching supplies, to hurry and advised the explorers to bring extra warm clothes in addition to their muskets and swords. As the men prepared for the trip, they seemed to be torn between savoring the adventure and fearing it. After a final prayer, they boarded the bobbing shallop, shielding each other from the cold blasts of winter air. Once clear of the ship, the shallop had to be rowed, for the northeast wind was too strong for sails. As the boat rounded Long Point, however, I could see her sails being unfurled and her oars raised. The evening service was composed mostly of prayers for the brave men and the success of their mission.

The next day I witnessed one of the greatest of tragedies. Mistress Dorothy Bradford, wife of Elder Bradford who was away on the expedition, was climbing down the rope ladder to board the longboat. Her foot slipped on the wet cordage, and she fell into the frigid water. I watched helplessly as she was washed away by the swift ocean current. I pitied the poor soul who had to tell her husband of his tragic loss.

The day following, a Friday, was equally sad. As heavy rains turned to snow, Master James Chilton died aboard ship, the first head of a family to pass away since leaving England. Adding to our sorrow was our concern about the shore party, for by nightfall the cold had become extreme. Aboard ship, many families huddled together for warmth. I covered myself with every piece of clothing I had.

The gloom aboard ship continued throughout the next few days. The weather cleared, but that did little to raise the spirits of the ailing passengers and crew. And we still had no word from the explorers.

On Wednesday, December 13th, after a full week ashore, the exploration party returned. Master Bradford threw himself face down on the deck when he heard of his wife's drowning, praying aloud there for more than an hour. When he finally stood, Governor Carver led him to his cabin.

I joined the anxious passengers who had crowded around the returned company to hear their story. Governor Carver, back from settling his friend down, was the first to speak. His words were frequently punctuated by coughs and sneezes from both the men of the exploring party, and the passengers who had remained aboard. His words were spoken with authority.

"Dear friends," he said, "I believe that we have at last found a satisfactory location for our settlement. It is the place that Pilot Coppin suggested to us earlier. During the last few days we spent a good deal of time surveying the area, and we found that it contains ample water and good soil for farming. It appears, also, to be well defensible. There is a crest of land where we can mount our ordnance for protection from hostile ships. If it is God's wish, we can settle there and build the community in that place that we have struggled these many weeks to find."

When the governor paused, I looked at the faces of the listeners. The gloom that had darkened their countenances for the last few days was replaced by the brighter look of hope. I, too, felt a rising sense of optimism. The governor continued.

"I am sure that all of you would like to hear of our actions. I shall let Captain Standish provide you with the details. My bones are weary from the exertions that this old body has been forced to endure. I shall now avail myself of the serenity found only in my cabin."

The governor, stooped from fatigue, slowly departed from the noisy crowd. Miles Standish, ever the military man, straightened and walked briskly to where the governor had stood.

He appeared confident, with dark, leather-like skin and the erect carriage of a warrior. He was still wearing his helmet and breastplate. Locks of bright red hair curled from under his metal headpiece, and matched the color of his pointed beard. A soldier by inclination, he had served Queen Elizabeth in Holland, supporting the Dutch Protestants against the Catholics from Spain. He was not a Separatist. It was his spirit of adventure that caused him to sail with us on the *Mayflower*. He spoke to us crisply, not as a storyteller, but as a military commander.

"I desire to begin my discourse with our departure from *Mayflower*," he began. "On Wednesday last, as you may recall, there were gale-like conditions when we embarked. As soon as we pushed off from the ship we were confronted with strong northeast winds. If we had raised sail, we would have been blown in a direction opposite from that we had planned to pursue. The sailors with us manned the oars until we got to Long Point, where the wind direction became more favorable. There, we were able to set some sail. Our intention was to travel directly across the bay to Pilot Coppin's destination, but the winds were too blustery. We sailed close to the shore, endeavoring to encircle the bay. As we departed Long Point, Edward Tilley and the gunner became very seasick, so…"

The gunner broke in. "We warn't the oney ones to get sick. We just had it worse."

Captain Standish ignored the interruption.

"We traveled about eighteen to twenty miles along the coast, but saw neither creek nor harbor. Since night was coming on, we retraced our path for eight miles hoping to find a suitable resting place. When John Allerton spotted a fair-sized bay, about three miles distant, we headed toward it. As we approached the beach on one side, we saw group of ten or more Indians crowded around a large black object on the ground. When the natives observed us, they all ran into the woods. We proceeded some six miles more along the coast, to avoid a confrontation, then put in near some sandy flats. On the beach, we built a makeshift stockade for protection, and lit a bonfire. We kept it burning all night and posted sentries to watch for Indian activity."

Stephen Hopkins interrupted. "I was one of the sentries, and we could see a fire burning about five miles up the coast. We figured it must have been the savages we saw earlier."

The captain cast an impatient glance at Hopkins, then continued.

"No one got much sleep during the night. In the morning, after our supplication to the Almighty and breakfast, Governor Bradford divided the group into two parts. The first, consisting of eight men, was sent back to the shallop to sound the harbor. The second group, of which I was a part, reconnoitered the area to find out if it was fit for settlement. Our party found that the soil was too sandy and the brooks in the area were too small. Continuing on, we encountered the location where we had seen the Indians. We discovered a partially cut-up whale on the beach. We concluded that that must have been what we saw the Indians doing. We saw their tracks and followed them along the beach and into the woods but never did see a living soul. After finding a sizeable pond, we continued deeper into the woods. At one point we discovered a deserted wigwam, located in the center of what appeared to be a large graveyard. Next to the tepee was a tall, wooden palisade. Inside the palings there were lots of graves, most covered by similar wigwams. Outside, in the open graveyard there were many smaller graves. These had no coverings, and were much more shabbily constructed than the ones inside the barricade. We came to the conclusion that the inner graves were where the important Indians were buried. After our discussion, Governor Carver suggested that we return to our encampment on the beach. When we arrived, we met the sailing party. They advised us that they had taken soundings, and the bay could, indeed, accommodate large ships."

Young John Howland spoke up again impatiently. "I was sailing wit' the others in the shallop, and we seen two big fat whales out in the bay. Must've been at least thirty feet long. I wanted to bring one back, but I guess there wasn't enough time, so they said."

Captain Standish smiled condescendingly, then continued.

"After comparing notes with the sea travelers, we collected wood for an all-night bonfire, and had supper. While eating we discussed the advantages and disadvantages of the place for a permanent settlement, and decided that, everything considered, it wasn't suitable. After our meal, we posted sentries and retired for the night. Around midnight, we were awakened by shouts from our sentries, yelling for us to get up and arm. We fired two musket shots and the noise must have scared the invaders, for we heard them retreating hastily through the brittle undergrowth. We talked over the incident, and decided that it probably was not Indians, but some wolves or foxes investigating us. By five o'clock in the morning we were up and about the encampment. Before eating, we fired our muskets to make sure that they had not frozen up during the night. We then stacked our loose equipment down by the shore and waited for the tide to come in so the shallop could be brought close by."

John Howland interrupted . "We was colder than the muskets, but... " The look from Miles Standish cut him off in mid-sentence. The military man turned back to his audience with a look of satisfaction, then continued.

"Some sixteen men placed their armor and weapons on the stack. I warned them that leaving the beach without their arms could be dangerous, but they insisted that they were safe. We all walked back to the encampment for breakfast. Our meal was interrupted by wild screams from the woods. One of our men had gone off to collect wood for the fire, and he returned on a run, crying out that the yells had come from hostile Indians nearby. As he spoke, a barrage of arrows rained down on us, but none, fortunately, found their mark. While those that had weapons were priming them, the ones who had left their muskets on the beach dashed back to get them. I was the only one carrying a flintlock musket. It allowed me to fire quicker than the rest who had matchlocks, so I was able to fire twice before the others could prime and load their pieces. Before they discharged their weapons, however, I ordered them to hold their fire and stand ready to defend our position."

I looked around at the group that was listening to the story being told. Each one had either fear or adoration showing on his face. Like some others, I worried about how deadly the Indians would be, and how we could survive in their presence. At the same time I felt great admiration for the brave men who had ventured onto the Indians' land. The captain hesitated while he lit his pipe. The short delay seemed to last for hours.

"We got to where our muskets were stacked," interjected Edward Dotey, one of the men who had run back to the beach, "and we got them ready to fire using the ember that I grabbed from the bonfire as we left. We thought we saw savages near the woods so four of us shot at them. We didn't have any more fire left to ignite our muskets, so we yelled back for help."

Captain Standish took a deep pull on his pipe, and continued.

"When I heard their plea," he said, "I called to the beach party to hold fast and protect the shallop. Thomas English knew a fire of some sort was needed to arm the muskets of the beach party, so he grabbed a brand from the bonfire and ran with it to the shore."

Master English, the runner, then added to the story.

"When I got there," he recounted, "the men took the ember and prepared their weapons. Soon, we heard shrieks from natives from all over. It seemed that they had surrounded us. We saw one Indian come toward us. Then he hid behind a tree. He shot three arrows and nearly hit one of our sailors. Our party fired three shots back at him, and I guess he was hit because he yelled and ran into the deep woods. We think that the rest of the attackers followed him, for it got quiet after he left. Mr. Hopkins here then had six men stay with him and guard the boat. The rest of us chased the Indians. We followed them for about a quarter of a mile but they were too fast for us. A couple of our men, disappointed at losing the quarry, fired a few shots in their direction. We then returned to the beach. There we found more than eighteen arrows on the ground, some tipped with eagle's claws, some with stag's horns, but most with sharpened brass. We kept them with us. We then boarded the shallop with Captain Standish. He had a few men walk along the beach, following our boat, to show the Indians that they couldn't scare us. After about a quarter of a mile, with no sight of Indians, we put in to shore, and took the walkers aboard. Within an hour the snow began to fall, and the freezing wind was driving it into our faces. We decided to continue our search anyway."

"That was a monumental mistake." interrupted Captain Standish. We were stunned by his admission, and waited anxiously for him to go on. He took another long puff and continued.

"We were sailing at the time in Cape Cod Bay. We were more than 20 miles from the Atlantic Ocean, yet the sea was so rough that it caused severe damage to the Shallop. Both of our rudder hinges broke apart. That left us with no means of steering. To make matters worse, the weather was getting increasingly wretched."

The Howland boy broke in again. "We was all scared, 'cuz we was being thrown about by the huge waves, and no way to stop it."

The captain ignored the comment.

"The steady wind was pushing us toward the dangerous breakers near the shore," he said, "and it was getting dark quickly. Fortunately, Pilot Coppin here had the good sense to order the crew to get oars in the water so that we wouldn't be driven onto the beach. The oarsmen were finally able to get the boat under control, and turn us around. It was a very close call. With their great strength, the sailors held the boat on a steady course using only the oars as the gale continued to grow in strength. We headed for a harbor, just north of us, with the aid of a little sail. Night came upon us, but Mr. Coppin, using only the wind direction as his compass, guided our rudderless boat toward two spits of land that he remembered had served to protect the harbor. But when we turned west to enter the harbor we faced an even greater calamity."

The long puff by the captain to heighten our interest wasn't necessary.

"The stiff wind snapped our mast into three pieces, allowing the sail to fall into the water. With great effort, the frightened men pulled the wet canvas back into the boat so that it wouldn't hold us back." Once more, the Howland lad interrupted the captain. "When the mast broke off, we was scared-er than before. It was snowin' hard, and it was black as tar out. We couldn't see nothin' anywhere. I started to pray real loud."

The captain, showed his irritation. He puffed hard then continued.

"The sailors pulled on the oars harder than ever, moving the boat slowly through the heaving water. Mr. Coppin's calls to adjust our course were nearly drowned out by the howling of the wind and the steady pounding of the waves against our fragile hull. Suddenly, for no apparent reason, the wind and the sea eased. It was as if the Lord had reached out and blessed us. We soon saw the glisten of sand ahead and knew that it was the shelter of the harbor that had saved us. We maneuvered close to shore and dropped anchor. Some of us, wary of Indians, stayed aboard for the night. I joined the majority of men who went ashore to escape the wet, cramped conditions on the shallop. We scoured the area for pieces of wood for a bonfire so we could steam the water from our soggy clothes and warm our near-frozen bones. After building a fire, we posted sentries to guard against intruders. We huddled around the burning embers. The snow fell steadily, and the cold penetrated our still-wet apparel. We tried desperately to sleep."

Young Howland, again. "We got so cold we thought we was going to freeze to death."

I saw Captain Standish puff harder. He continued.

"By morning, the snow was still falling. We spent the morning investigating our surroundings and found that we were on a small, uninhabited island. We spotted many varieties of trees, some we had not seen before. There were also a number of fresh-water brooks. Governor Bradford suggested we call the location, Clarke's Island, since one of our sailors, John Clarke, was the first to step ashore. In the afternoon, we baled out the shallop and spent much time drying our clothing with the heat from a large fire. We celebrated the next day, a Sabbath, by resting and offering prayers for our salvation. On Monday morning, December 11th, we re-boarded the shallop, departed the island, and circled the harbor, taking soundings at appropriate places. At one point we found what appeared to be a suitable place. It had a deep harbor—safe enough for the *Mayflower*. In fact, the harbor appeared large enough to hold a goodly number of sizeable ships. There were many convenient landing places along the beach. In the afternoon, we went ashore to survey the adjacent area. With each discovery we felt a bit more hopeful. We discovered many existing cornfields, fresh-water brooks, and large stands of timber, as well as ample flat land, suitable for building a settlement. It took us little time to acknowledge that we had finally found the place we had been desperately seeking. With new vigor we set sail for the *Mayflower*. As Governor Carver said earlier, we appear to have found our final destination, by the grace of God."

The Howland boy broke in. "We was so glad to find the rightful spot we hurried back through the snow to tell ya 'bout it."

I watched the faces of the listeners brighten even more as the words of Governor Carver were reinforced by the story we had heard from Captain Standish. Between the coughs and sneezes of our suffering group I could clearly hear quiet but unmistakable sobs of joy.

CHAPTER TWELVE

As the gathering was breaking up, Miss Priscilla came toward me. I could feel my heart pounding beneath my heavy clothes as she neared.

"Mr. Alden, sir," she said, looking up at me. "May I speak to you about my father?"

"It would be my pleasure," I responded. "I trust that your father is well?"

I noted a look of great sorrow on her face, and I felt deeply the desire to share her distress.

"My father's health is not good," she said. "He suffers greatly from the scourge that has befallen so many of our company. He has lately informed me of his request to you regarding the welfare of his family in the unfortunate circumstance of his becoming too ill to provide proper counsel. I should like to thank you for your generous assent, and to inform you that all of my family agreed there is no one better than you to carry out his wish. But if you feel that you would like to withdraw your offer at this time…"

I interrupted her forcefully. "Miss Priscilla, I consider it a great honor to serve your father, and under no circumstance would I recant my promise to him. As long as I breathe and have the strength to be of service, I shall continue to consider my promise a sacred trust. If there is something I can do for your family, even now, I am your humble servant. You have merely to ask."

"No," she answered, "not now. But the time may come.…Please know that my family appreciates your concern and will be forever in your debt."

"I do not consider it a debt, Miss Priscilla," I replied. "I am at your service no matter the condition of your father. Would that I had the opportunity to serve you, not only now, but far into the future."

With a blush on her lovely face, Miss Priscilla excused herself and walked slowly toward her cabin. She turned and smiled at me shyly just before she disappeared behind the heavy curtain that separated her family from the other passengers on the ship.

I stood there thinking that it is usually impossible to define the exact moments in our life when decisions are made that everlastingly affect our future, but I knew when I saw that smile on Miss Priscilla's face that two things were certain. The first was that I would remain with my courageous friends in America instead of going back to England. The second, of much greater import, was that I would one day marry the wonderful girl who had just graced me with her winsome smile.

The next few days were filled with the excitement of bringing everything that was on shore back to the ship, organizing all belongings for a smooth debarking at Plymouth, and praying that the site chosen will be fitting and final.

On December 15th, we weighed anchor, and Master Jones piloted the *Mayflower* out of the shallow harbor into the open waters of the Bay. With the shallop leading, the master set a course directly for Plymouth Harbor, a distance of about 24 miles. The strong Northeast wind was extremely unfavorable for us, and it was with great difficulty that the master brought the ship to a point six or seven miles from our destination. Sensing danger if he proceeded farther, Master Jones ordered that the *Mayflower* be put about. We reversed course and headed back toward open water. This action prompted many grievous utterances throughout the day, by both passengers and crew. All night the master tacked around, keeping the *Mayflower* out of harm's way. By morning the conditions had become more agreeable. The ship was pointed toward the two strips of land that marked the entrance to Plymouth Harbor. Just as we passed between the protective barriers, the wind shifted, strongly, back from the Northeast. It was our good fortune that we were, by that time, safely within the harbor.

"Truly an act of Divine Providence!" exclaimed Elder Brewster, when he became aware of our secure condition. "We were allowed to get into the harbor before the wind could cause us more distress. Surely it is a clear sign that this is where we should make our home."

The master moved his ship cautiously around the harbor to ensure that it was fit for winter docking. The passengers eagerly discussed possible landing sites and pointed to various locations on the shore. Just before dark, Master Jones, convinced that the harbor was deep enough and sufficiently clear of obstacles, chose his anchorage and secured his vessel. The settlers, fearing the unknown, showed no will to go ashore that night. Nor did anyone leave the ship the next day, for it was a Sabbath. Between services, many of the passengers readied their belongings in preparation for disembarking. Others stood on the upper deck, examining the shore, hoping and praying that the place selected could, with God's grace, provide a suitable home. I found myself joining in their prayer.

Early Monday morning, the crew cleared the shallop and made it ready to transport the first party of passengers ashore. Governor Carver cancelled the trip, however, insisting that an expedition first be sent ashore to determine if hostile Indians lurked nearby. Master Jones, four of his crewmen, and a group of settlers then boarded the shallop and made for shore. Before dark, the weary company returned. The usually laconic sea captain told us about their experience.

"We went from the ship directly to the coast," he said, "After securing the shallop on shore, we proceeded in a northerly direction for eight or nine miles. We never saw an Indian, or even a wigwam. We did come across some abandoned cornfields and plenty of woodlands. One of my sailors found a stream of fresh water and it looked like there are many others around. We pushed aside snow at several locations to check the condition of the soil. I'm no farmer but it certainly looked like fertile ground. I wouldn't hesitate to settle there if I were you."

The next day, the 19th of December, was also a day of exploration. One group of eight men went ashore in the longboat. A larger group sailed along the coast in the shallop. When they returned at nightfall, they told us of their adventures in detail. There were many of us on deck and we all listened with great anticipation. We hoped, and many prayed, that one company would give us encouraging news about finding a suitable spot for our new home.

Thomas English, a tall, thin, scholarly looking man who had been engaged in London to be master of the shallop, was the first to speak. He accompanied his words with many hand gestures to emphasize their import.

"I was aboard the larger boat with Master Jones," he said, "and we traveled close to the shore until we found a wide creek, which appeared to be navigable. We sailed inland for about three miles, since the tide was in. We calculated that a thirty-ton vessel could travel at high tide to where we were, but even our shallop, with its low draft, would run aground when the tide was out. At our location, we were confronted on both sides with heavy woods. These, we felt, would greatly hinder the use of the land for cultivation, for it would provide cover for marauding Indians. We also believed that we were too far inland for good fishing. Considering the circumstances, we decided that the area would not serve us well as a settlement. We did, however, name the waterway—Jones River—to honor all that the master, here, has done for our survival. Since we deemed it necessary to find a better location, we turned the shallop around and sailed back down-river to tell the others of our decision."

Some of the listeners groaned when Master English concluded his talk. Many looks of anticipation turned to looks of disappointment.

John Allerton, a brawny, light-haired man who was hired in London as a sailor, spoke next. He, unlike Thomas English, spoke in a monotone and used no animation as he described his group's venture. His expressionless face foretold the outcome of his exploration.

"We took the longboat back to the newly-named, Clarke's Island," he said, "to see if it would serve as a fit location for settlement. We hoped that its isolation would provide protection from the savages and its coast would afford a good place for the docking of ships. We soon discovered that the whole island was only two miles around—only two miles! We looked for sources of fresh water anyway and found only small ponds, and those likely to dry up in the heat of summer. We quickly discounted that place as a possible area for colonization and returned to the *Mayflower*."

No one else offered to speak. I could only hear sounds of water slapping the sides of the ship. I looked around at a sea of sad faces. Then, mumbling quietly, the group slowly disbanded.

Before retiring for the night, however, the leaders gathered in the Great Cabin with Master Jones. At the request of Elder Brewster I accompanied them. It was a noisy, cold, and crowded cabin I entered. The sounds of coughing echoed off the wooden walls of the dampish room. The ship's master called for quiet. He told the settlers, resolutely, that his patience had run out, and that he must get back to England. The Elders understood his warning and knew that brutal winter storms were coming. They also realized that their ability to work on their housing would be severely limited by the weather. They consulted with each other briefly and turned back to the group, voicing their promise to the master that on the next day they would make a final choice of location. It was obvious to me that everyone in attendance hoped that Christmas, only five days away, would not have to be celebrated between the decks of the foul-smelling, overcrowded ship.

The next day, following morning services, a large party went ashore to decide between two possible sites for the settlement. Just before nightfall, all but twenty returned to the *Mayflower*. Elder Brewster called for a meeting with the other leaders in the Great Cabin soon after he was back aboard. I stood next to him and watched as he drew himself up to his full height. He spoke in his most ministerial voice.

"We explored the two areas under consideration," he said, "to determine which one was better for our colonization. After viewing both locations we decided by voice vote to settle where we encountered the largest brook—the place that Captain Standish had so eloquently described to everyone a week ago. The site is on an extensive stretch of high ground overlooking the Bay. There, land has already been cleared and had been planted with corn no more than a few years ago. There is plenty of fresh water. On one side is a large hillock, from which all sides of the settlement, and the bay, are visible. This prominence would be ideal for mounting the many cannon we have brought from England. We left some twenty men ashore to secure the area and guide the party we shall send tomorrow to begin building our new settlement." When he paused, I looked around. Every face showed the same relief that I was feeling inside.

"Let us now retire for the night," the Elder continued, "for when we arise we shall commence the work that Providence has brought us to this land to accomplish. May He afford us His grace to complete our work according to His will."

As one voice, the assembly quietly said, "Amen."

I was awakened early the next morning by the howling of the wind and the uncommon severity of the ship's pitching brought about by heavy seas. I could hear the rain pounding on the heavy canvas that covered the openings in the upper deck. No match for the elements, they allowed water to pour onto the passengers and their possessions below without mercy. Master Jones ordered that three anchors be dropped to ensure the safety of the *Mayflower*, so severe was the weather. The storm delayed delivery of the provisions expected by the shore party at first light. It wasn't until eleven o'clock that the downpour lessened enough for the shallop, with the supplies, to leave the ship. Sadly, in the afternoon, Richard Britteridge, a single man, coughed his last as he lay on his wet bed of straw. His body was wrapped in canvas and placed on the top deck until the weather improved.

The next day, Friday, brought more stormy conditions. The passengers, wet, cold, and miserable, spent the day wringing out clothes, mopping the lower decks, and praying for better weather. Mary, wife of *Speedwell* passenger, Master Isaac Allerton, gave birth as the storm was raging. The happy event turned tragic when it was discovered that the baby was stillborn, possibly a consequence of the severe conditions aboard ship.

On Saturday, the weather abated and every man fit for work was brought ashore to fell timber and ready the land for settlement. The first trip of the shallop also carried the two canvas-wrapped bodies for burial. I planned to go ashore in the afternoon. On one return trip, Soloman Prower, a manservant of the treasurer for the settlers, Christopher Martin, was brought back. He was wracked with fever from exposure and, between coughs and wheezes, he related to us his experiences on shore.

"When we landed we was anxious to look around, and the night came on us, to our big [cough] surprise. It got so dark we couldn't see nothin' [cough] 'n then the rain began to fall, real heavy, [cough] 'n' we didn't have nuthin' ta eat 'sept one bite uv dried fish each [cough]. Nobody got much sleep at night, 'cuz the rain kept cummin' down [cough], soakin' us right through to the skin. We 'spected to see some stuff from the ship early in the mornin', but [cough] nuthin' showed up. When the sharrop finally cum we was all mitey glad. [cough] I wasn't feelin' too good, so I ast if I could go back to the [cough] ship, and they 'sez I could. Now [cough] I'm gonna go back to my bed, 'n' try to sleep [cough]." I coughed as I related this to show Soloman's distress. With a trail of water following him, the ailing lad shuffled back to his damp bed on the floor.

The next day, a Sabbath, began with rest and prayer, for despite the great need to build shelters ashore, no work was permitted on Sunday. About ten o'clock, young Soloman Prower coughed his last cough. Several of the crew ceremoniously wrapped him in canvas to await his final trip to land.

Shortly before noon, a series of wild shrieks from shore interrupted our devotions. I ran to the upper deck with many others, hoping to discover the source of the eerie cries. By the time I arrived on deck all of the strange sounds had ceased. Neither animal nor Indian could be seen on the snow-covered beach. Fearful and perplexed, we all returned to the services below.

The following day was Christmas, but there was no colorful celebration by the Separatists, for their religion forbade it. Every available man went ashore to continue the tasks of clearing land and hauling logs to where our town was being built. From morning to evening, we forced our tired bodies to work for the common good. As the sun was setting, we once again heard shrieks from the woods. Grabbing our muskets, which were primed and ready, we set out to find the source of the screams, but our cautious search revealed no sign of life. In near-darkness, I returned to the ship with most of the men. Twenty were left on shore, however, to guard the newly felled timber and sharpen the tools for morning use. Just as our boat neared the *Mayflower* an unexpected gale came upon us, making it extremely difficult to climb on board. The accompanying downpour prevented our seeing or hearing signs of the party on shore. Once we were aboard, there was an attempt by some of the non-Separatists to celebrate Christmas. Most seemed too weary to participate. And little enthusiasm could be generated for any activity at all, since there was only water to drink. Captain Jones, seeing the lack of cheer, decided to provide some.

"Men," he called out, "if it will spike the gloom all around us, I will gladly provide you with some libation from my private store. If you care to join me in my cabin, we will toast the King and commemorate this great day. Tomorrow you may slave some more, but tonight let us all be merry as befits our present condition."

I joined the men as they rushed aft with newly found energy. Even the violent pitching of the boat in the raging storm, did little to slow our advance to the master's quarters. Our merriment, however, was short-lived. Before all of our cups were filled we received the sobering news that young John Langemore, another man-servant of Treasurer Martin, had just died. He too was a casualty of the foul weather and the unhealthy conditions aboard ship. Master Standish told us that his body would be buried next to the three who already occupy patches of land on a hill, away from the shore and hidden from view. "His grave, like the others," he said, "must be concealed so that the Indians can't count how many are being taken from our company."

The blustery weather continued throughout the next day, preventing travel to or from shore. The men on board busied themselves with their tools, and the women spent the day cleaning their sleeping quarters, mending clothes, and tending the sick. I noticed that the settlers were showing increasing concern about the number of their company who were ailing. It seemed to me that every family had one or more members stricken with sickness. Men, women, and children were abed suffering from the cold, dampness, and the foul conditions all about us. I thanked Providence every day for my comparatively healthy condition and prayed often that Priscilla and her family would overcome the dangers that we were all facing.

The following day, Wednesday, the weather cleared sufficiently for the able settlers to go ashore. I couldn't help noticing that fewer were making the trip to the settlement each time we sailed. I was in the third boatload. We left the ship shortly after the sun's rising. As I headed for the area where timber was being cut, I encountered Governor Carver.

"Mr. Alden," he said, "Some of us are going to meet at the place where the logs are being stored to discuss plans for our township. We would appreciate your attendance at the meeting. You seem to have a level head on your shoulders and we could probably benefit from your sound judgement."

I answered that I was flattered by their opinion of me and would be pleased to join them in their deliberations. I walked to the meeting place with a light step. Governor Carver began to speak loudly to the group of ten men gathered on the beach.

"We are here, good friends, by the grace of God," he said, "and it is incumbent on us to build a settlement not only to serve our purposes, which are many, but to serve our Creator. We are called to build a proper center from which we can go forth and proclaim His message to this part of the world. This we shall do. To ensure survival, however, we first require a suitable place to mount our cannon, for defense is our highest priority. Captain Standish has suggested that we use that hilltop over there as a favorable position for our ordnance since it appears to afford a good field of fire. With its prominence, Indians would find it difficult to surprise us. Do I hear any objection to that location?"

No one spoke. The governor continued.

"Let us now discuss the layout of the township. What say any of you about a plan."

I heard considerable mumbling, but no one offered a suggestion. I felt obliged to speak.

"We need quick access to our cannon from where we will be housed, so I suggest that we establish a street, from the shore, where we will be unloading goods from the ship, westerly to the hill, where we must hie if trouble beckons."

"And we can build our houses along the street," Isaac Allerton added, "which would make it equally convenient to travel to the shore, or to our defenses."

"If we erect houses on both sides of the street it would make good sense, for it would offer a more compact defense," Captain Standish offered.

"Then we shall consider that as our overall plan," the governor said. "Do I hear any argument against this approach?"

"Who's gonna live where?" Christopher Martin interrupted.

"That we can decide at a later date," answered Elder Brewster. "Now, I suggest, we all join the felling parties so we may gather as many logs as possible before the weather hinders us from this most important work."

We spent the following days chopping down and shaping trees, making them suitable for construction. To minimize the number of buildings required for housing all of the settlers, the single men were assigned to individual families. With this disposition, Master Bradford, who was directing our activities, determined that nineteen homes were needed. Captain Standish and his wife, Rose, asked me to join their family unit, and I accepted their offer with great enthusiasm. To ensure that the workmen were not subjected to an unachievable task, the size of each plot was limited to 2¾ by 16½ yards for each person in the household. With these dimensions as a basis, we established the first street. This originated, as I had suggested, at the coast and led to the high ground where our cannon were to be located. We then decided that the first structure built should be a Common House, so that tools and other goods could be stored ashore, minimizing the time-consuming and sometimes hazardous travel to the *Mayflower* each morning and evening. We further agreed that this storage house should be near the beach. Before nightfall we laid the first logs for its construction. It was to be twenty feet square, with wooden sides and a thatched roof. To fill the cracks, we planned to use clay mortar, which was readily available from nearby pits.

The cold, wet weather continued. High winds added to the workers discomfort and brought great danger to the felling operation. Misfortune struck on the third day of the New Year. Shortly after we wet and tired workers returned to the *Mayflower* in the evening, we saw flames coming from the cornfield stubble on shore. There was little we could do but watch as the fire spread from field to field.

"Someone must have set it," Edward Winslow said, "The ground is too wet to ignite from a casual spark."

"But there's no one in sight," Governor Carver replied. "If there were anyone around, we could see them by the bright light of the fire."

With the same speed as it had started, I watched the fire die down and go out. It left the pungent smell of smoke hanging over our ship.

The next morning I accompanied Captain Standish to shore with four other men, before the main party disembarked. The captain wanted to be sure that there were no Indians around to ambush the workers. We searched the area, but only found a few old abandoned wigwams. We saw no Indians. We visited the burned cornfields, but on examination we could not identify the cause of the fire. The tree felling and hauling continued, as did the construction of the Common House.

The morning of January 8th was clear and sunny—a day to savor. Young Francis Billington, and Robert Coppin, one of Master Jones' two pilots, set off in the longboat to look for the large body of water Billington had seen in the distance from the masthead of the *Mayflower*. Upon their return, the younger Billington told us about their adventure.

"After leaving the mother ship, we rowed to the coast," he said. "We proceeded up a large stream, which had been named Town Brook by the governor because it flowed past the proposed settlement. We traveled about three miles and there found two large lakes. Fish appeared to be plentiful and the water was clear. In the woods we saw plenty of fowl, but dared not shoot at any for we felt that the single musket we had with us would not suffice for our defense, if Indians attacked us. Before returning, we traveled along the shore. There, we came across seven or eight abandoned wigwams. We made sure that we stayed well clear of them."

Many of his listeners chuckled at his last statement. I welcomed the brief show of humor. There had been little laughter during the previous weeks. The two explorers said that they considered their venture a great success. The group heartily agreed and suggested that the larger of the two lakes be named *Billington Sea*.

The day, however, was not a good one for Christopher Martin, treasurer for the settlers. He had recently lost both of his manservants through death and was himself lying weak and sweating in his bunk. When I passed by, his frail wife, Katherine, and Dr. Fuller, were by his side. The weary physician turned to me and whispered, "He has red spots on his skin, bleeding gums, and swollen joints. These are sure signs of scurvy. It is nigh time for bloodletting."

I responded to him in the same low voice. "We must send for Governor Carver at once. Master Martin is the only one completely knowledgeable about the settler's accounts. He must relate, quickly, what he knows to the governor, so that all information is not lost." I had no sooner completed my declaration, when to our surprise, Governor Carver came upon us.

"How fares Master Martin, doctor?" he asked.

"He appears to be beyond saving, Governor," Dr. Fuller said quietly. "I was preparing to perform a bloodletting as a last hope to save the man, but young Alden here thought it better to summon you first. It is an act of Providence that you have come so quickly."

Mrs. Martin, holding a white kerchief over her mouth to smother the sound, began to weep. I tried to comfort her with words of encouragement and hope, but it was to no avail. Tears flowed down her sallow cheeks. The Governor leaned over the ailing man and began speaking to him, gently, about the colonist's accounts. The overworked Dr. Fuller, nervous and distracted, pardoned himself and left us so he could minister to other of the ailing persons aboard ship. I remained with the grieving Mrs. Martin. Governor Carver familiarized himself with the dying man's accounts, prayed with him, and tightly held his hand for more than an hour as the treasurer slowly lost consciousness and took his final breaths. As the governor and I were leaving, Mrs. Martin placed her head next to her husband's and between sobs prayed for the salvation of his soul. We closed the door quietly.

The shallop, which was sent out by Master Jones early the same morning to search for fish, returned at nightfall with three large seals and a good-sized cod. Their success was greeted with great acclaim, for the ship's larder was nearly bare. That night, despite the sorrowful experience I had encountered earlier, I slept soundly.

CHAPTER THIRTEEN

The next day we were told that the Common House was complete, except for the roofing. Governor Carver determined that the great amount of work necessary to construct the settlement would progress faster if now, after the final thatch was added to the storehouse, the men were free to separate and build their own houses. The colonists agreed, and also decided that the Standish homesite should be the one closest to the ordnance platform on the hill so that, if the colony were threatened, the captain could arrive at the cannon mount in the shortest possible time. The heads of family units then drew lots for positioning the remaining households on the street. Work continued apace throughout the day.

The 11th of January was again a day of great distress. Elder Bradford was engaged in splitting logs near the shore. Quite unexpectedly his hipbone seized up on him, and his ankles began to swell. He called out that he was in great pain and needed assistance. John Hooke, his servant, and I escorted him back to the ship where he lay in bed in agony for most of the day. By evening, much of his pain had abated, but he was left weak and only just able to sit up. I sat next to him as he lay in bed mumbling, with reverence, about his dear wife who had drowned just one month before. As the spent candle flickered into darkness, Elder Bradford fell into a deep sleep and began snoring loudly. I left his cabin, assured that he would be of better spirit in the morrow. As I walked toward my quarters, I met Miss Priscilla. My heart began to pound as it always did when I was in her presence.

"How fares Elder Brewster?" she asked in a most caring way.

"He is sleeping soundly," I replied. Both of us remained silent for a long moment, then I added, "I pray that he shall be returned to good health in the morning. There are so many around who appear to have ailments much worse than his. It is a pity that these poor souls have come so far, only to be stricken at the end of their journey. But how fares your family, Miss Priscilla? I trust that they are well."

Her brown eyes showed that she was pleased with my interest in her family's well being.

"So far they have resisted the sickness, praise God," she replied. "But I wish that my father would lessen his exertions on the shore. He is a shoemaker, not a woodsman. I fear that if he continues to work at his present pace, he, too, shall suffer as the others."

"Shall I convey your concerns to him?" I asked.

"No," she said, smiling for the first time. "I am sure that your admonitions would cause him to press himself more. Although he thinks you an admirable man, I fain believe that he may not welcome your advice. He is as stubborn a worker as he is gentle a parent."

"I shall be guided by your advice, Miss Priscilla, for no one knows a father as does his daughter." I straightened up and looked intently at her face. Her smile was gone, replaced by her usual sad expression. I wanted to hold her close to me and comfort her. Instead, I verbalized my concern.

"Please remember, though, I remain your humble servant, and will do all in my power to help you and your family adjust to the present disagreeable conditions."

"And I thank you sincerely for your caring…John," she said, with a trace of a smile.

As I was about to profess that my heart was now in her keeping, she turned and walked away. All that night, I spent tossing and turning in my bunk.

Early the following morning, four settlers and I went ashore. The cold December wind chilled us, but the sky was clear. My assignment was to assist with the building of Captain Standish's house. The others, with sickles and two dogs, went to fetch additional thatch for the roof of the Common House. The sky grew increasingly cloudy through the morning. By afternoon the rain began to fall heavily. The downpour continued through that night and all of the next day, bringing delay to the construction work and misery to all of the workers. The weather cleared at dusk on the second day and I returned to the Common House area. As I approached the site, I saw two men, tired, soaked, and nearly frozen to death, appear from out of the woods. The builders quickly gathered around them. We provided blankets and brandy and prodded the shivering men for an account of what appeared to have been a harrowing experience. Peter Browne took a gulp of his brandy, and began. He hesitated often as he spoke.

"The four of us went in search of thatch," he said, "as the governor told us to do. About a half-mile from the settlement we found some, and cut enough for two large bales. John Goodman here and I stuck around to bind up the bundles. The other two men left us to search for more thatch."

One of the two searchers who had returned safely earlier interrupted.

"When we got back with the new load," he explained, "Peter and John was gone. We looked around and called out to them, but they didn't answer. We waited awhile, then when they didn't show up, we came back to the settlement with the bundled thatch."

Governor Carver recounted his response to the news that the two men were missing.

"When I heard about their dilemma," he said, "I became deeply concerned over their fate. Although the rain was heavy, I sought out four men to join me in searching for the two who had disappeared. We tramped through the woods but found no sign of them, so we returned to camp. I then organized a larger party. With them, I searched until dark, still without success. By that time we were thoroughly drenched and exhausted. I was wont to believe that the Indians had carried the men off and that there might be more savages around, so I had a secure camp set up and called off the search until morning."

Young John Crackston, one of the governor's search party, added, "We built a large bonfire on the beach, and tried to dry out, but we was still frozen and wet come morning."

Governor Carver ignored the youngster's interruption and continued to speak.

"We had hoped that the fire would be a signal for the lost men, but by daybreak there was still no sign of them. I then selected ten men, told them to bring their weapons, and we set out to scour the area for any trace of our missing brothers. We searched all day in torrential rain, but found no sign or sight of them so we returned to the construction site, tired and wet. There, I detected great fear in the talk among the settlers. Any mention of Indians seems to bring about uneasiness."

The Governor hesitated to catch his breath, and Edward Fuller, one of the men at the building site, eager to contribute, broke in.

"Just a short time ago, to our surprise, the two lost men staggered out of the woods. They were thoroughly soaked and looked exhausted. We thought it odd that John Goodman was wearing only one shoe, but he told us he had to cut it off his foot because his toes were frostbitten."

As the two weary souls sat on a log near the fire, shivering, two settlers, willing to face the rain unprotected, offered their coats for additional warmth. After draining the cups of warm tea that had been handed to them, the wanderers related the story of their travail.

John Goodman began speaking. His words were punctuated by the chattering of his teeth.

"Shortly after our two companions left us to seek out additional thatch, we finished binding the thatch we had. When we got hungry, we decided to eat some of the meat that we had brought along. There was nothing to drink, so we took the spaniel and the mastiff bitch and set out to find some drinkable water. After walking for a while, we came upon a large lake. The dogs were hungry, and when they spotted a deer in the woods close by, they ran after it. We chased the dogs for a very long time. When we finally caught up with them, we couldn't find our way back to the thatch area."

The listeners looked at each other and gasped. I understood their emotion for I have often thought about what it would be like to be alone in Indian territory. The still-shivering John Goodman continued.

"It was raining hard, and we had no protection, for we didn't bring our rain capes when we left the ship—it wasn't even raining then." This observation brought a chuckle from the group.

"By late afternoon we were completely lost and thoroughly soaked," he continued, "so we decided to look for an abandoned wigwam or something else to shield us from the downpour. We were frightened. We only had our sickles for protection. We knew that we had to keep moving to find some kind of shelter from the rain and biting winds or else we'd freeze to death. By nightfall we were too tired and wet to continue our search, so we curled up under a big pine tree. About midnight we heard the roaring of lions. Peter even thought he heard one come close to us. We both climbed trees to protect ourselves, but the wind blew too cold for us to stay up there. We came down and stood upright, leaning against a big tree, the shivering dogs beside us, for the rest of the night. Lucky for us, no animals or Indians showed up."

Peter Browne, still shaking from the cold, broke in.

"We were wet and hungry," he said. "We knew we had better find our way back or we would freeze or starve to death. We tramped through the thick woods and even waded through icy streams, but we didn't recognize anything like the route we had first taken. Fortunately, John here had the good sense to seek out some high ground, which we finally found in the afternoon. From the hilltop we could see the harbor, so we proceeded in that direction. As we neared the shore, we saw smoke from your fire and followed it back to here. We consider ourselves fortunate, for one more night of exposure would have brought us to our doom."

Governor Carver, in his usual scholarly voice, spoke.

"We are thankful that you have returned safely, gentlemen," he said, "but, remember, we are not in Africa. There are no lions here to my knowledge. The sounds you heard were probably wolves, a common threat to unarmed men."

Then, as he kneeled, he added, "Now, let us all say a prayer for your salvation. There have been already too many of our brothers who have crossed the divide. We must thank Divine Providence that you did not join them this day."

The group knelt on the soggy ground and offered thanks. I was pleased to join them. Before I returned to the *Mayflower*, I could see that the Common House had been completely re-roofed. I was told that many beds, brought from the ship, had been placed in the new building. Also, a goodly number of ill settlers, protected from the rain by canvas, had been brought ashore during the day so they could rest in the clean atmosphere of the finished structure. Although I elected to go back to the ship, most of the able men remained on land, housed in makeshift shelters. The next day was a Sabbath, and it was to be the first celebrated on shore by all of the passengers. I went early to my berth in the crew's quarters, weary from the day's hectic activities. Morpheus arrived quickly, but did not embrace me for long. About midnight, I was awakened abruptly by loud wailing and screaming, all coming from the upper deck. I rushed topside to find out what was causing the great commotion.

"Look, look!" one lady yelled as she wildly gestured toward shore. "Our settlement is on fire!"

"It must be the savages," another shouted. "They've probably murdered our people!"

Another screamed, "They've set fire to all of our buildings!"

I looked toward shore, and saw a small, but brisk, blaze coming from the Common House.

"'Tis a single fire," I said hopefully and calmly, "and I'm sure it will soon be attended to by the settlers on shore."

My words, however, were lost in the screams. Within the hour the fire died down and was gone from our view. With its disappearance, the screaming ceased, and the only light visible came from the ship's lanterns and the few stars that peeked through the dark curtain of clouds overhead.

At dawn, with a few other men, I traveled on the longboat to shore to see what had happened during the night. When we arrived at the Common House, several settlers rushed toward us, all anxious to tell the story of the fire.

"We was all pretty much asleep," blurted John Alderton, one of the hired seamen, "when a light from a candle lit fire to the dry thatching on the roof. We all fetched water from the brook with whatever pails we could find, and threw it up to the ceiling. Lotta people got wet, 'n' a heap uv clothes was burnt, but we finally got the fire out. No one got hurt. The place was real crowded with sick people, even the Guv'nor and Master Brewster was there in bed. Lucky no timbers was burned, only thatch. Lucky, too, there wasn't a big 'splosion 'cuz everyone's musket was in the building, and open kegs of gunpowder was there, too. Lot of the ailin' people got outta bed and helped us move the explosives outside. Coulda been one big bang, but there warn't."

Those on the ship who were able soon joined the group on shore for the first land-based Sabbath service, but the excitement of the fire and the burned condition of the Common House prevented the planned service from being held. At nightfall, many of the settlers and I boarded the shallop and returned to the ship.

The next day saw torrential rains. Little building was accomplished as no shipside workers were able to get to shore. Many of the following days were clear with sunshine, however, allowing great progress to be made on home construction.

On the 20th and 21st of January, quantities of food and supplies were brought ashore and stored in both the Common House and a small shack next to it. More ailing passengers were also transported to land. This brought great relief to Master Jones, who was waiting patiently to have his ship cleared.

The 22nd was a Sabbath, the sixth Sunday in the harbor. The weather was favorable, and the planters held their long-awaited service on shore in the Common House. Most of our prayers were for the many settlers who were sick, and for the souls of the departed.

The next week saw more supplies taken ashore and good progress made on the individual dwellings, although none was completed. On Sunday, under cloudy skies, we held the Sabbath meeting on shore again. Mistress Rose, wife of Captain Standish, was confined to her bed at the rear of the Common House. She was exceedingly ill and not able to participate in the service.

On Monday, despite frost and sleet, much of the settler's remaining goods were brought to shore. Progress was slow, but it was due to more than the weather. It was evident that a want of boats was also hindering the movement of supplies from the *Mayflower*. In the afternoon the skies cleared and the pace of unloading quickened somewhat. At dusk I visited the Common House to assist with the caring of the many settlers who were ill. The building was crowded with goods, beds that contained the sick and dying, and relatives trying to comfort their own. I threaded my way over to Captain Standish, who was next to his wife's bed. His eyes were swollen with the tears he refused to shed. Mistress Rose's eyes were permanently closed by death. He told me that she had a turn for the worse and had just taken her last breath. It was a sad sight seeing the captain, a man known for showing no emotion, close to weeping. After a long time, he looked up at me and said, "'Tis the Lord's will."

I remember responding softly, "Yes, I know."

Rose Standish was the eighth person to die that January. From the condition of others, both on the ship and on the shore, it was apparent that February's toll might be much greater. Every night I prayed fervently for the health of all of us, especially for Miss Priscilla and her family.

On the afternoon of the last day of January, Master Jones returned to the *Mayflower* with a number of fish. I joined the group listening to him tell of his day-long adventure. His voice was uncommonly upbeat.

"I took four sailors and went searching in the longboat for a good fishing area. As we neared Clarke Island, where our first landing in the New World was made, I sighted two Indians on shore. They were well painted all over, and both carried bows and arrows. I ordered the crew to row quickly to the island to confront them, but by the time we arrived, the savages had disappeared into the woods. I was fearful that we would be ambushed if we followed them, so we didn't. We continued our fishing expedition with some success, as you can see. Now we can all enjoy fish for supper. In light of our sighting, though, perhaps you should tell your leaders to better prepare for some kind of Indian activity."

As the settlers and crew dispersed, I wondered why we hadn't seen more of the Indians. Perhaps, I thought, they were gathering together to suffer us great harm. That evening, as we enjoyed a supper of fish in his dwelling, I shared my thoughts about the Indians with a despondent Captain Standish.

The next few days saw better weather, good progress on construction, and great concern all around about the increasing number of passengers in distress.

On the fourth day of February, the weather changed. A full-scale gale arose, subjecting the *Mayflower*, now light in the water due to lack of ballast, to a buffeting which nearly capsized her. Meanwhile, on shore, the settlers, despite the Sabbath restriction, worked hard to keep their buildings from destruction by the storm. In the afternoon, the winds diminished, and services were held. After our prayer meeting, Governor Carver announced that a small house, the first to be completed, was going to be commandeered to provide additional shelter for the sick because the Common House was too crowded.

Five days later, a chance spark ignited the roof thatch on the small shelter. The fire, as the one previous to it, was put out without harm to the timbers or the ill people it housed. Late in the afternoon of the same day, Master Jones and two crewmen went ashore in search of game. They returned with five geese and a large deer. He said the Indians had killed the beast and had cut off both antlers. When they came upon the site, the Indians were nowhere to be seen, and a wolf was eating the entrails. The furry predator ran when the men approached. The master offered the fowl to the sick settlers, keeping the deer for himself and his crew. The hungry settlers praised the hunter for his generosity.

Sadly, each night we endured more and more trips to the burial ground. Scurvy, bowel and lung diseases, and other wretched sicknesses were claiming the lives of both settlers and seamen. As the number of bedridden souls increased, the number of those capable of caring for them decreased. I spent many of my waking hours tending those in distress. Although I had no experience with woman's work, I fetched wood, made fires, dressed meat, clothed and unclothed the ailing, and even washed their smelly garments. I performed these necessary offices willingly and with as much good attitude as I could muster, as did the few others capable of doing so.

The 16th of February opened ominously. Dark clouds hung low in the sunless sky. In the afternoon, one of the colonists came running from the woods toward the settlement where we were working. He told us a tale that struck fear in the hearts of those who were huddled around him. Nearly bent over from exhaustion, he spoke breathlessly.

"I left in the morning to seek out ducks for our supper," he said. "In the afternoon, I was hiding in a little blind I had put together when I spied twelve Indians sneaking toward the settlement. I also heard loud noises away in the woods and figured that many more natives were nearby. I was sorely concerned for the safety of our colony. When the twelve Indians were out of sight, I hurried along another route back to camp to let you all know of my sighting."

On the same day, Captain Standish told us of his frightening experience.

"Francis Cooke and I went into the woods in the morning to fell trees," he related. "About noon we returned to the settlement to eat, leaving our tools back at the clearing. When we went back to continue our work, the tools were gone, no doubt taken away by the natives. We hurried back to tell the governor about the missing implements."

The two instances of Indian activity motivated us to assemble, take up arms, and prepare to withdraw to the Common House where we could better defend ourselves. We waited there in readiness, our weapons charged. No Indians appeared. The two encounters prompted Captain Standish, uncertain of the natives' intentions, to declare that we must immediately prepare ourselves for confrontation. Later, aboard ship, when told of the day's events, our leaders also showed great concern. After our evening meal, we convened a meeting in the Great Cabin and decided that all able men would meet on shore the next day to vote for a military leader and to make plans for our defense. After dark, we spotted a great fire back on land, where we knew the Indians to be. I slept little that night.

We held our morning meeting on shore as planned, but many passengers were not well enough to attend. Governor Carver put forward the name of Captain Miles Standish for military commander, and a majority of the colonists present voted for him. The Governor then gave Standish the title of Captain General, with full authority in all military affairs. Before our meeting was brought to adjournment, his first official action was thrust upon him.

Two Indians, their dark bodies painted with strange designs, appeared on a hill less than 400 yards from the place where we were assembled. They made signs for us to join them. We readied our arms, and awaited orders from Captain Standish. He motioned to the Indians to come across a shallow brook to where we were gathered. They remained in place. Noises from the woods behind the two natives indicated that there were many others with them, all hidden from view. The captain placed his musket on the ground as a sign of friendship, then he and Stephen Hopkins crossed the brook and cautiously moved toward the place where the two savages were standing. We watched as our two emissaries strode up the hill, proud and unafraid. We then heard even louder noises coming from the surrounding woods. Before the captain and Mr. Hopkins could get close to the Indians, however, the natives turned and ran back into the forest. We saw our men hesitate, then turn around, and come back to our meeting place. When they rejoined us, they explained that from the sounds coming from the woods, they knew that a large number of Indians were hiding there. They said that it would have been foolhardy to pursue them further. Captain Standish then insisted that we off-load our heavy weapons from the *Mayflower* as soon as possible. These, he noted, must be mounted in haste atop the wooden platform previously built for them, on the hill at the end of the street where we could command the ground all around. With an increased feeling for the need for security, we all returned to our work.

The next day, February 18th, was a Sabbath. We abstained from work, save tending to the needs of the sick on ship and on shore. Many were near death, and these were ministered to as best we could. Almost every night we made trips to the burial ground, carrying one or more of our company in rugs. The outlook for the future was to be bleaker yet. I heard whisperings that if the sickness continued as it was doing, the whole colony could be deprived of inhabitants come spring.

On Monday, aided by the settlers, the sailors unloaded from the ship one of the cannon brought over by the colonists. It was a Minion and it has a 3-inch bore. It is capable of firing a 4-pound shot for a distance of 360 yards. After placing it on the beach next to another Minion brought from the ship two weeks earlier, the settlers worked on their dwellings. The following day, we brought ashore the heaviest piece, a Saker, which has a 4-inch bore, and can fire a 6-pound shot. We also unloaded two smaller cannon called Bases. These have a 1¼-inch bore and can fire a half-pound shot.

We dragged all of the guns up to the platform on the hill, then mounted them on their wooden carriages as Captain Standish directed. The heavy Saker, weighing 1500 pounds, required every able man to hoist it onto its sled. We then all had to pull together on the rope that only inched the mammoth weapon along the muddy path. By late afternoon we were exhausted, but all of the ordnance was in position. Captain Standish, obviously proud of the achievement, felt obliged to fire the Saker to test it. He had the newly appointed cannoneer, Edward Dotey, charge the weapon with powder. Once this was done, and all observers were clear of the piece, the captain thrust a lighted match into the cannon vent. The roar was deafening, and it reverberated through the forest and the settlement. It was clearly a warning to the Indians that we were here to stay.

Master Jones soon joined us. He brought with him a fat goose he had shot. The settlers provided a crane, a mallard, and some dried ox tongue to complement the meal. Both passengers and crew prepared to feast atop the platform on the uncommon abundance of food. Our exuberance was short-lived, however. Thomas English, one of the sailors hired by the colonists, approached us as we were eating. His breathing was labored from his run up the hill and the poor condition of his health. He went directly to Governor Bradford.

"Guvnor," he said, "you are sorely needed at the ship. Master Mullins is lying near to death, and he is calling for you to take his directions as to his property." I accompanied Governor Bradford down the hill, past the many unfinished dwellings, and the partially completed stockade that was being erected around the settlement. The governor and I were then transported by the longboat to the *Mayflower*. Once aboard, we maneuvered between the many praying souls who were huddled in knots around their suffering relatives and friends. At Master Mullin's bedside were his two children, Joseph and Priscilla, and Giles Heale, the ship's surgeon. Alice Mullins, lay in a bed next to her husband, quietly weeping. Her frail fingers held a soiled handkerchief over her face in a vain attempt to mask her distress. Governor Bradford, bending low in order to hear the whispers of the dying man, slowly transcribed his final testament. The governor then requested that Master Jones and Dr. Heale witness the document. I felt an overwhelming desire to approach and comfort Miss Priscilla but did not do so, for I saw no way of meaningfully lessening her grief. Before the sorrowful night was over, Master Mullins died, as did three others, including Master William White, father of Peregrine, the lusty-lunged babe born in Cape Cod Harbor. Next day, services for the dead were held on shore, attended by all of the company fit to rise from their beds. We occupied the following two days with house construction and bringing four small cannon, called Patereros, to the governor's house where they were set up to command the cross streets at that location.

Sunday, February 25th, was cold and clear. We held Sabbath services on shore, but these were interrupted when news that Mistress Mary, wife of Master Isaac Allerton, one of the tradesmen, died aboard ship. She was overcome by a lasting grief from losing her stillborn child about two months earlier. Solemn services and burial were conducted for her the next day.

CHAPTER FOURTEEN

On Tuesday, sickness and death appeared to be everywhere. Even the seamen did not escape the afflictions. We had lost several petty officers, including the master gunner, as well as three quartermasters, a cook and a third of the crew. Many died from the cold or scurvy, others from lack of proper food or exposure to the unsanitary conditions aboard ship. Our loss in February was severe: seventeen died, the greatest number in any month so far.

On the first of March, the weather improved a bit. At one o'clock in the afternoon on the third of March, we heard the first thunder since our landing. It was strong, with great claps. Within the hour a heavy rain started to fall. Four days later, it cleared, and under sunny skies the first planting took place, mainly peas and beans. Many women planted the seeds they had sewn into the hems of their dresses when they were back in Holland.

Friday, the 16th of March, began with fair and warmer weather. All able men gathered on shore to conclude the establishment of Military Orders, which had been interrupted previously by the appearance of the two Indians on the hill. Just as we resumed the discussion of possible responses to native incursions, Francis Cooke shouted, "Indian!" and pointed to a solitary figure walking briskly along the street toward where we were gathered. The man's body was unpainted and he was unclothed except for a narrow leather band around his waist, which supported a small covering fringe. He walked tall and straight, his black hair falling long in the back. His left hand clutched a bow and two arrows, one with an arrowhead, the other without.

Captain Standish cautiously picked up his musket and went forward to meet him, for he did not want the Indian to enter any of the houses he was walking by. As the native passed the houses, the anxious occupants came out cautiously with their muskets and swords. Before the captain came face to face with the intruder, the Indian stopped, raised his right hand, and said in a friendly voice, and in broken English, "Wel-come, Englishmen!"

We were all thunderstruck by the appearance of the Indian and his use of our tongue. We crowded around him to listen to his words, for he was the first native who had made direct contact with us since we arrived in New England.

"Me, Samoset," he said. "Me Sagamore, Chief of Morattigans at Pemmaquid. Me not from this woods. Come from place called Maine. There, Englishmen do fishing. Fishmen teach me how to say your talk. Land be five days from here by walk. Much hard, if walk. Not by fishing ship. One day, if wind be good. Me come to here by Captain Dermer. He fishman from Maine. Sail his ship. Get to these woods eight months ago. Now need beer to bring heat to body."

Francis Cooke, eager to hear more, but obviously embarrassed by the native's lack of covering, removed his red-laced horseman's coat and gingerly placed it over Samoset's broad shoulders. Others fetched him some gin, a biscuit, butter, cheese, a piece of roast duck, and some pudding, all of which he downed greedily as we watched. He rested for a moment and then began to impart the information we were anxious to hear.

"Englishmen now make home," he said, "on land of Patuxet. That tribe all go to big woods in sky, many moons ago. Bad spirit make none left. Now, Nauset hunt here. Same ones shoot arrows to you from woods. They no like Englishmen—your Captain Hunt take many braves across big water like animal. Nauset say bad thing he did."

The settlers looked at each other in disbelief. Could an Englishman actually do such a thing?

"Soon you meet Massasoit," Samoset continued. "He greatest sachem of all. Meet Tisquantum, too. He speak better for you to understand. Both good friend to Algonquin. Both good friend to Englishmen."

The Indian then proceeded to tell us, in language sometimes difficult to understand, much about the surrounding area, what tribes were still around, how many were in each tribe, and who their leaders were. We were appreciative of all this information, but by dusk, Samoset was still talking, with no sign of departure. We tried to take it all in, but the labors of the day were taking their toll. Captain Standish suggested to the friendly Indian that he could spend the night on the *Mayflower* if he cared to. Our new friend quickly nodded his assent. The three of us walked to the beach to take the shallop out to the ship, but the tide, which was out, and the high winds at the shore, prevented the shallop from making the trip. Stephen Hopkins joined us and offered to lodge the Indian in his house, which we all agreed was a fine solution. Captain Standish posted a guard outside the dwelling overnight as a precaution.

In the morning, Samoset expressed a desire to return to the Massasoits. Governor Carver presented him with a knife, a bracelet, and a ring. Master Hopkins urged him to return soon with many Massasoits to trade trinkets for beaver skins. Captain Standish informed the Indian that if he returned with others, all bows and arrows had to be left at least a quarter mile from the settlement. Samoset nodded. Before walking away, he warned us again about the Nausets. He was not gone from us for long.

Early the next morning, a Sabbath, he reappeared with five Indians. They, too, were tall and strongly built. All five were dressed in deerskin. Four wore leather leggings and aprons. The same four had wide black stripes down the centers of their faces, from the top of their brown foreheads to their hairless chins. The other Indian, obviously the leader, was not so marked. He carried a cat's skin over his arm. Apparently heeding Captain Standish's admonition, none carried a bow or arrow. They brought four valuable pelts with them, which they wanted to trade. Being Sunday, the settlers refused to truck with them. The Indians then produced, to our surprise, the tools that had been taken from Captain Standish and Francis Cooke in the woods. We gave them a few trifles as thanks for their return. They began to sing and dance after their fashion, no doubt as a sign of friendship. The leader opened the leather case he had around his waist and pulled out some pounded corn. We supplied him with water as he requested. He mixed it with the corn and shared the resulting mush with his companions. He then took some tobacco leaves from a small bag attached to the case. When the Indians started to drink[4] the tobacco using a pipe that they had brought along, Master Hopkins motioned that they should leave and return another day. He asked them, too, to bring back more skins for trucking when they returned. The five clothed Indians left, but Samoset claimed he felt ill and was permitted to stay overnight at the settlement.

The next day continued to be warm, a trend that seemed to improve the survival of the ailing settlers. The burials began decreasing in frequency. Unfortunately, Alice Mullins, Priscilla's mother, who had been bedridden since the loss of her husband, was not spared. Her gentle soul passed on about midday to a more perfect place. Three other men and I carried her body, wrapped in her rug, to the hidden burial ground. Her young son, Joseph, was too ill to attend his mother's solemn service on shore. It was apparent, from the state of his health, that he would join his parents fairly soon.

I could no longer bear staying away from Priscilla. My heart weighed heavy with her grief. She was living with the Brewster family since the passing of her father, and I took time from my shipboard and ministering duties to seek her out. I walked to the Brewster house and rapped on the door.

"John Alden," she said when she saw me. "'Tis a pleasure to see you. Please come in." The thought of once again being next to her brought me a level of pleasure I had seldom experienced. I walked through the doorway with some hesitation. Priscilla was making soup. She was alone. I find it difficult now to describe the pleasing smell coming from the soup that bubbled in the blackened kettle hanging over the fire. As she bustled about the small room, I spoke to her.

"I have come to offer my sympathies for the loss of your dear father and mother. They were fine people, and I was proud to know them. The whole settlement will miss them sorely....How fare you, Miss Priscilla?"

She stopped and turned toward me. There was a look of sadness on her face. I felt the urge to embrace her, but restrained myself.

"I do as well as anyone who has lost those most dear," she said, her eyes filling with tears.

"But there are many among us who have had greater misfortune, and my heart reaches out to them. The thing that most concerns me now, I fear, is the condition of my brother, Joseph. He lies with the fever at the Common House, and good Dr. Fuller says that he knows of nothing that can bring him back to health. If I lose him, John, I shall be alone in this strange land. My sister, Sarah, and my brother, William, now in England, surely will not come here to join me, for they have their own interests back home. Perhaps I should return to England when the opportunity presents itself, for there are few here I now perceive as family."

I felt the exhilaration drain from my body.

"Miss Priscilla," I said with compassion, "there are many here who love...who consider you as family. There are many here who have also lost loved ones and need comfort. The kind only you can provide. I, myself, would miss you greatly. Pray, put the thoughts of leaving from your mind."

"But I am scarcely eighteen, John, and I... "

"Eighteen, indeed, Miss Priscilla," I interrupted. "With the wisdom of one many times older. I...the settlers need you sorely, and, I believe, they will not countenance your talk of leaving."

"Then I shall speak of it no further, John. I shall do as you think best, for I remember your pledge to my father that you will attend to our interests if he no longer can."

"That was my promise then, and it is, perforce, a pledge that I hold with greater strength today. I shall continue to care for you both, Miss Priscilla. That is, if you allow me to."

"Joseph and I require you to, John," she said, "And we thank you the more for your honoring your promise to my father at this time."

She may have requested that I stay and partake of her fragrant soup. Perhaps she said goodbye. For my part, as I left the house, I seemed to hear only the sweet singing of birds that were nowhere in sight, and the soft ringing of bells that seemed to come from heaven. I slept very well that night. Very well, indeed.

At some point during the night, however, one of the seamen sharing our quarters hit me in the head with one of his boots. He yelled that I was snoring so loud that nobody could sleep. I opened my eyes, threw his boot back at him, turned on my side, and returned to my pleasant dreams of Priscilla.

When I rose in the morning, I was still thinking about her. The weather was again warm, and the blazing sun was lifting itself slowly out of the water on the eastern horizon. I quickly downed my breakfast of mush, salted beef, biscuits, and cold water. Within the hour, I was in the longboat, headed for shore, where I planned to continue attending to the needs of the sick. When I arrived at the Common House, I was told that Samoset was still at the settlement, and that he had shown no inclination to leave. I spent the day doing what I could for the bedridden settlers.

Finally, on Wednesday morning, after three nights in town, the colonists told Samoset that he had to go. Before he left, he told us again to beware of the Nausets, and how disappointed he was that the Massasoits had not returned to the settlement with skins to barter.

Later in the day, we convened a third meeting in the Common House for the discussion of military orders that had been interrupted twice before by the appearance of Indians. After an hour of meeting, we heard women shouting outside.

"Indians! Indians!" one was yelling, and another, "There are three of them. They're going to attack the settlement!" We hurried outside, and saw the three natives standing boldly on a hill nearby. Whetting their arrowheads and flexing their bows in a threatening manner, they seemed to be daring us to come and fight. Captain Standish and Thomas Rogers, together with

Mayflower pilots Coppin and Clarke—all armed with muskets—strode toward them in a confident manner. The Indians thrust their bows forward in one last act of defiance, then turned and ran back into the woods. We once again abandoned our attempt to complete the establishment of military orders that we so needed to do.

Earlier in the day the ship's carpenter, weak from scurvy, had been persuaded to continue fitting out the shallop so it could carry furniture and goods to shore. The rest of the day was spent bringing the remaining items still on the *Mayflower* to the few completed dwellings and the storehouse. By evening everyone, along with all possessions, had been brought to land, leaving the ship ready to take on ballast and prepare for the journey back to England.

The next day Samoset returned. He brought four painted Indians with him. One was Tisquantum, the Patuxet we had been promised the previous day. Tisquantum claimed to be the last surviving member of the Patuxets, the tribe that lived on the land where our settlement was now being built. Tisquantum was called Squanto by the English. He told us an almost unbelievable story.

"Many years ago," he said, "Tisquantum and four Patuxet trapped by English Captain George Weymouth. He take us back to land across the great water. We all learn English talk, so can tell people about our woods, and how many braves hunt there. I spend nine years across great water. I meet there Captain John Smith. He promise to take me back to my land. Captain Smith good man. Honest man. He travel here to make map of coast. He sail me back to my people. He call my land, New Plymouth. He sail with other ship. That ship have chief, Captain Thomas Hunt, who come to my land to fish. Captain Smith tell Captain Hunt not go to home until he dry fish he catch. Fish used to truck for beaver skins. Captain Hunt, him bad man."

"Why do you say he is a bad man?" asked Stephen Hopkins. Squanto's face darkened, then he continued.

"He stay at Plymouth and say he want to truck with braves, but he put twenty Patuxet in irons, also Tisquantum. He then sail along coast and find seven Nauset. He put them in irons, like Patuxet. Sail all braves to Spain to sell for money. Most braves taken to Africa, but Tisquantum saved by good friars in Spain. They try teach me Jesus. Englishman take me to England. Stay with rich man there. Soon meet Captain Dermer. He say he make trip to my land. Tisquantum sail with Captain Dermer. When stop at Maine, Tisquantum find Samoset and sail to here. Tisquantum find no braves, only bones and old wigwams. All Patuxet taken away by big sickness."

"That must have been why there was no Indian settlement here when we arrived," Captain Standish said. "Now we know why for certain."

Squanto ignored the interruption. "Samoset and Tisquantum join Massasoits, who be friends to us. Now you settle on Patuxet land. Tisquantum now be friend to Englishmen."

Samoset then spoke, in a manner more difficult to understand. "Great sagamore, Massasoit, in woods by here. He with his brother, Quadequina, and many warriors. Samoset say to you before, he come, and now he has."

As the two Indians spoke, Massasoit with a single feather rising from his black hair, and many of his men, all fiercely painted, appeared on a hill nearby. They made no effort to approach. Squanto, fearing a confrontation, ran across the brook that separated us and up the hill to where the chief was standing. He briefly exchanged words with Massasoit and then returned, running, to where we were gathered.

"Great Chief wants speak to you. Says you send man to talk."

"If he wants to parley," countered Governor Carver, "let him come to us."

Squanto ran with the message back to the group of Indians. Our answer was apparently not acceptable to the chief. He remained defiant, still on the hill with his some sixty-odd braves. The atmosphere turned tense. We all knew that we had less than one-third the force the Indians had, and that even with our armor and muskets, we were no match for them in battle. Minutes passed. Both leaders stood firm. The tension increased.

Out of desperation, Edward Winslow, always the diplomat, asked to be allowed to approach Massasoit alone. Governor Carver refused his request. Master Winslow persisted. The governor refused again. Our men readied their muskets. Finally, Carver gave in to Master Winslow's request and instructed him to tell the chief that we want peace and that we would like to trade with him. He also called for food, drink, and trinkets, which he gave to Master Winslow to bring to the Indians. The gifts included a knife and a jeweled earring for Quadequina, and two knives, a jeweled pendant and some brandy for the leader. We watched anxiously as our courageous envoy walked alone across the brook to meet with Massasoit. The sachem appeared to be pleased with the gifts. He communicated to Squanto that he wanted to truck for Master Winslow's sword and corselet. After a long discussion, and still not being able to convince our representative to make the trade, the great Sagamore, with twenty of his men, came toward us. I could see that the Indians carried no weapons. Quadequina remained on the hill, holding Master Winslow as hostage. Captain Standish and Isaac Allerton led a group of six men, all armed with muskets, to the side of the brook to meet and salute the chief and his party.

It was a strange sight, indeed, to see our heavily bearded contingent, all rigged out in military finery and looking as martial and formidable as possible, greeting the much taller and more powerfully built, beardless, Indian band. Captain Standish, at least three heads shorter than Massasoit, moved to the right of him. Then he and *Mayflower* mate Andrew Williamson, with the rest of us bringing up the rear, escorted the Indians down our single town street, strutting proudly past small groups of astonished spectators.

All of the Indians were dressed alike in deerskin with heavily painted faces. Some were decorated in black, others in white or yellow. Massasoit alone had a red face and wore a long, heavy chain of white bone beads around his neck. To the chain were fastened a knife in front and a small leather tobacco pouch behind. He was also the tallest of the group and appeared to be a solemn and dignified man, sparing of speech and grave in manner. He offered six of his men as hostages for the safe return of Master Winslow. Once at the settlement, we hastily furnished a partially completed house with a green rug and cushions to provide a suitable meeting place. Shortly after the sachem had settled on the cushions, and we had crowded around Captain Standish, we heard a blaring of horns and a rolling of drums coming from the street. Through the single window, we could see Governor Carver and a squad of armed settlers approaching the house. The governor entered alone, his face solemn and his demeanor authoritative. Massasoit promptly rose and kissed the governor's hand. Carver reciprocated, then smiled. He called for a portion of meat and a pot of hard liquor. When they came in on a wooden tray, he took a drink, toasting the leader. Massasoit took the pot and downed a substantial quantity. His eyes soon began to water, and he started to sweat profusely.

As Captain Standish, a few of the armed settlers, and I watched from the sidelines, the two leaders sat and ate. Using Squanto and Samoset as interpreters, they negotiated a treaty of peace that was favorable to both our sides. First and foremost, they pledged not to cause harm to one another. Also, if the peace were broken by an Indian, this person was to be sent to Plymouth for punishment, and, likewise, if the offender were a settler, his punishment was to come from the Indians. Indians were to leave arms behind when visiting, and the colonists were to do the same on their visits. They pledged, too, that if either side were attacked unjustly by outsiders, the other side was to provide assistance immediately. The terms of the agreement were slowly transcribed by Governor Carver. He signed the finished document and handed it to Massasoit. The chief assured the governor that the pact would apply to all tribes under his control. He then had Squanto read the document to him in its entirety. He nodded as each condition was read to him then, with a great flourish, made his mark.

It was a friendly meeting, and the agreement that was reached was far beyond our expectations. When the formality was over, the sachem, in an imperial manner, rose and left the house. With fitting ceremony, again to the sound of horn and drum, the chief and his men were escorted by some of us to our side of the brook. The governor and Massasoit again embraced. Master Winslow had not returned, so Captain Standish held the Indian hostages. Massasoit and the rest of his party then crossed over the brook and soon disappeared into the woods. Squanto and Samoset remained with us. Moments later, Massasoit's brother Quadequina and a company of Indians appeared. They came over the brook and approached us. Quadequina called for Squanto, then spoke to him in a language none of us could understand.

Squanto turned toward us. There was a look of anxiety on his face. "Quadequina say he want party, like Massasoit," he said.

"Then so he shall," declared the governor. He called for some food and drink. The meal was accompanied by loud and discordant music from the drums and horns of the relieved settlers. The Indians seemed to delight in the sounds. After two hours of enjoyment not seen since we arrived at Plymouth, Quadequina called upon his braves to return with him to their temporary home. Soon after they left, Stephen Hopkins pointed to the woods and called out, "Look, here comes Goodman Winslow!"

We all turned and watched as the Indian's sole hostage walked toward us. We then released the Indians we had held. From the woods beyond we could hear the sounds of the Indians setting up camp, at a distance, we supposed, of less than half a mile. Captain Standish, equally trustful and cautious, assigned a group of settlers to stand watch through the night.

CHAPTER FIFTEEN

The next day, Friday, March 23rd, was a fair day. Most of the snow was gone, and we could hear the birds squawking over their territorial rights. A few Indians came to visit us early in the morning, seeking food and drink. They indicated that Massasoit⁵ would like some of our people to visit him. Captain Standish and Master Allerton elected to go and see the chief. The Indians visiting us stayed and wandered around the settlement until ten in the morning. Before they left, the governor filled a kettle with dried peas from our supply and gave it to them to take to Massasoit. In the afternoon, Captain Standish and his companion came back to the settlement. Many of us gathered around to hear them tell about their stay with the Indians. Master Allerton began.

"We were greeted cordially when we arrived. Women and children were about, all curious to see our faces and our garb. Families lived among the trees. Wigwams dotted the grounds, and shelters were being built of branches and leaves. We were escorted to the Sagamore's hut, where he greeted us with good cheer. We sat on the ground and enjoyed the shelled nuts given to us. Massasoit offered us a pipe and tobacco, which we smoked, as did he and two of his braves."

Captain Standish, looking pleased, continued the story.

"They did not speak a word we could understand, but our visit was friendly. We certainly gained a new vision of Indian life. We can perhaps now consider them more friendly than heretofore. I was sorry that I didn't have my musket, for another demonstration to them of the weapon's power would add assurance to our newfound belief in their friendship. Allerton here told me that would have been a bad idea." I saw both adventurers smile at each other.

All who heard the story agreed that there was no apparent threat in the Indians' attitude toward us, and we could, perforce, treat them less like hostile savages.

Captain Standish called for a fourth meeting to once and for all address the subject of military orders and perhaps enact some laws with which to govern our new colony. The settlers who were able gathered in the Common House. When discussion of both matters was complete, we took a vote to elect a governor for the coming year. Master John Carver, who was elected governor for the *Mayflower* passage, was elected to his first full term on land.

Squanto, who was staying with us, had left alone at noon on the same day to fish for eels. He returned at nightfall with all he could carry. He explained to us how he waded into the water and caught the slippery fish using only his hands. Some of us expressed doubt about his ability to catch eels that way. Anyway, we cooked the catch for supper. They were all quite fat and sweet to the tongue.

The next day, Saturday, was as sad as the previous one had been joyful. Mistress Elizabeth, wife of Edward Winslow, died in the Common House, as did Oceanus, the babe born during the Atlantic crossing. He was the son of Stephen and Elizabeth Hopkins, whose other three children remain with us.

Of greater consequence to me was the passing, that same day, of James Mullins, brother of Miss Priscilla. She, then, was the last of the Mullins family alive, and my pledge to her father to care for surviving members of his family bore heavily on my mind. I found it difficult to share my sorrow with Priscilla because I sensed her grief was far beyond any I had ever known. When I approached her and offered my simple condolence, she requested that I help carry her brother's body to the hidden gravesite on the hill. Three settlers and I brought the young boy's remains to the burial site and placed them in a spot next to his loving parents. I passed the rest of my day thinking about Priscilla and watching, with sadness, the *Mayflower* crew bring ballast, wood and water to the ship in preparation for its return journey to England.

The next day was a Sabbath, the fourteenth in our new land. Most of our prayers were for the many dear friends and relatives lost since we arrived. The weather, gratefully, continued to improve, as did the physical condition of the settlers and crew.

I spent the next few days tending to those among us still ailing, assisting with the building of dwellings, and joining the hunting parties in search of game. When I had time I would stand on the beach where I could see sailors on the *Mayflower* overhauling the rigging, loading ballast, and stowing the wood and casks of water. I wondered if I would be missed by the crew, since there would be no cooper on board for the voyage back to England.

On Thursday, Master Jones tried to persuade all of us to return with him, for he feared for our safety if we stayed here in the wilderness. Not a single person gave in to his solicitations, nor did anyone appear to waiver in their resolve. As the ship neared departure, though, I could sense increasing anxiety in the brave company that had decided to remain. I, too, felt some fear, but this was quickly dispelled by what I perceived to be great courage and determination on the part of others.

CHAPTER SIXTEEN

On Sunday, we spent the full day in prayer. Many of the ship's crew participated. Even Master Jones and his officers joined us as their labors allowed.

Most of the settlers and I spent Monday and Tuesday aiding the crew load their remaining supplies. None of the fancy lumber, furs or other items promised to the Adventurers in London who financed our trip was available, although a few skins and roots were put aboard for our sponsors as a token, indicating the promise of the riches to come.

Late on Wednesday, I shook hands with the departing sailors and said my farewell to Master Jones. I struggled to hold back tears as I said my many goodbyes. Looking around the beach I could see similar responses by the other settlers and crew as they tendered their farewells. I saw promises being made, letters being passed, and friends' and relatives' names being transcribed. At dusk, the crew was seated in the longboat, with oars held steady just above the foaming water. Master Jones reached out and shook the hand of Elder Brewster as a final gesture. The oars were then dipped into the sea, and the longboat moved slowly away. We could hear the sailors singing their nautical ditties as they moved closer to their ship. Everyone on shore was aware that they were watching the final trip out to the *Mayflower*. Such was the day before the leaving of our last link with home.

Early the next morning, Thursday, April 5th in the year of our Lord, 1621, I stood with the brave group of settlers on the shore of Plymouth, New England, watching the sails on the *Mayflower* being set for its departure. As the good ship turned toward the harbor entrance, we saw her ensign being raised. When it finally stood atop the mainmast, fluttering in the stiff breeze, we saw a great puff of smoke coming from the side of the ship. Moments later, we heard the sound of her cannon, bidding us a final goodbye. Shortly after, behind us on the hill, our own ordnance fired a loud salute. It seemed to be a fitting response to the ship's parting shot. We watched for over an hour as the *Mayflower*'s hull grew smaller and smaller, finally becoming a dot, with a bit of white sitting on top.

When the spot disappeared below the horizon, and only the sails were visible, I joined the others and ran back to the gun platform, which was at a higher elevation. This location afforded a view of the fast disappearing vessel for a longer time. Before long, the sight of the sails was gone.

I shared the feeling of abandonment that the other settlers were obviously experiencing. For a long time I stared at the empty stretch of water. When I turned, I saw that most of the men were on their knees, with hats off and heads bowed. Here, I thought, were some of the few souls that had survived the curse of winter and were yet well enough to view the departure of the ship that had brought them to this unknown frontier. From the original group of 102 passengers, only about half remained. Buried next to those who hadn't survived were half of Master Jones' shipmates. There was no doubt that our greatest challenges were still ahead. The ship we had just seen disappear from our view was no longer available as a shelter. It was also our last connection with England, and home. Now the nearest friendly colony, Jamestown, in the territory of Virginia, was hundreds of miles away, and our greatest threat lurked nearby, hidden in the woods. I pondered, too, over the tragedies that had befallen us since we arrived, and the many blessings that Divine Providence had bestowed, which allowed at least some of us to survive.

While surveying the kneeling multitude, my eyes fell upon Miss Priscilla. She was standing with her head bowed, her eyes closed, and her palms pressed firmly together in prayer. I walked to her side and stood silently, admiring the depth of her beauty. Beside me was the one I cared about the most, I thought. Courageous, capable, gentle, and caring. I could feel my pulse pound as never before. After a long time, she opened her eyes.

"John," she said, "you startled me. Did you watch the ship go?"

"Yes, Miss Priscilla," I answered softly, "and it is a sad day for us all. I pray that we survive its leaving."

"Of course we shall," she countered. "With God's help, and sturdy men such as you to protect us, our life shall be as one day we had dreamed it to be."

"Miss Priscilla, may I be so bold as to tell you of how I have often dreamed it to be?"

"You would honor me by doing so," she said. I detected a welcome sincerity in her reply.

"My dreams have always been frequented by your image," I began, hesitantly. "Your inner strength and great beauty live with me day and night. I chop down trees for you; I build houses for you; I tend the sick for you. I even picture you across from me when I eat at my table. Your visage never leaves me, nor do I wish it to."

"Why, John Alden," she replied, "you make more of me than I warrant. For sooth, I have been courted by many men—even the stalwart, Captain Standish asked for my hand after Rose, his good wife, died. But no one has ever spoken to me as eloquently as you just have."

"I pray that I have not offended you, Miss Priscilla, for that is not my intention. I shall leave at once if you so desire."

"You flatter me, sir. You do not offend me. Please stay and tell me more of your dreams."

"Of a surety, I fear that I may speak words that you will find too arrogant."

"I cherish every word you utter, John, so please tell me what is in your heart."

"My heart…my heart is brimful of your presence, Miss Priscilla, as my mind is likewise full of thoughts of you. Would that you had similar thoughts, and also visions such as mine. I see our lives bound fast together, through endless time. My hope and dreams are only with thee, Miss Priscilla, for in this body, they no longer dwell."

"John…I have watched you daily and have never seen one cast in such a gentle mold. I, too, would welcome our joining together, for this has been a dream of mine since we first met. But I fear I have little to bring to our union, save the ten pounds my dear father left me in his will, and the seventy pairs of shoes he brought from Holland to use in trade."

"Miss Priscilla, I challenge any man to measure that as little."

"There shall never be another man so richly loved as you, John, for now you possess not only your own heart but forever mine as well."

"Miss Priscilla, you are as cherished as any maiden ever has been. You have, this day, made my every dream come true."

"Perhaps you would like to kiss my hand, Sir John, since you have so eloquently asked for it."

"Milady, with this kiss, I seal our betrothal. You bring me happiness beyond belief."

"As you also bring the same to me, dear John. And please address me in the future as Priscilla, for as of now, we perhaps are strangers no more."

"If such do pleasure you, Miss...that is, Priscilla, so shall I call thee. I will now work diligently on the completion of your family's house, which has been sore neglected since your dear father joined the multitude who are now with their Maker. When it is finished, we shall be married together by Elder Brewster, and I shall then have a suitable home for you, my bride."

"Your every wish is as mine, John. May I now take leave of you and announce the engagement that I have so fervently prayed for, for longer than you can imagine?"

Reluctantly, I bade my new fiancée farewell. I kissed her gently on the lips as I had so often dreamed of doing, then watched her walk—nay, skip—down the hill, to inform whom she would of our newfound joy.

CHAPTER SEVENTEEN

The last of the settlers have walked slowly back down the hill toward the settlement, and I now stand here in the early afternoon alone, jubilant over Miss Priscilla's decision to be my wife. I am at the same time fearful of the danger from the loss of so many of our company. There remains, today, such a small part of our original group from England.

But now I must overcome the past and savor the new hope that infuses us. The weather is improving daily, the Indians appear not to be as savage as we first feared, and seeds are being planted for the food we have been so deprived of this winter past. Although many that came with us are now with their forefathers, there still remains a sturdy lot of survivors who wish to build a new colony, a solid foundation from which the Good News of God can be spread to the natives on these shores. For we are truly planters, and, if our Lord looks with favor upon us, our seed shall multiply and establish, forever, a land of freedom to which all men and women can come and flourish.

Yea, at this time I would gladly surrender all of my worldly possessions if I could but fathom what Divine Providence has planned for our future.

EPILOGUE

The *Mayflower* left Plymouth harbor on April 5, 1621. Master Jones had kept her there for five months, considerably longer than he had expected, to provide shelter for the settlers who had few buildings to protect them from the fury of the New England winter. He also delayed his departure because more than half of his crew had died from the same maladies that had befallen the settlers, and he didn't want to cross the Atlantic undermanned during the stormy months of January, February, and March. The *Mayflower* reached England on May 6, 1621. It was a relatively rapid voyage, taking less than half the time it took to sail to New England. She had a refit at her home port and returned to merchant service for a short time. Master Christopher Jones died in March of 1622, probably from the aftereffects of his trip with the Pilgrims. He had married, eighteen years earlier in 1603, a second wife, Josian, widow of Richard Grey of Harwich. She inherited his portion of ownership of the ship. It was held in port while her husband's will was probated, a period of years. The ship deteriorated during that time and was valued, in 1624, together with "one suit of worn sails" and her fittings, at a bit over £138. Due to its poor condition after such a long period of disuse it was probably cut up and sold for firewood, then a valuable commodity.

Despite having the *Mayflower* for protection, forty-seven, or almost half, of the settlers died from the cold, malnutrition or scurvy while the ship remained in New England. Included were thirteen of the original eighteen wives. However, twenty-one of the children under sixteen survived. It is likely that the parents, especially the mothers, sacrificed themselves to keep their children alive. Of the twenty-four original households, four were completely eliminated. Only four remained untouched.

The peace agreement consummated with Massasoit, who died more than forty years after the *Mayflower* landed, lasted throughout his lifetime and continued for some years afterward, although some Indian tribes not under his control threatened the settlement during that period.

Squanto remained with the colonists and eagerly taught them how to trap animals, plant, fertilize, and fish. Without his caring attitude, it is doubtful whether the fledgling settlement would have survived its second winter. In 1622, however, Squanto was charged by the settlers of duplicity and was nearly put to death in accordance with the terms of the original peace treaty. Both sides, however, showed compassion and agreed to let him live.

Governor Carver died shortly after the *Mayflower* left for England. William Bradford was elected to the fill the vacancy and was re-elected to the office no less than thirty times.

Captain-General Miles Standish remarried. He wooed Bridget Fuller by correspondence while she lived in England. He then sailed there and brought her back to Plymouth. She was the widow of Edward Fuller, one of the settlers who had died earlier. Fuller had hoped to bring Bridget to America when the settlement was established. With Bridget, Standish had four sons. He and his family moved to Duxbury, a few miles from Plymouth, in 1632, when the new town was first settled. He died there in 1656.

Priscilla's young man in Leyden, Jacques de la Noyes, later changed to Delano, married another soon after the Mullins family came to Plymouth. In November of 1621 on the *Fortune*, the first ship to arrive after the *Mayflower*, his brother Philippe came to court Priscilla, but she was betrothed to Alden. Philippe fought in the Pequot War. He married Hester Dewsbury in 1633. Their son, Thomas, got John Alden's daughter, Rebecca, pregnant and there was a shotgun wedding. The carnal couple were banished to the wilderness and lived in a house on land John Alden gave them. John and Priscilla's wedding was the second performed in New England.[6] John and Priscilla had eleven children, and over fifty grandchildren. The first three or four years of their marriage were spent in Plymouth, where some of their children were born. They then moved to Duxbury. The site of their first house, in Plymouth, is marked today with a marble slab. The house in Duxbury, where John Alden died, still stands and is maintained as a National Historic Site.

During his lifetime Alden served as assistant to the governor, deputy governor, and acting governor. For several years he was treasurer of the colony. He was also a representative from Duxbury and served on the Council of War during King Philip's War. He surveyed highways and served as an arbitrator for disputes between the townships. John A. Goodwin, in his history *The Pilgrim Republic* called him "a brave, sincere, and honorable man, worthy of a place in the front rank of the fathers of New England."

Alden was also a humble man. A few months before he passed away, he listed his occupation in a deed of land as "cooper."

John Alden died in 1687 at the age of 88. He was the last survivor of the signers of the Mayflower Compact. It is believed that he has had about a million descendants, with over 50,000 living today.

For more on John Alden, the Pilgrims, and their settlement at Plymouth, read the books listed in Appendix A.

PHILIP

Indian King

PHILIP

INDIAN KING

From the village of his childhood,
From the homes of those who knew him,
Passing silent through the forest,
Like a smoke-wreath wafted sideways,

Where he trod, the grasses bent not,
And the fallen leaves of last year
Made no sound beneath his footstep.

And the melancholy fir-trees
Waved their dark green fans above him,
Waved their purple cones above him,
Sighing with him to console him,
Mingling with his lamentation
Their complaining, their lamenting.

Ye who love the haunts of Nature,
Love the sunshine of the meadow,
Love the shadow of the forest,
Love the wind among the branches,
And the rain-shower and the snow-storm,
And the rushing of great rivers
Through their palisades of pine-trees,
And the thunder in the mountains,
Whose innumerable echoes
Flap like eagles in their eyries,
Listen to these wild traditions…

Selected verses from *Hiawatha*
by Henry Wadsworth Longfellow

PHILIP

INDIAN KING

Prologue

It was exceedingly good fortune for the Pilgrims in 1620 that they landed at Plymouth after their adventurous voyage across the Atlantic Ocean. The location they selected for their settlement was in an area that had recently seen a plague that severely affected the native inhabitants. Few Indians were left near Plymouth to prevent the English from occupying their new settlement. It is likely that the devastation to the native population was from diseases brought from Europe by the explorers and traders who had traveled earlier to New England. With limited resistance from the remaining Indians, the colonists were able to establish a foothold in the new land. Most historians agree that it is doubtful the colony could have survived without the wholesale decimation to the tribes from the widespread epidemic that had affected most of the Indian population around Plymouth.

Metacom, who was given the name Philip when he was a young man, was the son of Massasoit, sachem of the Pokanokets, a small tribe of Indians living south and west of Plymouth. Massasoit, known by the Indian name Osamaquin, was also the chief sachem of the Wampanoag Federation, a larger group that included many tribes including the Pokanokets. The chief sachem was chosen by the tribal leaders. Their selection was based on the candidate's wisdom and ability to bring diverse groups together. The position was not permanent. It lasted only as long as the leader was able to rule with compassion, fairness, and authority. The Wampanoags at the time of the Mayflower landing numbered about four hundred "braves," who occupied the entire wooded area between the Plymouth Colony and Narragansett Bay. Philip became chief sachem in 1662, after the deaths of his father and his older brother. Philip is most remembered for initiating the first major attacks on the English settlements that were struggling to survive in early New England. Historians also believe that the fifty-five-year period of peace that ensued as a result of an agreement negotiated on March 21, 1621 by his father and the Pilgrim leader John Carver was terminated by Philip's actions.

This fictional account, in the words of Philip, explains why he initiated his campaign against the settlers, who were once his father's friends. It also relates how the war named after him expanded to involve most of the outlying New England settlements and how the final fighting ended. All of the major events described actually occurred. They are recorded in works by contemporary writers and historians of the period.

* * * *

In addition to knowing the conditions that brought about King Philip's War, it is worthwhile to understand where this historic event fits into the series of religious and territorial conflicts that occurred in New England before and after the landing of the Mayflower at Plymouth harbor in 1620.

Years before the Pilgrims came, the French and English in northeast America were struggling for the rights to the fur trade flourishing at that time. Hostilities in the newly colonized areas began in 1613 at Mount Desert Island in Acadia, a French territory in what is now northern Maine. There, Captain Argall, sent by his English patrons in Virginia to eliminate the French presence, bombarded the French settlement at Saint Sauveur. His men then landed and decimated the colony. To show their disdain for Catholics, they also cut down a cross that was erected by a small colony of Jesuits that Madame de Guercherville, a pious French noblewoman, had sent overseas to proselytize the Indians. That incursion was the first recorded clash in America between the Catholic French and the Puritan English. The fighting in Acadia ended in the same year it had begun, but other confrontations between the two European powers continued in New

England for the next hundred and fifty years. Most of them involved native Americans.

Shortly after the arrival of the Pilgrims, some seven years after the Acadia incident, Governor John Carver of the Plymouth Colony and the Wampanoag leader Massasoit signed a peace treaty. That historic agreement covered the actions of the Pilgrims and Massasoit's people, and it lasted for more than forty years, until well after the chieftain died in 1661. Small engagements did take place, however, between the settlers and some tribes not governed by Massasoit during that period of relative peace.

The continental rivalry between the two European powers continued unabated during much of the seventeenth century as did the encroachment of Indian territories by land-hungry English settlers who arrived from across the "great sea." With each new deeding or taking of land by the colonists, resentment built in the Indian community and it became only a matter of time before open hostilities would occur between the newcomers and the native Americans.

Major fighting in New England directly between the English settlers and the Indians began in 1637 with the start of the Pequot War. That particular engagement lasted one year, but the wars in North America between the French and the English continued until 1763 when Canada was finally ceded to England. Throughout most of the intervening period, each side befriended Indians to assist in the nefarious deeds performed against the other side. Both sides participated in the slaughter of innocent women and children. There were no real winners in these conflicts, only great losses of life.

History has provided the following names and dates for the wars that occurred in this full century and a half of upheaval in the northeast region of the North American continent known as New England. The individual periods of war were usually defined by some hostile act at the beginning and some treaty, surrender, or death at the end.

1637–1638 The Pequot War
1675–1676 King Philip's War
1688–1698 The Ten Years War
1703–1713 Governor Dudley's Indian War
1722–1726 Governor Dummer's Indian War

1744–1749 Governor Shirley's War
(also called the French and Indian War)
1755–1763 The Last French and Indian War
(called the Seven Years' War in Europe)

This story begins on the morning of August 10, 1676. Philip is on a small parcel of land located in a swamp on the Mount Hope Peninsula[7] in Narragansett Bay. He is being pursued by English forces led by Benjamin Church, an aggressive and resourceful army captain.

CHAPTER ONE

My Indian name is Metacom, though some prefer to call me Metacomet or Pometacom. As I sit here uneasily on a rock in the woods on land that I once considered my home, I am anxious to tell the story of how I got to this place and of the forces that brought me here. English soldiers have killed or captured most of my family and friends, and are now searching the area for me. This may be my last opportunity to let everyone know how my people were treated by the newcomers from across the sea. The white man will surely tell his story, but mine must be recorded also. If it is not, it will likely die with me and the true history of the Indian struggle in New England will never be completely known.

I was born thirty-eight years ago at Montaup, a small Indian village at the head of the bay near where the Narragansetts have their home. Members of my tribe, the Wampanoags, which once numbered about 20,000 but because of the recent great sickness was reduced to about 1200, lived on the peninsular where Mount Hope is located. Most of the wigwams my people live in are built with small poles fixed in the ground, bent and fastened together with bark of trees, oval or arbor-wise at the top and covered with bark or mats made of sewn cattails or woven bulrushes. They are constructed in this fashion so that they can be moved easily when my people relocate to areas best suited for fishing or hunting. My family's shelter was larger than most, and it was fitted out in a manner worthy of the head of our tribe, for my father was Chief Massasoit, great sachem to the Wampanoags and respected leader of our people. He was much admired for his gentle manner and fair judgment not only by our tribe, but by others as well. Even the white men who first landed at Plymouth quickly came to respect his wisdom and desire for peace.

My brother Wamsutta was born a few years before I was. I also had a younger brother, Sonconewhew, and a younger sister, Amie. She married Tuspaquin, chief of the Narragansetts. As the elder children of a sachem, my brother and I enjoyed the many benefits allotted only to us. We were allowed to run free and not be bound by the longstanding tribal rituals that other young Indians were forced to participate in. We also had the advantage of being trained in hunting and woodcraft by my father's older brother and experienced counselor, Quadequina. He taught us the ways of the forest animals and the habits of the fish. Under his guidance we grew to love the woods, and like all Indians we believed that the wonders of nature belonged to all people. My father's younger brother, Akkompoin, was my personal counselor for many years. He taught me about Indian customs and the ways of the English. He also taught me how the English recorded time and how their days are numbered. Akkompoin, who was well into his sixties, was killed last month by the colonists.

We Wampanoags are in a federation composed of many tribes. We exist within the larger group of Algonkian people who live throughout the area. We all speak similar languages and share common cultures. In the spring we plant corn, beans, tobacco, and gourds. Our women tend all the crops except for tobacco, which is the responsibility of men. We believe that the provider of our food is the great god Cautantowwit, who lives in the southwest where good, warm weather comes from. We also believe that the crow, especially revered by us among all animals, is Cautantowwit's messenger.

All creatures are sacred to us, and we only kill what we can eat or get clothing from. We hunt bear, moose, deer, wolf, squirrel, rabbit, fox, and beaver. After the slaughter of any animal, we offer thanks to its spirit. In the case of the beaver, for example, after we take the meat and fur, we take its bones and return them to the stream where the beaver lived. That way we believe its spirit survives. It is with these beliefs that I spent my early years in Montaup.

My older brother, Wamsutta, and I were allowed to sit in on many of the meetings our father had with our braves, representatives from other tribes, and the Englishmen. We were privileged to hear our father render justice when disputes occurred and negotiate agreements between his followers and the newcomers from across the water. We loved our father and were proud of his displays of fairness and gentleness. It was at one of the tribal meetings that I first heard of the white man's lack of similar qualities. I was quite young when I heard a discussion about the honesty of the new settlers. Our father, the Great Sachem, told a shocking story.

"When I was young brave as my sons here," he said, "I heard story of strange ship that dropped anchor in great bay near woods of the Patuxet. It was English ship with white man named Hunt as chief. He say to our people he come to truck with Indians. Before going back to sea, his men capture Indians and take them aboard his ship to be sold across the sea for money."

The thought of the poor braves being taken from their own land and sold as slaves has never left me. Nor have the many visions of the white man's brutality I have seen since. At another council, my father told a more devastating story—one about the destruction of the entire Pequot nation.

"Some moons before my son Metacom was brought to me," he said, "English sea captain named Stone go up big river of Connecticuts to truck with Indian. After he and his men go ashore and get drunk with firewater some Pequot braves take hatchet to them. After they do this, braves fear English be angry so send wampum to colonists. Pequots say Stone die in revenge for injury he cause to Indian. English accept story. When another captain die soon later at hand of braves, English Captain Endicott with seventy men sent to Pequot territory to show Indians the strength of colonists. His men and other captains with him shoot Pequots. Shoot braves, squaws, and papooses. Also burn corn and destroy wigwams. They do this in many woods where Pequots stay. Pequot braves are good warriors, and with Sachem Sassacus they fight back. Try to save tribe from English guns. Soon braves from Mohegans and Narragansetts join white man to fight Pequots. Together they destroy tribe. Some Pequots run to west, but most die. Many made to be servants for white man."

Upon hearing this distressing account, I remember hearing my father's counselors calling for war.

"The colonists get stronger every day, Great Sachem," said Quadequina. "What they do to Pequots they do to us."

Another counselor added, "They soon take our country from us. We must dig up hatchet now. We are strong enough to send English back over the great water."

Massasoit raised both of his hands and called for quiet. He looked around and slowly proclaimed:

"I am friend to white man. They friends to us. They have much guns and powder. Promise to use it to keep Narragansetts and other tribes from taking our territory. I have made treaty with white man. I must not break it."

The vision of any of my people being made to suffer at the hands of the colonists made me angry. Although I was still a young man, I wondered when the killing would stop. Not soon, I was to find out as time passed.

115

My father also told stories of atrocities by the Indians like the one that occurred the year before the Pequot war. The Tarrantines, a tribe in Maine, went to war there against the local Penobscot tribe. After defeating them and with increased boldness they moved south as far as Narragansett Bay, destroying Indian villages and killing men, women and children along the way. I was told that so many natives were killed before the warring tribe returned to Maine that the survivors were unable to bury all of their dead.

My father's stories sickened me and made me lose trust in both white men and some Indians.

CHAPTER TWO

In the English year 1661, my father's spirit was taken away to the court of Cautantowwit in the southwest. All of our tribe mourned his passing, and representatives of many other tribes shared our grief. Medicine men danced their wild dances for many days after he was laid to rest in a place of honor at the Pokanokets' burying grounds. By the time my father left us, all of the good men who had founded the original Plymouth Colony had also died. The agreement of peace that Massasoit had made with them had never been broken. Now, however, new men rule the colony. Their generation does not share the wisdom and humanity of the previous one.

My brother, Wamsutta, was made chief sachem of the Wampanoags after the death of our father. Our new leader had recently married Weetamoo, the squaw sachem of the Pocasset Indians, a friendly group of Wampanoags living near our Great Hope Neck homeland. Many representatives of other tribes joined us in the celebrations of my brother's coronation. Once again, the feasting and dancing continued for many days. While the partying was in progress, I went hunting in the woods. I was then nineteen years old. As I was following fresh deer tracks, my father's faithful friend Tobias approached me and said that my brother wanted to see me at once. I hurried back along the narrow path to our settlement. I found Wamsutta in his wigwam. He was alone and uneasy.

"Brother Metacom," he said, "I with some other braves go to Plymouth after the next sunrise to speak with the Englishmen. They want me to make same agreement of friendship they had with our father. I want you to come with us. Words spoken in our woods are more and more those of the white man. To survive, we must be as them. It is time we receive names as the English have. We will ask their court to give them to us."

I nodded consent and immediately began preparing for the trip by packing some food and supplies. The forty-mile trek took us two full days. When we arrived at Plymouth the colonists greeted us with great respect. The settlers provided us with roast turkey and a delicious apple drink. Wamsutta and his braves carried on their business with the leaders of Plymouth, and my brother ended up agreeing to continue our father's treaty of peace. While their negotiations were being held, I moved around the village under the watchful eyes of the inhabitants. I saw many things that astounded me. The heavy coats that were worn, the odd way the white man washed his body and his clothes, and the way he built his cabins—solidly, with square logs and a roof of thatch. Many other things were strange to me as I wandered the straight streets of the fortified town.

I rejoined Wamsutta in the afternoon. He brought me to the wooden-frame house of a man he called a magistrate. We knocked on his heavy door. A stooped old man in a long, black coat greeted us. He had a wrinkled brow and a short, trimmed beard. He inquired of our reason to meet with him.

"We want English names," Wamsutta answered in his most commanding tone. The words made the magistrate laugh, but we felt that it was not a laugh of derision.

"I would be glad to oblige you if that is your wish, Chief." he said, "Please come in."

We entered his house cautiously. It had wooden furniture and a brick fireplace. Metal pots hanging from bars over the coals must have contained food, for the wonderful smell of cooking meat filled the room. When my brother and I stopped looking around, the magistrate asked us to sit.

"And what shall you two be called?" he asked.

"You choose," Wamsutta replied. "Need English names for me and brother."

The intelligent-looking Englishman standing before us closed his eyes and scratched his head. After a short while, he again looked at us.

"Because both of you young men appear to be strong and fearless," he responded, "you shall be called by the names of two of the great kings of old. He looked at Wamsutta solemnly. "You, Chief, shall heretofore be called Alexander, and I hope that you may conquer your world as your namesake from Macedonia conquered Greece hundreds of years ago." He then turned to me. "You, my boy, shall heretofore have the name Philip. He was the father of Alexander. He was also a hero. Both men were great warriors, and I hope that their courage may be transferred to the two of you."

The new Alexander, and I, the new Philip, walked tall as we left the magistrate's house. Our father would have been proud, just as he used to be when he had fatally shot an arrow into a large deer in the forest. We returned with swift steps to our home at Mount Hope. The trip back took only one day and one night.

Word came to us shortly after our return that the continuing festivities for our new leader worried the officials at Plymouth. They mistakenly believed that our celebrations were councils of war. Even though Wamsutta had just traveled to Plymouth to renew our father's treaty of friendship, the colonists feared that he was now planning hostilities against them. We had continually tried to let the colonies know that we were not preparing for war.

Wamsutta, like our father, often traded parcels of our Indian land in exchange for English weapons, utensils, coats, and wampum[8]. Most of our transactions were with Roger Williams, a clergyman who earlier had been banished from Plymouth for being too liberal-minded about Indians. He had set up the colony of Rhode Island, and for additional land he and his people traded much-needed arms, powder, and ball with members of our tribe.

After less than a year of Alexander's rule, the leaders at Plymouth Colony, troubled by our selling of land to the people of Providence and fearing that we were really conspiring against the people of Plymouth, sent messengers to our leader with the demand that he travel again to Plymouth. This time it was to assure the court that the rumors of our unfriendliness to the colonists were not well founded. When the couriers arrived, they found my brother fishing with some of his braves. Alexander told them that he would come when he had finished his fishing. The messengers showed great disdain. They returned, seething, to Plymouth without Alexander. Word soon came to our councils that the Plymouth government viewed Alexander's reply as disrespect and that they would be sending Major Josiah Winslow with some soldiers to enforce their demand for my brother's attendance at Duxbury, a small village near Plymouth. Although Major Winslow was the son of the early governor of the colony, his feelings for the Indians were not the same as those of his tolerant father. When the party arrived at Mount Hope, the Major's manner was haughty. He commanded my brother to accompany him immediately to Duxbury. My brother answered that he was feeling ill and asked that his travel be delayed for a short time. I watched helplessly as the major pointed his musket at Alexander's chest and ordered his soldiers to seize him. Despite my brother's protests expressing his ailing condition, two of the major's men bound his hands.

"Philip, stay here and be leader until I come back," he shouted to me as the military contingent marched him away. Those were the last words I ever heard my brother speak.

CHAPTER THREE

While Alexander was at Duxbury, I had much to do with the day-to-day business of the tribe. Akkompoin, younger brother of Pokanoket and chief councilor for Alexander assisted me in many ways. Together we discussed what land we could afford to trade for English products and weapons. Alexander had sold many pieces of our land and the Pocasset land of his wife, Weetamo. In our selling of land, Akkompoin and I agreed to again favor Roger Williams, head of the friendly settlement to the west of us. That leader had been good to my father and to others in our tribe ever since his banishment to Rhode Island. Although our selling of land to him infuriated the government at Plymouth, his trading of weapons to us was of great importance. The advantage of guns over our bows and arrows was considerable, and more and more of our braves were clamoring for muskets with which to hunt and protect themselves. The Englishmen at Plymouth refused to sell us similar muskets for fear that we would be using the weapons against them at some time in the future. Some Plymouth colonists did secretly sell arms to us in spite of the restriction, but not in the quantity we could get from our trading with Roger Williams.

As day after day passed, I became increasingly concerned about Alexander's welfare. I had received no communications from him since he was forcibly taken away, so I prepared to send a messenger to Duxbury to determine his situation. I thought about going myself, but I remembered the last words from our new sachem telling me to stay and attend to the affairs of the tribe.

Akkompoin and I were discussing our options when Annawon, one of Alexander's party, and two other braves approached us on the run. All were sweating profusely and breathing heavily.

"Our Great Sachem dead!" one brave shouted.

Another brave screamed, "They murder your brother!"

I was shocked. "What is it you say? You speak about Alexander?"

"Yes." The visibly troubled Annawon said in a solemn voice. "He die on way back from meeting with white man. After leaving Duxbury, Great Sachem want to go to Marshfield to see friend, Josiah Winslow. He become very sick there, and need come home. We carry him but he die on way back to Mount Hope. Now braves are carrying him here. We come back fast, to speak to you about your brother."

"Why do you say white man make him die?" I demanded.

"We each have different thought why him die," Annawon responded. "Me think him was bad sick when him go on trip. Him refuse to ride on horse to Duxbury as white man do. Say must go on foot same as his braves. Get worse sick from big trip. Him die near Cohannit[9] River on way back as we carry him. Me think him die from too much trek."

Another brave shook his head and interrupted. "Me think white man poison sachem when drink on peace pipe. Chief Wamsutta too strong to die from making trek to see white man."

Annawon held up one hand to silence the brave. He spoke slowly. "Me think him become weak from way treated by white man. They show him no respect. Make him leave as hostage both sons who traveled to Duxbury with him. Bad way white man act. Make Great Sachem give up spirit."

No matter what had actually killed Alexander, I felt the leaders at Plymouth were to blame. Once again they showed their hatred for Indians, and I vowed that somehow, some way, I would avenge my older brother's death.

After a period of mourning for Wamsutta during which our warriors again performed tribal dances, his body was buried on the same hill as that of our father. My personal grieving was cut short when the council leaders came to me to announce that I had been chosen to replace my brother as great sachem of the Wampanoag Federation. I was pleased to accept the new role, but wondered if I was fit to take on such responsibilities. The long nights of feasting and ceremonial dancing that followed my selection brought closure and re-energized the tribe. I finally felt the strength to act forcefully like my father and brother. Believing that my new position warranted it, and that it would dispel any thoughts by others to question my authority, I conferred on myself the title of King. Soon after the celebrations, my councilors and leaders from other tribes met with me to share their views about our relations with Plymouth Colony.

"Chiefs and braves say it time to fight white man," Awashonk, squaw chief of the Sekonnetts stated flatly.

"This is no way to act with English," I countered. "They have many guns and men. Fighting them now is bad for Indian. We must stay in peace as my brother and father wanted."

"But we must not let white man keep taking our woods," said my councilor Monashum. "Soon we have no woods to hunt or space to grow food. Too much has been taken from us already."

I took some time to consider the opinions of my companions, then declared we would not fight the colonists at that time. I told them that the English, with their apparently unlimited supply of men, guns, powder, and ball, were much stronger than we were. I thought that perhaps we would have a more favorable outcome if we could get other tribes to join us. Then the fight would be a fight of equals.

CHAPTER FOUR

On August 6, 1662, about a month after my selection as great sachem, the leaders at Plymouth sent a messenger summoning me to appear before their General Court. The subject of their concern was my selling of land to Providence Colony. I took Akkompoin, my uncle and closest advisor, along with Pawsaquens, Nuncompahoonet, and other councilors with me to the hearing. When we arrived at Plymouth, an armed military guard escorted us to a large wooden meetinghouse. Inside the single, windowless room candles flickered on the walls. At one end of the chamber the Plymouth leaders and armed settlers were seated. I assumed that these were the men who would judge us. On the other end of the barren building were empty seats facing the unsmiling members of the English tribunal. Once we were all seated opposite the colonists, an official convened a session of the court. The obvious leader, an elderly gentleman in a long black coat and a white wig, stood and addressed me. His loud voice echoed off the bare walls of the chamber.

"Sachem Metacomet, or Philip, if you prefer, we are greatly disturbed by your selling of land to colonies or people other than to this court at Plymouth. Such sales must not continue. If we are to remain as friends, you must agree that this practice will not go on. It is our intention that this court henceforth shall be made aware and approve of any sale of land by you or your people. On our part, we agree not to settle on Indian lands or to otherwise cause you trouble." After a meaningful pause, he continued, "Do you understand these terms and do you agree to them?"

I knew that to disagree would provoke the members of the tribunal to perilous action, so I nodded.

The leader continued. "We have prepared a written agreement that reflects these terms—one that will be valid for seven years. We would like you and the representatives you select to sign it now as a symbol of your good faith."

"You say it is for seven years?" I asked, wondering what will happen after the contract expires.

Ignoring my question, the leader went on.

"During that time you will sell no land without our consent. Do you agree?"

I looked at the faces of my companions. They were void of expression. I could tell from their bearing that my councilors understood what I already knew. We sign, or suffer the indignities and probably the muskets of the colonists. Again I nodded agreement. We slowly rose one by one, walked to the table in the center of the room, and made our marks on the parchment.

CHAPTER FIVE

Before the end of the first year of the treaty, I was alerted that several members of my tribe were planning to sell a tract of land to some colonists without my approval or that of the Plymouth Court. I realized that there was no way I could control all of my people, but as representative of the Wampanoags, I wanted to demonstrate my personal commitment to the terms of the treaty, so I had one of my interpreters[10] prepare and send a message to Plymouth. I well remember its wording.

King Philip desire to let you understand that he could not come to the Court, for Tom, his interpreter, has a pain in his back, that he could not travil so far, and Philip sister is very sick.

Philip would entreat that favor of you, and aney of the majestrats, if aney English or Engians speak about aney land, he pray you to give them no ansewer at all. This last summer he maid that promis with you, that he would sell no land in 7 years time (except that approved by the English court), for that he would have no English trouble him before that time, he has not forgot that you promise him. He will come as sune as posible he can to speak with you, and so I rest, your verey loveing friend, Philip, dwelling at mount hope neck.

To the much honored

Governor, Mr. Thomas Prence,

Dwelling at Plimoth.

For the next few years no land was sold by my people to anyone except the Englishmen, and in return Governor Prence made sure that we were treated fairly by the colonists.

The year after I wrote to Governor Prence, I married Wootonekamuske, a Pocasset princess. She was the younger sister of Queen Weetamoo, the wife of my dead brother, Alexander. My new wife was a beautiful squaw and she presented me with a fine, strong son the following year.

I remember writing to officials at Plymouth in 1665 asking if I could buy a horse for my personal use. I was pleasantly surprised when they gave me a large black stallion free of charge. I proudly rode the fine animal for many years. I thought at the time that maybe all Englishmen were not evil.

Five years after signing the seven-year treaty, in 1667, the Englishmen saw fit to violate the contract they had forced me to sign. Settlers from Plymouth established the town of Swansea on land that belonged to us at Great Hope Neck. Such closeness threatened us and removed more of our hunting grounds. I watched with great distress as the settlers built houses and a church and cleared many of our trees to make room for farms and pastures. Some of my hunters were sentenced to English jail for trespassing on what was rightfully our land and other of my people were harassed and shot at by the encroaching colonists. These actions were especially disturbing because before the Englishmen came, we Indians believed that all land was to be shared. The English belief that land could be owned as personal property was foreign to us, but we were forced to accept the English position. With great restraint by my people, however, our part of the land agreement continued to be kept. I made sure that all of our land sales were approved by the Plymouth Court for the full seven-year term of the agreement.

In 1667, the same year Swansea was established, I was summoned again to Plymouth to answer charges made by some Narragansetts that I was plotting against the English colony. This demand was doubly troubling since it was the English who had broken our land agreement. When I arrived in Plymouth, I was told that the court had been advised I was conspiring with the French and the Dutch against the English. The accusation was not true, of course, and I vociferously insisted on my innocence. I told the court that the Narragansetts who delivered the message were telling lies. After much discussion, the Plymouth Court finally accepted my reasoning. After I again renewed my father's treaty of peace and paid a fine of forty English pounds, I was permitted to leave. We defiantly took back our muskets, which had been taken from us on our arrival and held by the colonists during the proceedings.

After my return to Mount Hope, I made a point of visiting Canonchet, great sachem of the Narragansetts. He was about my age, with a tall, strong build and a regal bearing. He had straight black hair closely cropped along the sides of his head. The single eagle feather he always wore was stuck up in the back of his roach, the high crest of hair at the top of his head. He wore only a small covering of deerskin, and leather moccasins. Canonchet was made chief sachem when Miantonimoh, his father, was taken prisoner by the Mohegans, and then put to death on the advice of the English.

We two young leaders had always had mutual respect for each other. Although the Narragansetts had been hostile toward us in the past, the treacherous actions of the English had brought us together. When I confronted Canonchet with the Plymouth charges, he denied that his people had made them.

"My friend," he said, "we have recently been united in our distrust of the Englishmen. It would not be wise for us to harm you or your tribe at this time when our only way of saving our land is by acting together." I believed him and told him so. He continued in a determined tone, "I will seek out the ones who have made these false accusations and deal with them as our Indian law provides."

We then discussed our weakened position with regard to the settlers. We agreed that conditions must not stay that way. Together we made plans for a unified strike against the white man. This action was intended to completely eliminate the English threat or at least to reduce the unjustified English encroachment on our lands. We discussed a plan of attack and other details— the increased use of our bows and arrows instead of our muskets, in order to conserve balls and powder, and sources of the necessary food and water. We talked well into the night about ways to accomplish our mission.

CHAPTER SIX

In March of 1671, seeing the town of Swansea expanding more into our territory every day and watching our braves become increasingly agitated, some of my councilors called for a meeting. I listened to their convictions as I sat in a chair-shaped rock formation at the foot of Mount Hope. I considered this natural seat as a kind of throne from which I addressed members of my tribe in our meetings.

My councilor, Samkama, spoke firmly. "Great Sachem," he said, "We must show the white man that we are yet strong. Our braves say they are ready for war. They practice with their guns and perform their war dances. You must explain to them the reasons you have for not attacking Swansea and starting fight with English."

I feared for the lives of all my people. I knew that we were still not ready to engage the settlers in combat. I continued to feel that if we could hold off until I could get other tribes to join us, we might then be able to confront the white man militarily.

I faced Samkama squarely. "Say to the braves who are thirsty for war to go to Swansea and show their guns but do not fire them. Perhaps such a scene will convince the white man that we are prepared to fight. This might discourage him from taking more of our woods. We must remember what the medicine men tell us: the party who is first to bring death will not win the war."

Later that evening when I was alone, I asked our god, Cautantowwit, to restrain the braves from doing more than I had ordered. The next day I found out from my councilors that my wish had been granted. Although my braves had gone to Swansea and proudly displayed their muskets, they didn't fire them. The war I feared had been averted once more.

In the year 1671, seven years after we signed the seven-year treaty, we believed that we were finally free to sell land to others. We began negotiations to accommodate the desires of the Rhode Island colonists. Plymouth soon learned of our plans, however, and they considered our actions as tantamount to initiating a war. They asserted that the original contract I signed did not specify the seven-year period of enforcement as I was led to believe. They told me that it specified no time limit whatsoever, but we were not educated enough in English writing at the time to see the deception—another trick of the white man in their continuing effort to deceive our people.

In April of the same year, soon after our display of arms at Swansea, Plymouth sent a message to me at Mount Hope. They feared that our Swansea actions were the start of hostilities and claimed that my land sales were in violation of our earlier agreement. They commanded me to appear at a meeting on the green at Taunton. That was the settlement that we called Cohannit, some twenty-five miles away from Mount Hope. I immediately assembled my councilors and we headed for the meeting place. We arrived, seventy strong, at Two-Mile River, a few miles from the center of town. From there I sent two of my men to find the Englishmen and bring them to us for the meeting. Soon after, two Englishmen, James Brown and my friend Roger Williams, walked toward us. My men stood tall and displayed their muskets.

"Governor Prence would like to know why you will not come to the green," stated Mr. Brown. I ignored his question and spoke in a dignified manner, "I am now here. Have your governor come to me."

After an uncomfortable silence, the Englishmen turned to speak to each other then stared back at me without saying a word.

"How many of your men are at Taunton?" I asked, my eyes narrowing on their faces.

Realizing that I was suspicious, they offered to stay as hostages if I would go ahead to the green. I agreed and took all of my men except three. The two Englishmen stayed behind, guarded by my three braves. We walked cautiously away from the group. When we came to Plumbley Hill, about halfway to the Taunton Green, I could see many Englishmen assembled in the open space. Each had a musket and a long sword hanging by his side. We continued walking slowly down the hill but stopped and took cover at a mill close to the green. I sent one of my braves over to Governor Prence to tell him that he should come to meet me at the mill. The governor sent a messenger back with the proposal that we come together in the meetinghouse that faced the green. He also proposed that, as a sign of friendship, we stack all of our guns outside. I sent back a message of agreement, and we proceeded to the wooden building. Once inside the large but nearly empty structure, my people gathered and sat on the floor on one side of the room. The Englishmen sat in wooden chairs on the other. Along with Governor Prence there were other Plymouth officials and representatives from the Massachusetts Bay Colony.

Their spokesman presented me with the accusations and demands that I had expected. I was told that my tribe was conspiring with the Narragansetts, and that this must not continue. When I was allowed to speak, I denied that I was planning an attack. I spoke firmly, protesting the trampling of our corn by the English cows, horses, and pigs. When I finished, I was assured that the destruction by their animals would cease. But their condemnations continued. Their constant charge about my conspiring with the Narragansetts fatigued me and left me confused. I was finally worn out. I confessed that I had done wrong, knowing that I had spoken with Canonchet. I even stated that the English were my friends although I knew the opposite was true.

The leader produced a new treaty. He held it up for all to see and demanded that we sign it. The agreement required me to confess my folly for not abiding by the laws of Plymouth and the King of England as I had previously agreed. It also demanded that I renew my pledge of faithfulness to the colonies. In addition, it required us to turn over to Plymouth all of our guns—those we carried and those possessed by the entire tribe. I looked around at the determined faces of the colonists and realized that I had no option but to sign. We were far outnumbered by the gallery of threatening English soldiers facing us.

I believed at the time that the Massachusetts government would be fairer than Plymouth in their negotiations with us, so with determination I addressed the court.

"I will sign this new treaty only if I can conduct all future business with the people of Massachusetts Colony."

The Plymouth leaders spoke among themselves, then their leader replied.

"We feel that if we both adhere to this agreement, there will be no reason for you to do business with our friends to the north. But if that is your desire in the future we agree to your condition."

Believing that I had freed our tribe of control by the overbearing Plymouth government, I walked to the table where the document was resting and signed my mark. I then turned and nodded to four of my councilors: Tasover, Capt. Wispoke, Woonchapanchunk and Nimrod. They moved silently to the table and made their marks. Then, William Davis, William Hudson, and Thomas Brattle, the English representatives who had witnessed our signing, added their signatures on the parchment. The smiles that I witnessed on the faces of the colonists as I left the room made me angry, but I knew that their treachery was no match for ours.

Reluctantly we collected our seventy guns and slowly stacked them inside a nearby house. I promised to send the rest of the tribal guns when I returned to Mount Hope. I knew in my heart that I would never do this. Our braves needed the weapons for survival—both for food and protection. Dejected, we left the English and headed home. We knew that our people would consider us as traitors because of the agreements we felt forced to make. When we arrived at Mount Hope, I immediately gathered and addressed my people. I told them that we would send no more guns to the English. To this day we haven't. In June, the Plymouth Court ordered that since I had not sent the promised weapons, the seventy guns we had surrendered there were to be permanently confiscated.

A few weeks after our meeting at Taunton, I learned from a friendly colonist that the Plymouth government was sending a letter to the Massachusetts government requesting assistance from them in all disputes with the Indians. The message was reported to have ended with the threat that if assistance were not provided, Plymouth would send out its own soldiers to reduce me to reason. Two days later, James Brown, an English representative, came to Mount Hope and ordered me to appear at Plymouth on the thirteenth of September. I asked him about my position with the government of Massachusetts, and he said that his only mission was to bring me back to Plymouth. I insisted that I would instead travel to Massachusetts to meet with the governor because I believed that he was a fairer man to deal with. He warned me that if I didn't come with him to Plymouth, he would send a military force to Mount Hope to forcibly bring me back. Fearing that I would have to travel to Plymouth as my brother had, I told the man with conviction that I would not return with him. Incensed by my refusal, he walked to his horse, mounted it, and sped away. I immediately packed for the two-day trek and left for Boston alone. I was determined to convey my views to Governor Leverett before he made up his mind about assisting Plymouth. As I moved quickly along the leaf-strewn paths between the settlements on the way to my destination, I thought of the many arguments I would make to convince the governor of our willingness to abide by English law.

When I arrived at the governor's residence, his ambassador advised me that although Massachusetts was sympathetic to my cause, all decisions were in the hands of Plymouth. I insisted on talking directly to the governor. I finally convinced the representative of my resolve, and he led me to the door of the governor's office. When I entered the richly decorated room, the governor was seated at his large desk. Three other men who were sitting in front of him turned to face me. I apologized for the interruption then told the governor that the agreements by my father and renewed by my brother and me were for friendship and not for subjection. We were not subjects of the Plymouth government, I emphasized. I admitted that I had violated the Taunton treaty, but I said that was because I had not had the time to gather all of our weapons together. The governor demanded an explanation about my apparent preparations for war. I was able to convince him and his associates that I had no evil intent and no such plans. The governor said he understood my position, but that what his ambassador had stated about Plymouth's authority over me was true.

"Then I must speak with your king!" I remember shouting. "I myself am a king and I will deal with no one but one of equal authority!" Governor Leverett was surprised at my demand. He spoke to me in a fatherly fashion.

"King Philip, since I am not the King of England, and he is many miles away, I will advise him of your wish to confer with him. Meanwhile, I will review your situation with the officials at Plymouth to see if we can perhaps together resolve the problems you appear to have with them. I am sure that we all want peace and I will do all in my power to achieve that end."

The governor's assurance did little to settle my mind, and I returned home knowing that my request to speak with the king was as futile as getting the English to acknowledge their unfair treatment of my people.

In late August, after I had devoted much time to the affairs at Mount Hope, I learned from one of my messengers that Governor Leverett had traveled to Plymouth earlier in the month. He had joined with Governor Prence and the governor of Connecticut to confer about my situation. A friend of my tribe attended the meeting and sent word to me that the Plymouth governor had produced a list of charges against me. His complaints included my lack of cooperation with English authorities, my refusal to surrender the rest of my tribe's guns as I had agreed, and the significance of my meetings with other Indian tribes. All of these actions, he said, could only be interpreted as acts of war.

A few weeks after learning about Governor Prence's accusations, I received a command to attend yet another meeting at Plymouth. The rider who brought me the message assured me that representatives of all three colonies would be in attendance, so I complied with the summons. I knew I would be subjected to the same accusations and threats as before, but I felt that with Massachusetts in attendance I would get a fair hearing.

I arrived in Plymouth with my councilors on the twenty-fourth of September. As expected, I was presented with a long list of grievances. The list included the charges Governor Prence had previously made, as well as the following: that I had refused to come to court when summoned, that I had made war plans with other Indian tribes, that I tried to win the favor of the governor of Massachusetts by twisting the truth, and that I had been rude to two Englishmen. The hearings relating to all of the charges continued for five full days. The constant repetition of the accusations left me completely bewildered. Before the meeting concluded I was ordered to sign yet another agreement—one that made me acknowledge that all of my people were subjects of Plymouth and the King of England. In addition the document stated that I could make no war without the permission of Plymouth, and that I had to have the court's permission before I could sell any more land. I was also made to promise that I would pay to the government of Plymouth the sum of one hundred pounds over a period of three years. Preposterously, I was also to furnish the governor with five wolves' heads each year as tribute. The most detestable provision was that in the future I could consult only with Plymouth about our differences. Recognizing the harm that would come to my people if I didn't sign, I made my mark at the bottom of the agreement as did my councilors, Wocokon, Uncompaen, and Samkama. My younger brother, Sonconewhew, also signed. When the deed was done, I vowed to myself that I would never pay tribute to any Englishman, and to this day I haven't.

CHAPTER SEVEN

When we returned home and I told my people what the agreement we had just signed at Plymouth meant, they accused me of cowardice. At a meeting of my councilors shortly after, I sat on my throne at the base of Mount Hope and argued with my people that I had had no other choice to make but to agree to the terms of the English document. But I assured those gathered that I had never planned to actually comply with the new demands of the colonists.

"Then we must make war," said Woonchapanchunk. "It is time we bring end to white man's demands."

"Yes, Great Sachem," added Annawon. "We must wait no more. It is time to face the white man and teach him that we too share the land. Wherever we go, the white man say we break his rules and are punished for it. They even treat you as bad Indian, Great Chief. You are forced to hurry to Plymouth whenever they say. They make you sign treaties that make us give up land we need to grow crops and hunt in woods. They even try to take away our guns."

"There are many tribes to join us, King," Monashum said. "Pawsaquens and Peebe have count with me number of braves who would fight with us. Queen Weetamo has three hundred Pocasset braves and Squaw Sachem Awashonks has three hundred Sakonnett warriors. We have three hundred and Nipmucks have many more. Even Canonchet will bring Narragansetts since we now friends. Now is time to dig up hatchet, Great Sachem. We have already waited too long. The white man gets stronger while we do nothing."

Of course, I knew that my councilors were right. Every day that we did not engage the Englishmen they were getting more powerful and more aggressive. I was certain that I could no longer continue to hold back my people, nor could I convince the white man to give back the lands that he has stolen from us.

"I will send messengers to our friends," I said. "We must entreat them to join us in our cause for we can only succeed if we join together in this fight. I will myself go to see Canonchet, for he must be part of our war as he promised. Even though Narragansetts kidnaped my father, Massasoit, many moons ago, that tribe is now our friend. Canonchet has the braves we need if we are to win the fight with the white man."

I hesitated and looked around at the anxious faces of my councilors. I said, "Tonight I say to all of our warriors, 'Time has come to dig up hatchet.'"

CHAPTER EIGHT

For the next four years, the English had little official communication with us. I sincerely hoped that they were adjusting to our presence and not preparing for war. I restrained my followers from overt acts of violence so that there would be no excuse for the Plymouth government to attack us. I continued to visit my English friends around New England and even began to dress more like them—white shirt, cloth breeches and all. I corresponded with the English through my interpreter. I remember in detail the contents of one letter that I had written in May of 1672 and had delivered by a messenger.

> Philip, Sachem of Mount Hope
> To Captain Hopestill Foster of Dorchester
> Sendeth Greetings.
>
> Sir, you may please to remember that when I last saw you at Wading River, you promised me six pounds in goods. Now my request is that you would send by this Indian five yards of white or light-colored serge to make me a coat; and a good Holland shirt ready made; and a pair of good Indian breeches, all of which I have present need of.
>
> Therefore I pray, sir, fail not to send them by my Indian and with them the several prices of them; and silk and buttons and seven yards of trimming. Not else at present to trouble you with only the subscription of
>
> King Philip
His Majesty at Mount Hope

Early in 1674, after a period where there was little provocation on either side, Plymouth lifted the ban on the sale of guns to us. We had been getting arms in secret anyway, but this made it easier to obtain the weapons we would surely need to withstand an attack by the English. During this period of relative calm, I sent emissaries to many tribes around New England soliciting their support in the event of a confrontation. In secret talks Canonchet and I agreed that war was inevitable—that the English will continue to take our lands by fair means and foul to further satisfy their needs to expand. After lengthy discussions, the Narragansett leader and I were in accord that we must be the ones to launch an offensive if we were to succeed in restraining the English. We planned for a first encounter in 1676. This two-year time delay would allow us to secure the aid of the many tribes unhappy with the treatment they, too, were receiving from the English. We knew that it would take that much time to convince the different tribes to forget their petty differences and join together. We believed that only by uniting with us would they save their land and probably their lives. We tried to keep all of our negotiations secret for fear that the English would become aware of our intentions and strike us before we were prepared. Our only chance of success lay in having our first attack come as a complete surprise. Of course, during that period of disguised friendliness, our spies kept us informed about the English preparations, which were becoming more and more evident. We learned that the settlers were building fortified houses and organizing an army. We were also advised that their Benjamin Church was traveling to many outlying Indian tribes hoping to get them to side with the colonists in the event of hostilities.

We were not, however, destined to be the ones to establish the exact time of the onset of violence. That was determined by an unrelated incident, which acted as the spark—the spark that finally ignited the flames of war.

CHAPTER NINE

John Sassamon, the Christian Indian whom my brother and I had maintained as our interpreter and scribe for more than ten years, was found by my councilors late in 1674 to be secretly appropriating land for himself and his heirs by falsifying records in transactions between the colonists and our tribe. It was an act that made me lose complete trust in the man, despite the fact that he had usually acted faithfully during his term in my employ. When I became aware of the facts, I sent him away summarily. He retired at Assawompsett, a twenty-seven acre tract about twenty miles east of here. In January of 1675, he traveled to the Marshfield home of Governor Josiah Winslow. He told the governor that our Federation was plotting with the Narragansetts and that together we were planning to start a war with the English. Within hours of his return from Marshfield, members of my council told me about his meeting with the governor.

"We must stop the traitor before he does more harm," demanded Tobias, my favorite councilor.

"We must not let him continue to betray us," added Mattashunnamoo, Tobias' son.

I listened to their pleas for punishment, but I mildly protested that Sassamon had been a good interpreter for me and that was to his credit. I defended him for a while, but I knew that my advisors were right, for what he had done was detrimental to our plan.

"Yes, we must treat him as one who has acted against us," I finally said. "You must bring him here to receive the punishment that Indian tradition requires."

Before anyone was sent to get Sassamon, I was told that a group of friendly Indians had spied his hat and gun lying near a hole in the frozen surface of Assawompsett Pond. Apparently, the group searched around and found Sassamon's body underneath the ice. Believing that he had drowned accidentally, they buried his body on the shore nearby. From friends I also learned that when Plymouth heard of Sassamon's death, they questioned the theory that he had died accidentally. They sent a party to dig his body up. When they examined it, it was evident that Sassamon had been murdered, for they found that his head was badly bruised and his neck was broken. When the news became public, a Wampanoag Indian named Patuckson visited Governor Winslow and told him that while he was observing from a nearby hilltop he saw three Indians kill Sassamon. He identified the men as Tobias and his two sons. Later, I learned that the three accused Indians— who were my friends—were captured and bought to Plymouth for trial. Although there were six Indians on the jury, all members of the tribunal declared that my councilor and his sons were guilty of the crime. Despite the fact that our treaty with the white man called for Indian crimes to be punished by Indians, the three who supposedly had killed Sassamon were sentenced to be hanged by the English on June 8, 1675. The condemned men loudly insisted on their innocence, but the death sentences were not revoked.

One of my councilors who attended the event told me that on the appointed day, before a crowd of cheering white men, Tobias and Mattashunnamoo were hanged from a makeshift wooden gallows. When it was young Wampapaquan's turn to swing, he added, the rope broke or slipped from his neck when he dropped, allowing him to live. After falling to the ground, the condemned man yelled that he had no part in the killing. He admitted that his father and brother had killed Sassamon. He insisted that he was not an accomplice. The court reprieved him, but it was of no ultimate consequence. Within the month the English hanged him anyway.

I protested to the Plymouth authorities about the whole affair, even telling them that their only witness, Patuckson, owed a gambling debt to one of the accused so his declaration was surely a lie. They refused to discuss the matter, promptly turning things around and blaming me for Sassamon's death because of the way I had dismissed him. Of course, Plymouth had no proof of my involvement, so they dropped all charges. The whole incident further inflamed my braves, however, and I could sense that it would not be long before I would lose complete control of their actions.

On June 14, less than a week after the hangings, Queen Weetamo, squaw sachem of the Pocassets, and I both received messages from Plymouth that called on us to help reduce the level of hostility that the colonists knew was rapidly building among us. Soon after I got my letter, colonists Samuel Gorton and James Brown came to me with a plea from Governor Winslow to meet with him and settle our differences. My warriors wanted to kill the two messengers, but I prevailed upon them to let the men return to Boston. The attempts by the government of Massachusetts to lessen the feelings of contempt we had for the English had little effect. Neither the queen nor I provided a response to their pleas for reconciliation.

On June 15, Benjamin Church, acting as an English emissary, visited both Weetamo, queen of the Pocassets, and Awashonks, queen of the Sekonnetts, to try to convince them to condemn me and seek the protection of the English. My informers told me that his mission was not successful, either.

My spies also advised me that on June 16, Church traveled to see Governor Winslow. He informed the governor about his failed approaches to the two women leaders and suggested that the Massachusetts government provide the two tribes and their leaders with a safe haven as a reward if they remained neutral. I learned that the governor declined to give Church an answer. He did, however, make him a captain in their military.

On June 17, my warriors began performing war dances at Mount Hope. They continued with their animated and noisy activities for two weeks. While this hectic display was going on, John Easton, deputy governor of Rhode Island, visited me. He implored me to enter into further negotiations with Plymouth so that war could be avoided. I told him that it was the colonists that had created the conditions that had brought us to our present state of distrust. Mr. Easton, a Quaker who believed in nonviolence, protested, saying that the state of affairs was the fault of both parties. He suggested that we come together to bring about a truce or any agreement that would avoid the spilling of blood. I felt that my listener might understand our position better if I explained to him the reasons for our growing resentment. I remember clearly the words that I expressed to him on that day:

> The English who came first to this country were few and forlorn. They were poor and did not know the ways of the woods. My father, Massasoit, was sachem of the Wampanoags. He treated them in a kind and friendly manner. He gave them land to plant and build upon. With Indian assistance the English colony flourished and grew. As time passed they took possession of a large part of my father's land by means fair and foul. But he remained loyal to them until he died. Then, my brother became sachem. The Plymouth

government harassed him into an early death. Then I became sachem. The English disarmed my people and took away even more of their land. Today only a small part of our territory remains. I am determined not to live until I have no country.

Mr. Easton, still hoping to avoid direct conflict, protested that the English were too powerful to be overthrown. Though I tended to agree with him, I felt that events had gone past the point of meaningless deliberation. The colonists were continuing to take our land, and my warriors were too focused on confrontation. Mr. Easton left, unsatisfied. I knew then that war was soon to come.

Deputy Governor Easton, with the hope of yet getting me to change my mind, sent a message to me after he returned to Rhode Island. In it, he said that a letter from Plymouth had arrived declaring a state of emergency in the colony. It notified the leaders in Rhode Island that there were to be no more negotiations with me, or my councilors. It further stated that because of our resistance to their entreaties for peace the colonies were preparing for war.

On June 18, some of my men, without my knowledge, seized some settlers who had come onto Wampanoag land to retrieve horses of theirs that had strayed. When I learned of the men's capture, I had my people release the Englishmen and return their animals, for I wanted Plymouth to have no excuse to advance into our territory. This show of leniency further inflamed my warriors and their war dances became increasingly more frenzied. Fearing that their activity might bring the start of hostilities, I sent messages to many of my English friends at Swansea telling them that they should leave for safer settlements as soon as they could. I assured them that I had no wish to hurt them but my warriors might if war were to break out.

On June 19, some of my braves, in an act of bravado, vandalized the home of Job Winslow in Swansea when he was away. When they returned to camp, they told me about their adventure and said that they had harmed no one.

On June 20, I was informed that another group of my pent-up warriors had ventured to the outskirts of the same settlement and had looted and burned two unoccupied houses. The cautious owners must have left earlier for the safety of the nearby garrisons. On their way back to Mount Hope, a few of my emboldened warriors entered the home of the Salisbury family. One of the returned braves told me his story.

"When we get to house, no one is there," he said. "We surprised when owner and his son appear. Even more surprised when boy raise musket and shoot one brave. We all run from house carrying injured man and return to Mount Hope. He die from wound soon after our return."

My warriors felt that the killing by the white man was the provocation they needed for war. As a river overflowing it banks, it unleashed the pent-up anger that my braves had been holding back only because of my reluctance to resort to violence. The warning from our medicine men that a war could not be won by the side that kills first was now of little consequence.

CHAPTER TEN

My spies advised me that the Swansea settlers' first act after the show of violence was to send a messenger to Plymouth Governor Josiah Winslow at his home in Marshfield to report on what had taken place. A friend of mine close to the governor informed me that on June 21, the governor had sent orders to the towns of Bridgewater and Taunton to send a force of seventy men to Swansea immediately. He also had ordered the settlements to send about a hundred and fifty more men to a rallying point in Taunton the next day for the rapid reinforcement of the men he was sending to Swansea. In the afternoon, he wrote to the Massachusetts governor in Boston advising him of the uprising. He requested that the governor do what he could to prevent the Narragansetts and the Nipmucks, both of which were under Massachusetts jurisdiction, from joining my Wampanoag forces. I was also told that Governor Leverett sent him a reply, assuring him that he would cooperate fully with Plymouth.

The first contingent of seventy men ordered by Governor Winslow to go to Swansea arrived on June 21 as planned, according to my informers. When they arrived, the soldiers discovered that most of my braves had left the town to return to Mount Hope. Many of the people of Swansea, responding to the arrival of the troops, left the confinement and shelter of the Miles and Browne garrisons and cautiously moved to the less congested settlers' houses that could best afford them protection.

Governor Winslow, hoping that prayers might bring peace, ordered that Thursday, the 24th of June, be observed as a Fast Day in Plymouth Colony. It was to be treated as a Sabbath, and no work was to be done. My warriors saw this pronouncement as an opportunity to create more havoc without interference, since most of the settlers would be attending church services. Without my knowledge, groups of my braves traveled to Swansea and other nearby settlements. According to reports given later to me, my vengeful warriors ambushed some families in Swansea who were returning from worship services. One settler was killed from the first volley of fire from my braves, and other colonists were wounded. Another settler who had sent his wife and child ahead to the Miles garrison while he gathered up some belongings was shot dead by my braves as he was leaving his house. His wife ran back to assist him, and my men also killed her and her young son. Two other men left the same garrison house to get water from a well, and my men killed them. They also shot and killed a sentry who was standing near the supposedly well-guarded stronghold. Two other sentries near there were also badly wounded by my braves. These acts of vengeance disheartened me, but did not surprise me.

Other braves who returned later that day, informed me that at Mattapoiset, about fifteen miles west of Mount Hope neck, my men observed a group of colonists retrieving corn at a distance from the Bourne garrison house where most of the settlers had gathered for safety. Firing from behind bushes, my warriors killed eight Englishmen including, I was told, the boy that had shot my brave the day before.

The next morning one of my men related to me that after dark the previous evening, two settlers from the garrison house in Swansea headed to the nearby town of Rehoboth to get a doctor for the two sentries that had been wounded earlier in the day. He said a fellow brave killed both of the couriers.

These were incidents I had no part in provoking. But I knew that since my people spilled the blood of the colonists, it meant that the war I had so earnestly tried to delay had finally been thrust upon me.

CHAPTER ELEVEN

My eyes—the friendly Wampanoags disbursed throughout the colonies and other tribes—kept me up to date about the intentions and movements of both the colonists and the Indians. Most of my information came from these trusted informers. They risked their life daily, and I owe much to them for their dedication to our cause.

Major William Bradford, son of the former governor of Plymouth, was ordered by Governor Winslow to organize the group of reinforcements that he had sent to Taunton. Bradford's objective was to proceed to Swansea and have his men join the troops that were already there to defend the settlement from further Indian incursions. Benjamin Church, the newly appointed captain, was selected by Bradford to command an advance guard, whose mission it was to scout ahead of the main force traveling to Swansea and make sure that the way was clear for them.

Church, a colonist from Rhode Island, lived near the Sakonnet Indians. A friend of Awashonks, Squaw Sachem of that tribe, he knew our woods and was familiar with our type of fighting. He was also our friend until he found that we were preparing to resist by force the English taking of more of our lands. He was a proud man, aggressive in nature and considerably more knowledgeable in the ways of the Indian than were the other colonists.

During his march to Swansea, his small company encountered no resistance. When he arrived at his destination, he posted guards at garrison houses and other substantial homes where settlers had gathered for safety.

I was told that Governor Leverett of Massachusetts, heeding the urgent request from Governor Winslow of Plymouth to use his influence to keep the Narragansetts and Nipmucks from joining my forces, decided to send missions to many of the tribal leaders to try to prevent a full-scale war. Captain Edward Huchinson, Seth Perry, and William Powers traveled to Providence where they sought the assistance of Roger Williams in their dealings with the Narragansetts. The men met with four leaders of that powerful Rhode Island tribe—Pessacus, Ninigret, Quinnapin, and Queen Quaiapen. After considerable discussion, the four sachems assured the visitors that they would not assist me in my rebellion. After I heard of the statements made by the Narragansett leaders, I still believed that when the opportunity presented itself, the Narragansetts would come to my aid despite their statements to the Englishmen. The governor's envoys apparently felt that they had accomplished their task nonetheless, and returned home.

One of my English informers attached to Captain Benjamin Church's group told me about another attempt to isolate me. Governor Leverett had ordered Captain Matthew Fuller to take about forty men and travel to Queen Weetamoo in the Pocasset territory, an area located directly across the bay from my home at Mount Hope. Captain Church and his men were included in Fuller's party. The force divided when the men arrived at the Pocasset shore. Fuller took one group of twenty men, but when he had a minor skirmish with some of my braves he immediately headed back to Swansea. Church, with the second group, spotted Indian tracks and followed them to a field where he saw two Indians gathering peas. When he called to them, they ran into the nearby woods. Church's soldiers pursued them into the woods but there the Englishmen came under fire from the Pocassets. Church was apparently determined to continue the chase, until he saw a massive concentration of Indians on a distant hill, ready to come after him. He ordered a retreat toward shore. The group, holding off a superior number of attackers, slowly withdrew. Church's small band continued to repulse many Indian advances as they waited on shore. Just before dark, a sloop commanded by a Captain Goulding rescued the besieged Englishmen from the beach and brought them back to the safety of their fellow countrymen. When I learned about Church's actions from my informer, I was troubled by the attack, yet was pleased that not one of Church's men was harmed, for, I felt, every Englishman killed increased the hatred against our tribe by the white man.

To appeal to me directly, Governor Leverett ordered Captains Thomas Savage, James Oliver, and Thomas Brattle to Mount Hope. As the group approached Swansea, the men came upon the mutilated bodies of the two Englishmen who had been sent to Rehoboth from the Miles garrison to get aid for the wounded sentries. My braves had brought the dead couriers to a spot that the white man was sure to pass. There, they had mounted the bodies on poles. Despite the frightful sight, the three officers ordered their men to proceed to Swansea. When they arrived, they were quickly informed about the grisly details of the other Swansea attacks. All of the fear-stricken men hastily returned to Plymouth, believing that it was useless to try to convince me that if I engaged in a full-scale war with the English I would surely lose.

During the bright moonlit night of June 26, I was sitting on my throne at the foot of Mount Hope conferring with my council. To everyone's surprise the light of the moon began to dim. As the strange blackness continued to obscure the moon, it grew darker around us, and the shifting shadows all around appeared to be intruders. I could sense the increasing unease of my councilors. Chief Annawon was the first to speak.

"This darkness is a sign from the white man," he said. "It warns us that we must not attack his houses any more."

The night grew even darker, and my councilors' mutterings became louder. I could sense the fear building around me.

Cheemaughton said, "Our great god, Cautantowwit, must be unhappy with us. We need more dances to comfort him."

Other of my councilors strode back and forth, no doubt believing that the end of their world was near. Within an hour, it was as dark as a black bear's fur. The only glimmer of light came from the small partially obscured stars blinking above us. Three of my councilors stumbled away from our meeting place to their wigwams and families. Others, stunned by the rapid loss of light, began chanting in low tones. One brave called out for a medicine man, but the only sound we heard in return was the wind rustling the leaves. It was an anxious time. My soothing words did little to calm the frightened men. I grew concerned about their future ability to fight.

Within an hour, the light slowly began to return, bringing all objects back into view. The woods gradually appeared to lose their threat, and activity by the remaining men resumed amid many sighs of relief.

"What make moon disappear?" I remember one of my councilors asking.

"It is not a warning," I answered. "Great Sachem Massasoit once said that even the sun goes away sometimes but comes back soon." Repeating the sage words of my father did little to convince my council that the sudden darkness was not a message to be heeded but a natural event. Our meeting was over for the night.

CHAPTER TWELVE

On June 28, Captain Bradford's men waiting in Swansea were reinforced by even more forces—a foot company led by Captain James Cudworth; a cavalry company led by Captain James Prentice; another cavalry company led by Captain Daniel Henchman, all from Plymouth; and a foot company from Boston led by Captain Samuel Mosely. My spies, who were posing as guides to the soldiers at Swansea, informed me that the leaders spent their time making preparations for a joint attack on Mount Hope while awaiting the arrival of their commander, the newly-promoted Major Thomas Savage, who was coming from Boston with his two small units of cavalry.

Before the major's arrival, many of the men at Swansea began to show impatience. Captain Cudworth, recognizing their anxiety, allowed a small group of horsemen to scout the nearby Indian territory. Benjamin Church was among them. Before traveling very far into the wooded area, the anxious soldiers came under ambush by a group of my braves. One Englishman was killed and another wounded. Without waiting to regroup, the surprised company hastened back to the safety of their companions in Swansea. Captain Church's courageous call to his men to continue fighting and not run away went unheeded.

When I heard about this incursion onto the Mount Hope Peninsula by English soldiers from Swansea and their rapid retreat, I expected that a much larger force would very shortly be invading our homeland. I called for a quick meeting of my councilors and instructed them to prepare all of our able people for evacuation of the peninsula over the next two days. We knew that there would be less chance of entrapment if we moved to Queen Weetamoo's large Pocasset territory on the mainland, east of us across Mount Hope Bay. I sent messages to the Pocasset leaders asking them for additional canoes to help us cross the bay. With the assistance of the Pocassets, we were able to evacuate our entire tribe of about three hundred braves plus women and children, by June 28. I knew, however, that the evacuation gave us only temporary respite because the disappointed English forces were sure to pursue us with an increased lust for our destruction.

On the 29th, Major Savage arrived at Swansea as expected. I was informed that the number of soldiers who accompanied him, added to the men already assembled, brought the total force to about five hundred. I learned later that the major ordered a full-scale attack on Mount Hope Peninsula, to begin early the next morning. He no doubt hoped that a surprise attack on our settlement would decimate my warriors and eliminate us as a fighting force. My spies told me that it was noon and raining when the first troops crossed the narrow bridge that separated the town of Swansea from Indian land. The combined force then proceeded to search for signs of Indian activity. After passing the outlying houses of the settlers, many that Indians had burnt to the ground, the soldiers that led the advance were confronted with a hideous sight. Mounted on poles positioned along the road were the heads of the eight Englishmen that my braves had killed earlier during the Mattapoiset raid.[11] My messengers said that Major Savage's men, although shocked by the sight, proceeded warily along the paths that led to our encampment. To their surprise, they encountered no Indians along the way or in the area where our tepees were still standing. My informers noted that the soldiers explored the whole peninsular without success before returning to Swansea.

On July 1, Major Savage ordered his men to build a fort on the northern part of Mount Hope Peninsula near the Kickamuit River. He had probably hoped that the structure would allow his men to command the area and prevent me from returning to my homeland from the north. I later heard that Benjamin Church wanted the soldiers to continue to pursue my people into Pocasset territory after they found us missing at Mount Hope, but that he was overruled by Major Savage. It is likely that such a move, if undertaken, would have been successful and would have destroyed my warrior forces. Thankfully, the white man's delay was much to my advantage. It allowed me to cement my relations with Weetamoo and plan my next tactic.

I believed that if we remained too long in the Pocasset area it would be a fatal mistake. I felt that we could be easily blocked from traveling north toward the Taunton River, which was our only means of escape to friendly territory. I feared that if we were cut off, we would probably be subjected to an attack by a large army, with no place to go. With these thoughts in mind, I ordered all of my people to prepare for a long trek north. My hope was that our evacuation could be completed before the English could mobilize their forces and move them into a position to prevent our escape. I knew the trip would be dangerous, but I knew of no other option to save my people.

As my braves and squaws were assembling for the move—gathering food, weapons, and supplies—I sought out Weetamoo, squaw sachem of the Pocassets.

"Queen Weetamoo, sister of my beautiful wife, and once the wife of my murdered brother," I said, "I fear for your life, and that of your people. The English say that they protect you, but their promises have only left a trail of blood. Join me and my people. We will move together to the north. There we will both find safety with friendly tribes."

Weetamoo listened thoughtfully as I spoke about the large areas of land that the English had taken from us without our consent or adequate compensation. I told her of their unjust establishment of the settlement of Swansea at Mount Hope Neck and how their animals overran our farms and destroyed our crops. I saw tears in her eyes when I related how members of my tribe were treated unfairly and put in English jails after false accusations by malicious colonists. Our talks continued for a number of days.

We were interrupted constantly by messengers who advised us of actions that had taken place at other locations. They told me that some Indians had attacked Taunton on June 27. They said that many houses were burned there, and that John Tisdale, owner of one of the torched houses, was killed. I was pleased to hear that the warriors hadn't harmed any of the Leonard family who lived in Taunton. I had visited them often and they were my friends. Mr. Leonard had often allowed us to use his forge to repair our guns. I had earlier requested that no harm be brought to his family.

I also learned that on July 9 some of my men attacked Middleborough, burning most of the houses and destroying livestock and many of the colonists' crops. The settlers, having traveled earlier to Plymouth for safety, were spared. I was also advised that the Nipmucks under Sachem Totoson had attacked Dartmouth on the same date, and that on July 14, Nipmucks, led by Sachem Matoonas, attacked the town of Mendon. Six colonists were killed there, and cornfields and several buildings were destroyed.

By the time my discussions with Queen Weetamoo ended, she agreed that her people would also suffer at the hands of the English. She consented to have her Pocassets join me in our flight to safety, and together we announced our plan of escape to our anxious people.

Our two tribes assembled quickly, with a minimum of commotion, to flee our precarious position before the white man could block our departure. We had to leave behind about a hundred women, children, and elderly whom we feared would slow us in this necessary move. I later found out that Captain Benjamin Church had persuaded the group that couldn't accompany us to surrender, promising them no harm. They were subsequently turned over to Plymouth authorities. I was told that at a Council of War on August 4 the Plymouth government decided to sell all but a few of my helpless people into slavery. That was one more atrocity that strengthened my resolve to fight the English.

CHAPTER THIRTEEN

We left the Pocasset territory undetected and slowly moved toward the Taunton River. We soon learned that several hundred soldiers led by Major Savage had entered the swamp in our pursuit. Not finding us there, they began to move northward in our direction. Upon hearing the news, my younger brother, Sonconewhew, one of my best war leaders, volunteered to protect the rear of our party as we moved toward safety.

On July 18, fearing that the English were gaining on us, he positioned himself with a number of braves behind bushes ringing a clearing that we knew the soldiers would have to travel through. When the white men did appear in the open space, my hidden men opened fire. They killed five soldiers and wounded several more. The startled military contingent regrouped and then returned fire. Their volleys killed three important members of my Wampanoag council. I also suffered the loss of Sonconewhew, my dear brother and chief war captain.

With the coming of darkness and its illusive shadows, the English feared they would start shooting each other so they returned to their camp. Their hasty retreat and reluctance to press their advantage allowed us to continue our movement northwest. We encountered no additional soldiers during the rest of our trek to the shore of the Taunton River. When we arrived there we rested while our strongest braves cut down trees and reeds to construct the rafts necessary for us to cross the river. As I waited for the floating platforms to be completed, I reflected on the bravery of my brother. His untimely death further strengthened my determination to fight the English.

By the 26th of July all of our people had been transported to the other side of the river by the makeshift rafts. I planned to lead our people westward to the north of Swansea, then over the large exposed plain north of Old Rehoboth, across the Pawtucket River, and past an area called Nipsachuck about twelve miles north of Providence. From there it was not far to where friendly Indians had their home. I hoped to join the aggressive Nipmucks whom I knew were already attacking English settlements on the western frontier of the Plymouth region. By July 30, we had passed safely over the Old Rehoboth plain, crossed the Pawtucket River and were making our way to Nipsachuck. There, we planned to refresh ourselves. We arrived on the 31st of July. We spread out over the open area and made camp so our people could rest.

While we had been traveling away from the Pocasset swamp, messengers occasionally informed me of the white man's movements. I learned that English forces from Providence and Old Rehoboth, together with allied Mohegans led by Oneco, were pursuing us, aiming to prevent our uniting with the Nipmucks. I was not informed and had no way of knowing at the time, however, that the enemy was already close to our encampment at Nipsachuck and were observing us from behind the foliage.

On August 1, a combined force of about two hundred and fifty English troopers attacked our position just after daybreak. They charged out of the woods from two sides with frightening yells and with muskets blazing. Some of my men were barely awake, but everyone ran for his weapon to repulse the fierce attack. With great courage my men stood firm against the onslaught. When the white clouds of gun smoke settled, it was apparent that we had resisted the assault. But the bloody battle had cost the lives of twenty-four of my warriors including four more of my captains. To escape from a possible second attack, I commanded everyone to hurry into the nearby woods. Once we reorganized, I told my men that rather than risk a second attack, we would continue on our way toward our objective, friendly Indian territory. Our rapid retreat forced us to abandon much of our equipment. As we departed the area, we could see in the distance the English and their Mohawk friends ransacking what we had been forced to leave at the campsite. The rampage had ended by nine that morning. Wasting no time mourning our losses, we proceeded along the Blackstone River toward the Nipmuck camps. I later learned that a Captain Henchman and his reinforcements arrived at Nipsachuck from Providence to join the other forces soon after the fighting was over, but neither the English nor the Mohawks continued to pursue us until the next day. The delay provided us with the time to travel far enough away from Nipsachuck so we couldn't be caught again.

On August 3, our combined party of Wampanoags and Pocassets split in two. Weetamoo wanted to move to the south to join with Ninigret and his Niantics, part of the Narragansett tribe. He had earlier assured her of safety. After cordial farewells, I had my people move northwestward so that we could join forces with the Nipmucks to continue our battle against the white man. Although that tribe was fighting on its own, I felt that by our fighting together, we would stand a better chance of resisting the English attacks.

After our separation from the Pocassets, I learned that a week earlier Captains Hutchinson and Wheeler together with Ephraim Curtis and about twenty-five militia and native guides left the Boston area on orders to go to Nipmuck country to secure the promise of allegiance to the English cause from that tribe. The military forces arrived in the settlement of West Brookfield on August 1. As they continued their march toward New Braintree, Muttaump and his Nipmuck followers ambushed the troops and killed eight English soldiers. Although Hutchinson and Wheeler were wounded, they led their remaining troops back to Brookfield where they joined the twenty families who were gathered in a tavern, the most secure structure in that settlement. Muttaump and his warriors followed the retreating soldiers back to Brookfield and proceeded to burn the houses and slaughter the livestock there. Edward Huchinson, no relation to the captain, was the first settler killed in Brookfield. Later, settler Harry Young peered out of a window, and was shot dead. One of my informers saw how Sam Prichard tried to sneak out to summon aid and was also killed. Nipmuck Indians mounted his head on a pole in front of the garrison, so all of the settlers could see it. I was also told that tribesmen, unable to get the colonists to surrender, shot flaming arrows at the tavern, but the occupants quickly extinguished the fires. The Indians then loaded a wagon with straw and other combustibles, lit it on fire, and pushed it next to the building. When an unexpected downpour extinguished the fire, the Nipmucks continued their assault with muskets and arrows. They burned the remaining houses in the settlement. The defended tavern and one half-built house escaped destruction. The raid on Brookfield lasted for two days. I was told help arrived on August 5 for the besieged Englishmen. In the late afternoon, Major Simon Willard with about forty-eight horsemen rode into the village, surprised the Indian attackers and quickly joined the colonists and soldiers in the tavern house. By morning, the Nipmucks, believing that they could do little more damage than had been done, moved back into the woods. My Wampanoags had taken no part in the Brookfield fighting, but hearing about the Nipmuck successes made them more eager to engage the English themselves.

We heard about the Nipmuck engagements on that same day that forty braves and I joined the Indians at Menamset, the Nipmucks' main camp.[12] When the warriors finished telling us their stories about the Brookfield fight, I praised the leaders for their successful attacks. I had little to offer them as tribute so I took off my mantle, which was made of much wampum, and cut it in three parts with my knife. I offered each of the three chiefs one part of the valuable mantle as a tribute to the bravery shown by them and their warriors. My people then refreshed themselves and secured more powder and ball. The next day we left Menamset and continued our trek westward toward other Indian camps along the Connecticut River.

As we were proceeding along the well-traveled paths, a messenger arrived and told me that many Praying Indians in the Boston area—those who had exchanged their native beliefs for the English God—had made an offer to fight on the side of the English. The leaders in Massachusetts refused to allow their participation in the fight against me and instead made arrangements to isolate and transport them to Deer Island, a secure reservation in Boston Harbor. I was advised that most of this group, made up of neutral Nipmuck and Massachuset Indians, then escaped from the English and planned to join my forces in the West. The news excited me, and I felt that my hope to unite the tribes against the superior forces of the English was finally becoming a reality. Later, other messengers from Boston informed me that the Massachusetts government, suspecting that the powerful Narragansetts might also join my warriors, decided to use force to prevent that from happening.

CHAPTER FOURTEEN

O n August 15, I arrived at an Indian camp near Hatfield together with forty warriors and some women and children. My braves immediately began their war dances to renew their fighting spirit. Meanwhile I conferred with the Nipmuck leaders—Monoco, known to the white man as One-Eyed John; Shoshonim, known to the white man as Sagamore Sam; and Muttaump. Both Monoco and Muttaump had recently returned from taking part in the devastating attacks on Brookfield. All three sachems were anxious to continue raiding the English settlements, and we agreed to join forces. We decided that the isolated villages along the Connecticut River were ripe for attack. The sachems pleaded with me to direct the engagements from afar, for they valued my leadership and didn't want my life expended in a battle they knew I would insist on leading. After hours of controversy, I consented to the wishes of my councilors. I knew that with my crippled right hand I would be no match in combat with an agile English soldier.

I lost the use of my hand a number of years ago when one of my braves gave me an English pistol. He had gotten it from a Rhode Island settler, trading much wampum for it. I thanked him for the gift and immediately loaded it with powder and ball to test its ability to compete with our larger muskets. I fired it at a tree some distance from me and was much pleased when I saw the bark of the tree shatter. I then loaded it with a larger charge of powder to see if I could hit a tree at a greater distance from me than the first one. I carefully took aim and fired again. The powder ignited and the gun exploded in my hand, ripping the flesh from my fingers. I covered the open wound with wet leaves and hurried back to camp. There, our shaman asked the spirits to repair my injured hand. For two months one of our medicine men applied herbal mixtures to my injury. Today my scarred hand resembles a rigid claw, but it provides me with enough function to serve my needs. When I wave it during my animated discussions with my councilors, it provides assurance to them that their leader is strong and can withstand both pain and misfortune.

CHAPTER FIFTEEN

While at Hatfield, I learned from messengers that soldiers from Boston and Connecticut had gathered at Hadley, and that they had been joined by some Mohegans who wanted to act as scouts. We were sure, however, that we knew trails that would allow us to avoid contact with the enemy scouts as we traveled to the settlements we intended to raid.

On August 22, Monoco and Shoshonim with a group of Nipmuck braves traveled a long distance to the east and attacked the settlement at Lancaster, killing seven Englishmen and burning one house.

On August 25, the neutral Norwottocks, part of the Nipmuck tribe, fled their camp on the western bank of the Connecticut River above Northampton when they found out that English troopers from Hatfield were approaching with orders to disarm them. The Indians halted at Hopewell Swamp in Whately and ambushed the soldiers. The Norwottocks killed nine, but lost an equal number. The swamp battle was over in three hours, and the remaining Norwottocks, pleased that they were able to hold on to their weapons, made their way to the Indian camp at Hatfield and told us of their experience. They gladly joined our warriors in the fight against the white man.

On August 31, with some of my Wampanoag warriors and a greater number of Nipmucks, I secretly crossed the Connecticut River and advanced toward Deerfield. We attacked the unsuspecting settlement on September 1. We killed one colonist and burned many of the houses and barns there. By evening we had re-crossed the Connecticut River and were traveling toward Squakeag[13], the most northern settlement in the Englishman's western territory.

There we burned many houses and killed eight settlers.

On September 4, as some of my jubilant braves were returning to our camp at Peskeompskut, they encountered English troops. The soldiers led by Captain Richard Beers were traveling from the colonist's fort in Hadley to assist in the evacuation of Northfield. Firing from ambush, the combined force, which included Pocumtucks and Nashaways, killed twenty-one soldiers including Captain Beers.

When we returned to camp after the Squakeag encounter, a Nipmuck who had just returned from spying at Hadley, entered my shelter. Still breathing hard, he addressed me.

"Colonists now preparing to send Captain Lathrop with soldiers to Deerfield to get corn that was left there after attack," he said. "They have orders to bring corn back to Hadley."

I thanked him for the information, then relayed the news to the Nipmuck leaders. On September 18, as Lathrop and his men were returning from Deerfield with the fully loaded carts of corn, they were ambushed at Muddy Brook by a force of Nipmucks led by Monoco and Shoshonim. Only sixteen English soldiers were able to escape from the bloody battle that followed. The corn that they were carting was brought back to Peskeompskut by our warriors, for our people were also in great need of food.

On September 26, the Agawam Indians destroyed William Pynchon's mill in Connecticut. Pynchon, an army officer, apparently was determined to avenge the destruction of his property so he gathered a large force of military men at Springfield. They left that settlement to join other soldiers stationed at Hadley. This combined army raided one of our camps north of Hadley on October 5.

The Agawams who lived around Springfield realized that without Pynchon and his men the English settlement was no longer strongly defended. They immediately attacked poorly protected Springfield, killing three Englishmen and burning thirty-two houses and twenty-five barns. Most of the settlers, aware of the imminent attack, found safety in the three well-defended garrison houses in Springfield.

On October 19, Muttaump with eight hundred warriors attacked Hatfield. My informers told me that to lure the English soldiers away from the garrison houses, Muttaump ordered his braves to build a number of large fires a few miles away from the settlement. Captain Mosely, in command at the time, sent ten men to investigate the source of the giant columns of smoke. Five of them were killed by Muttaump's men who fired from hiding places in the nearby woods. Four other soldiers were wounded and captured. The remaining soldier was seen racing back to the garrison house. Muttaump then divided his men into three units. One approached the settlement from the center and the other two from the sides. Heavy fighting took place. The braves were repulsed three or four times. Muttaump finally conceded that the settlement could not be taken. He and his followers returned to camp with his prisoners. He told me about his engagement shortly after he secured guards for the captured white men.

When I heard the news of this attack and our other recent successes, I was jubilant. I believed that if we could get the additional help of the Narragansetts and the Mohawks, we could force the English from our lands. But first, I had to convince the two powerful tribes to actively join me in my fight. At that promising time, I had no way of knowing that events that were to occur over the next few months would completely destroy my hopes and vision of a land again open and free.

CHAPTER SIXTEEN

During the second week in November, most of the Nipmucks prepared to travel to the Indian fortress at Mount Wachusett.[14] In the winter, both the English and the Indians retired to remote quarters since neither side cared to fight in the snowy weather. Group movement was difficult due to the snowdrifts and ice; and the defoliated woods offered little ability to hide.

As the Nipmucks assembled their gear and food for their winter stay at Wachusett, I prepared for trips with some of my sachems to cement relations with the Narragansetts in Connecticut and the Mohawks in Albany. The Mohawks were part of the Iroquois Federation, a group of tribes that had little inclination to join me in my fight, for many were friendly to the English. I felt confident, though, that the recent showings of the white man's brutality would do much to convince the Mohawk sachems that to survive, their tribe must fight alongside my Wampanoag warriors. As I was gathering the necessary provisions for my extended trip, messengers brought me disturbing news. They told me that on November 12 the three English colonies had voted to raise a thousand men to invade the Narragansett territory and subjugate that tribe so that they would be unable to join me. Rhode Island, although not included in the three-colony commission as a result of the Indian-friendly actions of founder Roger Williams, nevertheless had agreed to supply boats to transport the English army across the waterways needed to be traversed to get to where the Narragansetts were encamped. General Josiah Winslow of Plymouth had been appointed commander of a combined army composed of five hundred and forty Massachusetts men commanded by Major Appleton, a hundred and fifty-eight Plymouth men commanded by Major William

Bradford, and four hundred Connecticut men commanded by Major Robert Treat. The well-respected Benjamin Church, who was apparently dissatisfied with the way that the commanders were pursuing the war, had opted to act on his own. I was told that out of respect for his achievements, he had been given the title of Special Assistant to General Winslow and the opportunity to select the men he wanted to lead.

On December 6, I left the camp at Peskeompskut with some of my ablest sachems and braves to visit Canonchet at his Narragansett homeland in Rhode Island. I was anxious to warn him of the English army buildup and persuade him that the time was ripe for his active participation in our fight with the white man. There was light snow on the ground, but the weather was clear and we were well supplied for the grueling trip.

On December 8, when we were a distance from camp, my scouts informed me that English troops were moving toward where I planned to go. To avoid running into the soldiers, I returned to Peskeompskut. Over the next two weeks, as I pondered my next move, messengers kept bringing me increasingly distressing news of the events occurring in Rhode Island. I felt that my alliance with the Narragansetts, a tribe much larger than the Wampanoags and Nipmucks combined, was becoming a less likely reality as each bit of information arrived.

On December 9, I learned that the Massachusetts and Plymouth army contingents had assembled at Rehoboth, across the Seekonk River from Providence, then were ferried to Providence by the complicit Rhode Island boatmen.

By December 11, all of the English soldiers were situated at Wickford, their advance base. I was advised by informers that while waiting for additional forces to arrive from Connecticut, small parties from the groups already at the English encampment advanced into the woods to try their luck at capturing or killing unsuspecting Indians. Benjamin Church with his handpicked followers captured eighteen Narragansetts. Other groups of soldiers captured thirty-nine more. All of the seized Indians except one were sent back to Boston. I later found out that the captured Indians were sold as slaves. The retained Indian, a Narragansett named Peter, apparently saved his own life by offering to lead the English to his tribe's encampment.

On December 15, while the two armies at Wickford waited for Major Treat and his Connecticut force to join them for their attack on the camp of Canonchet's Narragansett tribe, yet another Narragansett, Stonewall John, appeared at the English camp with a supposed offer of peace from Canonchet.

I was told that Major Winslow, suspecting treachery, sent him back to bring the appropriate sachems to Wickford in order to conduct proper negotiations. When Stonewall John requested that English soldiers accompany him back to protect him, the cautious Winslow sent only a small party along. A short distance from Wickford, concealed Indians fired on the unsuspecting soldiers, killing five. The remainder scurried back to their base camp to tell of Stonewall John's trickery.

On the evening of the same day, a party of Narragansetts attacked the stone garrison of Jireh Bull at Pettaquamscut, just south of Wickford. Indians killed fifteen of the seventeen people housed there. They completely destroyed the house. They were prevented from additional killing and destruction of property because Major Treat with his three hundred and fifteen Connecticut troops and one hundred and fifty Pequots, on their way to join Major Winslow at Wickford, surprised them at the scene.

On December 18, the English soldiers from Wickford and Major Treat with his Connecticut soldiers gathered at Pettaquamscut. The combined force prepared for a quick advance into Narragansett territory from that nearby settlement.

On December 19, the soldiers, led by the traitor Indian Peter, entered the swamp area where the sprawling village that sheltered about 3,500 Narragansett braves, women and children was located. There were about six hundred wigwams standing on the camp's six-acre tract. The Englishmen were initially confounded by the strong palisade fortification they encountered. I was told that they seemed inclined to return to camp until Peter showed them one wall that had not been completed. Its narrow opening had a single tree trunk lying flat on the ground, the top of which was the only path to the inside of the village. A small group of soldiers immediately charged single file over the downed tree toward the single opening. They were met by a blast of fire from the Indians inside. Two captains and most of the attacking soldiers were killed before they could enter the well-guarded enclosure. A second group attacked, only to be stopped again by Indian musket balls and arrows. This assault cost the life of another captain. A third attempt was made by sending a continuous flow of soldiers through the opening. Three more captains were killed and another wounded, and many additional soldiers were fatally wounded, but the opening was breached. Once inside the palisades, the English soldiers opened fire in full force, killing many Indians including women and children. They set fire to the wigwams and huts including those sheltering frightened squaws and their helpless children, most of whom were burned to death. High winds carried the flames from wigwam to wigwam, roasting the screaming occupants as well as destroying food stored within the makeshift shelters. Witnesses told me that Benjamin Church called out to save the supplies, but the ruthless soldiers continued to set fire to every wigwam.

Some Narragansetts, seeking to flee from the advancing Englishmen, pulled down a few of the palisade poles near them and escaped into the woods. With a small group, Church followed the Indians through the snowy terrain, but turned back when he was hit by balls from Indian muskets. The wounds apparently weren't life threatening. Church then gave up on the chase and returned to the village, which was completely engulfed in flame. Canonchet, together with a number of Sachems and other braves, had made a successful escape from the camp.

I found out later that Major Winslow, after a contentious fight with his officers about whether it was safe to travel back to Wickford in the falling snow, commanded his troops to return despite the freezing weather. The swamp fight was over, but according to my informants, it had claimed the lives of more than ninety soldiers including half of the company commanders. The one hundred fifty-two soldiers who were wounded in the attack had to be supported or carried along the perilous route back to camp. Fifty of them died along the way, and twenty-two more died soon after they returned to Wickford. The toll on the Narragansetts, however, was terrible. My messengers estimated that over 1,500 Narragansett men, women and children were killed. Upon hearing the news of the slaughter at the Narragansett camp, I knew that my hope of support from that tribe was doomed. My only salvation then was to convince the Mohawks and the other tribes in the west to join me.

CHAPTER SEVENTEEN

It was early January when I set out westward with many of my sachems and braves toward Scattacook, a friendly Indian village about twenty miles north of Albany. Once there, I was determined to persuade the leaders of the local tribes to stand side by side with me in my fight against the English settlers. The trek, which would have taken less than a week, actually took over three weeks due to the wintry conditions. The snow, often falling heavily, obliterated the trails and at times made forward movement impossible. Although I heard little complaining from my companions, I knew that most were homesick and wished that they could be spending the winter back with their families at Mount Wachusett.

On January 22, we arrived at Scattacook. I held talks with the Mahigan and Abernaki leaders for many days. They finally agreed to join forces with me, for they too were aware of English encroachment of their lands. I also contacted local Dutch and French representatives, since both of their governments despised the English. From them I was given assurance that their countrymen would provide us with food and weapons. Their promises brightened my outlook since I knew that the two governments would spare no effort to help us in our struggle. When I revealed my plan to travel south to speak with the leaders of the powerful Iroquois Federation, especially the Mohawk tribes, about joining us, one old Mahigan sachem warned me against it.

"No parley with Mohawks," I remember him saying. "They sign treaty of peace with Governor Andros in Albany. Will not fight against white man. Mohawk no like Wampanoag or Nipmuck. Mohawk make war, not peace with your tribe."

I thanked him for his information, but I knew that without the aid of the strong Mohawk tribe we would stand little chance to free ourselves from English domination. After many days of celebration over the joining of the Mahigan and Abernaki tribes with our own and the helpful offers of the Dutch and French, I gathered my party together and headed south. Two Mahigan warriors joined us to show us the way to the Mohawk camp. The heavy snowfall we encountered made it difficult to follow the correct trails. It was only the skill of the two Mahigan guides accompanying us that kept us on a proper path. On our third day away from the Scattacook village, as we proceeded with great difficulty through even higher drifts, three Mahigan braves on horseback appeared out of the white curtain of snow in front of us.

"We come from Mohawk village to give you warning," one said. "English governor tell Mohawk sachems that Wampanoag and Nipmuck bad medicine. Mohawks there dig up hatchet. Plan to fight, not help you. You go back to Scattacook. You safe there."

After consulting with Annawon and other of my councilors, I decided to continue on to Mohawk territory despite the threatening message we had just received. Without the support and active participation of the Mohawks, I knew that our forces would be no match for the English, who were regrouping and preparing for attack according to information I had received. I was determined to proceed with my plan and told my leaders to prepare for the trek. The next day proved how wrong I was in my decision to continue south.

CHAPTER EIGHTEEN

Two miles from Albany we encountered an extremely dense forest growth that we had to move through to reach our destination. It was nightfall when we reached the woods and the snow was falling, so I directed my men to find shelter among the trees for the night. I posted sentries and found a suitable spot myself for bedding down. The wind howled throughout the night, but the thick pine overgrowth provided some shelter from the heavy snow. Just before dawn I was awakened by the sounds of musket fire. I heard one of my braves shouting: "Mohawks! We are being attacked by Mohawks!"

In the dim light I could see muzzle flashes. They were coming closer and closer. Noise and smoke were everywhere. Not knowing how many warriors were attacking us, I gave the order to seek shelter deeper in the woods. Soon, far into the woods, we formed a defensive line against the attackers. We fired with great accuracy from behind the trees, finally repulsing the Mohawks. I could plainly see them in the first morning light, retreating to the south. Following this surprise attack, it took much time to bury 40 of my brave warriors in the frozen ground.

My vision of having the Mohawks fight by our side against the Englishmen was over. With a heavy heart, I reluctantly led my courageous but disheartened men back to Nipmuck country and home. Our difficult trek through the wintry weather was made even more cheerless by the memories of our lost comrades and our defeat at the hands of the Mohawks.

On March 12, 1676, the remnants of my party and I arrived at the Nipmuck camp near Northfield. We were met with their loud cheers and lively dances. The celebrations going on were in honor of their own successful attacks on many English villages. The distressing news about my failure to get the Mohawks to join us did little to dampen the enthusiasm of the tribal leaders. The sachems told me at great length about their victories.

On February 10, Nipmuck parties had attacked Lancaster. Despite warnings to the English leaders from the Christian Indians, James Quanapohit and Job Kattenanit, the colonies did little to fortify the town. The inhabitants gathered in the five garrison houses and saw their houses burned. Many tried to flee when the raiders began to set fire to the fortified garrison houses. The attackers killed the settlers as they tried to leave the flaming buildings. The Indians counted thirty-seven townspeople dead. When Captain Wadsworth with his soldiers arrived from Marlborough, the raiding party left, taking along the town's livestock and twenty-four prisoners. One of the prisoners, a Mary Rowlandson, wife of the village pastor, was carried off with her wounded infant daughter in her arms. She had lost her sister, a brother-in-law, and a nephew in the melee and had been wounded herself in the side. She was kept alive by the Nipmucks for the ransom she would bring. Later, on two occasions, I met this brave woman. She told me about her experiences and how her infant daughter had died. I remember complimenting her on her bravery.

On February 21, Medfield, about twelve miles from Boston, had been attacked at daybreak. Eighteen settlers were killed as they sought refuge in the garrison houses. Forty or fifty houses and barns were burned before help arrived. The Nipmuck and Narragansett warriors escaped to the north. They burned a bridge over the Charles River to prevent the soldiers from following them.

On February 25, the tribe attacked Weymouth. There, eight houses were burned, but no people were killed.

While I remained at Northfield, messengers brought me news about other successful raids against the English settlements.

On March 12, Tatoson and his Nipmuck warriors traveled all the way to Plymouth where they attacked Clark's garrison. They killed eleven people, and before leaving, the braves confiscated guns, ammunition, and English money.

On March 13, Monoco and his warriors attacked Groton, burning sixty-five houses and killing one settler. Two others were killed later that day when the Nipmucks ambushed some of the settlers fleeing from the town.

The next day, Quinnapin and other Nipmucks attacked Northampton, killing eleven colonists and burning the same number of houses. Only the coming of a contingent led by Captain William Turner, commander of the garrisons in the river towns, prevented the complete destruction of Northampton.

The slaying of colonists was not only an activity for men. On March 15, two Englishmen traveling from Marlborough to Sudbury were waylaid by a band of vengeful Indian women. Both men were killed and cut to pieces by the irate squaws.

When the Nipmucks attacked Warwick, no one was killed, but the town was completely destroyed.

On March 26, a Sabbath, Agawam warriors attacked settlers traveling from Long Meadow to Springfield to attend church. One man and one woman were killed. Two women and two children were taken as prisoners.

On the same day, Nipmucks attacked Marlborough. Most of the houses in the town were burned while the owners were at church.

On that Sabbath in Seekonk, Rhode Island, a vengeful Canonchet and his Narragansett braves trapped Captain Michael Peirce and his company of sixty-three soldiers and twenty Christian Indians. Peirce lost fifty-five of his men and eight of his friendly Indians.

The next day, the same Narragansetts attacked Providence. They killed several colonists and burned fifty-four houses. Roger Williams, because of his friendship with the Indians, was left unharmed though his house was one of those destroyed.

On March 28th, Nipmucks attacked Rehoboth. They burned sixty-six houses and many barns and buildings.

I took pleasure in these successes, but I also knew that without the Narragansetts or Mohawks at our side, we could not prevail against the white man. The English colonies seemed to have an unending supply of soldiers and arms. The Indian tribes, on the other hand, were losing warriors in numbers that could not be replaced. Our need for food was also of great concern. While we were waging war against the white man, we were neglecting planting, catching fish that were then running in the streams, and hunting animals that we needed for food and clothing. Many of our victories had provided food during the winter, but I knew that in the coming months we would need to have our own supplies.

CHAPTER NINETEEN

In early April, Shoshonim approached me. "Me say, good to let our hostages go," he said. "That way English will treat braves better if they are captured."

I disagreed with him. I believed that the English would not for any reason lessen their lust for Indian scalps. The truth of my belief was borne out shortly thereafter. Shoshonim, without my knowledge, released a number of his hostages to gain favor with the colonists. The old sachem was captured soon after his show of kindness. He was hanged without a trial, in front of a cheering crowd.

Later in April, Canonchet, who had returned to his homeland to get seed corn for planting, was captured at Stonington. The proud Narragansett was one of our best leaders. To the end, he defended his actions and his honor. On orders from the English, he was shot to death by Mohegan Sachem Oneco and two Pequot sachems.

On April 21, about five-hundred warriors from different tribes and I participated in an attack on Sudbury. Although we killed many soldiers and settlers during the fight and in later ambushes close to the settlement, we were not able to completely destroy the garrison houses that housed the inhabitants. It was an important victory, but it was also our last joint encounter against the English.

There were many other individual raids, some close to Boston, but none with a coalition of tribes. On May 11, Tuspaquin, one of my sachems, traveled to Plymouth with other Wampanoag warriors and burned eleven houses.

I knew that our men were extremely tired and hungry, and their desire to fight was far less than their desire to return home. I began to hear more of English victories than successful Indian raids.

The following week, Captain William Turner with his forces attacked Peskeompskut, our camp on the Connecticut River near Deerfield. At the time it held mostly women and children. The surprised victims there were either slaughtered by the soldiers or sold into slavery.

I believed that our women who normally do the planting, were being targeted by the English soldiers. As more and more squaws were captured or killed, our ability to feed ourselves in the future became of enormous concern. I felt helpless to correct the situation, and I, too, was overcome with great weariness.

Meanwhile, under the constant urging by English governments at Albany and Plymouth the Mohawks attacked many of our camps, killing Narragansetts and Wampanoags wherever they could find them.

Also to my dismay, Massachusetts officials, recognizing the superiority of Indian tracking and fighting techniques, finally allowed the Christian Indians—who had been confined to secure reservations around Boston—to join them in the war. Their participation removed many of our advantages, which up to that time were critical to our ability to frustrate the English soldiers. With Indians at their side they learned to follow trails, survive in the forest, and shoot at us from behind protective foliage.

On July 2, John Talcott and his soldiers attacked a Narragansett camp in Rhode Island. They killed thirty-four men and ninety-two women. The next day they killed or captured sixty-seven more Indian men, women, and children who had come out of hiding to seek peace.

The news of this slaughter reminded me again of the English woman, Mary Rowlandson, who was not killed, but taken captive during a raid at Lancaster. I had met her twice while she was being held for ransom, and each time she told me about her experiences in captivity. On the second occasion, I gave her an English shilling for making me a fine cloth cap for my son. I later invited her to eat with me, and we shared a cake that I fried in bear's grease. Her captors allowed her to accompany them on their travels, and she was eventually set free for a ransom, unlike many of our squaws and children who were captured by the white man and immediately killed.

Later in July, I received news that the great Nipmuck leaders Monaco and Matoonas were captured and killed. I finally had to face what I had long refused to accept—that the tide of war had turned against us. My dream of joining the tribes and overwhelming the English was gone. I felt I had but one option—to return to my homeland to join my squaw, Wootonekamuske, and my nine-year-old son.

On July 30, as I headed for Mount Hope, soldiers commanded by the persistent English captain, Benjamin Church, spotted me in the woods near Bridgewater. I eluded them by hurrying into a nearby swamp.

The next day, English soldiers surprised my aged uncle Uncompoin near the Taunton River and killed him before he could escape. That same day, soldiers raided a large Wampanoag encampment and took many prisoners. I was devastated when I was told that my squaw and son were among the Indians captured.

On August 1, as I was resting on a stump on the banks of the Taunton River, English soldiers on the other side saw me and began to shoot at me. I hurried into the woods and again escaped.

On August 3, an English scouting party found my ally, Weetamo, squaw sachem of the Pocassets, drowned in the Taunton River. She had slipped off a raft as she was fleeing from a search party. She had made it only about halfway across the river. Messengers told me later that the English had mutilated her body and had her head mounted on a pole on the Taunton green.

On August 6, my good friend, the great Nipmuck leader Totoson, was found dead in the woods by English soldiers. My spies told me that they thought he had died from a broken heart.

As I carefully continued on foot back to Mount Hope, I was in great despair. My braves continually caught up with me to give me the news of Church's successes. He had captured one hundred thirty Wampanoags in one encounter and even more in another. Sometimes gaining only a few captives, overall he substantially reduced the number of warriors available to fight.

Once I arrived back in my camp in the swampy area near Mount Hope, I held many meetings with my remaining faithful braves. During one discussion, the brother of Alderman, a member of Weetamoo's Pocassets, offered the suggestion that we surrender to the English. I knew that such a move would mean death to me and most of my followers. Believing that the idea of giving up could only have been offered by someone who was on friendly terms with the white man, I jumped up and plunged my knife into the heart of the traitor. As he lay in our midst, dead, I solemnly stepped back and asked if anyone else had similar thoughts. Everyone present stood tall and assured me that our fight was going to last to the finish. I found out later that Alderman, brother of the Indian I had killed, had left camp the night before to visit Benjamin Church. He apparently had offered to lead Church to us, if he could be assured that he would not be harmed. Church must have agreed to his terms.

Early on August 12, as most of my men slept, Church, with a military contingent, apparently surrounded our camp. Awakened by an alarm from a sentry and suspecting an attack, I called to rouse my men. When I began to hear the firing of muskets, I told my braves to disperse and prepare to fight. Although only partially dressed, I grabbed my own gun and ran deeper into the woods. I knew that I was the main target of their attack because my informants told me that Church had promised his superiors he would pursue me to the death.

I didn't realize how far I had run until I came to the edge of the swamp. I decided to rest. The sound of gunfire had almost stopped and I hoped that it was a sign my men had repulsed the surprise attack. I considered going back to find out how my braves were faring, but I felt I would be walking into certain death if Church and his men were still scouting the area.

CHAPTER TWENTY

In the semi-darkness, I am now sitting on a large rock—a refuge from the muddy ground all around me. The sunlight is now just beginning to show through the leaves, casting eerie shadows throughout the woods. It is difficult to tell whether the shapes in the distance are men or twisted branches. I had better continue on my way before the sun brightens the landscape if I am going to escape from the English soldiers as I have so often done in the past.

Hark! What's that noise behind me. It sounds like the latching of a musket. I mustn't take the time to turn around. I'd better run.

What's that hiss!

No time to look. That noise can only mean a misfire—a flash in the pan. I'm safe again…I'd better race away from here like a hunted deer.

What's that! Sounds like another latching…

EPILOGUE

E arly in the morning of August 12, 1676, Philip was spotted by the Englishman Caleb Cook, and his companion Alderman.[15] The two scouts had been sent out by Church along with others to search for the elusive Philip. When the two men found the Wampanoag sachem, both raised their muskets and fired at close range. Cook's musket was damp, and it misfired. Alderman's gun didn't. He shot two balls into Philip's back. One ball hit him directly in the heart and the other just above it. Philip died instantly. His body fell forward onto the miry ground, his musket beneath it.

Alderman then ran to tell Church the good news. Church hurried to the site of the killing, and when his whole force was assembled around him, he told them that Philip was dead. Some Indians pulled Philip's body from the mud and dragged it to a dry upland. Church described the sachem as "a doleful, great, naked, dirty beast," and declaring that Philip had caused many an Englishman's body to lie unburied, ordered a native executioner to decapitate Philip and quarter his body. He then directed his troops to hang the pieces, except Philip's head and one hand, on trees throughout the woods. The Indian's head was carried to Plymouth where on August 17 it was marched through the streets. The English then impaled the head on a tall pole outside the Plymouth fort, where it remained for twenty-four years. Philip's twisted hand was given to Alderman. He put it in a jar and preserved it in rum. For a long time afterwards, Alderman traveled around, showing it to inquisitive settlers for a small fee.

Following the death of Philip, the English began to rout out the remaining pockets of Indian resistance. Most of the tribal leaders were either killed or executed. Some lesser tribal members were able to hide until the fighting was over. Others fled to outlying regions including New York and Canada where the native Indians welcomed them.

In a sentence demanded by the Plymouth government, the English sold Philip's wife, Wootonekamuske, and their nine-year-old son to slave traders from the West Indies in March of 1677. Quinnapin, chief lieutenant of the Narragansett leader Canonchet, was executed on August 25. Annawon, councilor to Massasoit and Alexander, and Philip's old but capable war leader, who led the Wampanoags—who were not captured or killed with Philip at the final battle at Mount Hope—out of the swamp, surrendered on August 28. He was sent to Plymouth where he was executed. Philip's brother-in-law, Tuspaquin, surrendered to Benjamin Church on September 6 after receiving assurance that he would not be killed. The Plymouth government overruled Church and beheaded the Indian brave. Tuspaquin's wife and son were sold into slavery.

With the death of Philip and most of the other Wampanoag, Nipmuck and Narragansett leaders, the colonial governments focused on rebuilding their settlements and clearing the small pockets of Indian resistance still remaining. As the English became stronger and the Indians less of a threat, military leaders became more aggressive in their treatment of the native Americans. Many officers committed acts of unbelievable atrocity, exemplified by one particular action of Major Richard Waldron.

On September 6, 1677, Waldron and his men were joined by about four hundred more troops at what is now Dover, New Hampshire. On the same day, about an equal number of Abernaki Indians arrived at Dover hoping to sign a peace treaty. Waldron encouraged the Indians to feign a military engagement with the English. As part of the ruse he had the Indians gather together and fire all of their guns into the air at the same time. Without loaded arms to defend themselves, the Indians were immediately surrounded and disarmed. Over half were sent to Boston where they were either executed or sold into slavery.

Other more limited skirmishes occurred in New England in the years after Philip's death. In 1677, many English were killed or taken hostage when renegade Indians raided Deerfield and Hatfield on their way to Canada.

The last open battles occurred in Maine. By August of 1677 hostilities there too had ceased, and a peace agreement, the Casco Treaty, was signed on April 12, 1678. That document, signed by the English and the Abenaki Indians, formally ended hostilities in Maine, and essentially ended the New England conflict known as King Philip's War.

The bloody war was the most destructive in New England's history. About 2,500 colonists died and about 6,000 Indians were killed, wounded, or sold as slaves. Over half of the ninety English settlements then in existence in New England underwent Indian assault. Many of those were destroyed completely. Only a few were left untouched.

As with many wars, this war was essentially a fight for land. The Indians wanted to hold onto the woods that they had hunted and fished in for thousands of years. The colonists wanted the same land for the needs of a population that was rapidly expanding due to the influx of English immigrants. The white men, with greater weaponry but lack of experience in wilderness fighting, came close to losing the battle on many occasions. With their superior resources and assistance from friendly Indians, however, they were eventually able to claim victory. When King Philip's War was over, the remaining natives were disbursed throughout the territory and made subservient to the white man. With the final battles, the threat of a united Indian rebellion in New England was forever ended.

Bloody struggles directly between the English and the French—most with Indian participation—were soon to begin. Those hostilities and their tragic consequences were destined to continue for almost a hundred more years.

****

Some historians conclude that Philip was weak and cowardly. The Reverend William Hubbard wrote soon after the war was over that Philip was "a savage Miscreant with Envy and Malice against the English." About 1850, Samuel Drake, an antiquarian, writing about Philip, stated that "there is ample testimony of his cowardice; being always the first to fly when he fancied his Enemies near."

Other writers saw him as a man of unbelievable courage and cunning. Washington Irving, author of the beloved *Rip Van Winkle* and *The Legend of Sleepy Hollow* noted in his book *Philip of Pokanoket* that Philip was "the most distinguished of a number of contemporary Sachems who made the most generous struggle of which human nature is capable, fighting to the last gasp in the cause of their country, without a hope of victory or a thought of renown." Irving ended his biography of Philip with the following: "He was a patriot attached to his native soil, with heroic qualities and bold achievements that would have graced a civilized warrior."

Perhaps the evaluation of Philip by Professor Douglas Leach in his book

Flintlock and Tomahawk best summarizes the true nature of the Indian leader. He wrote:

"It has long been recognized that Philip was not the great leader he was once assumed to be. The struggle of 1675–1676 bears his name because he started it, and during those fateful months of war he was accepted as the symbol of Indian resistance to the white men, but once the conflict had spread beyond the bounds of Plymouth Colony, Philip lost his control of the situation. Other tribes and other leaders began to fight against the English, and they had their own ideas and their own ambitions. There is no evidence that Philip ever exercised supreme command over the various warring tribes. Instead, he seems to have sunk into the position of a leader among many leaders. So far as we can tell, he played no part in the great battles that occurred after the summer of 1675. Some writers have even charged him with cowardice, although it is difficult to see how a coward could have retained the loyalty of so many brave warriors."

One may conclude from the many writings about Philip that he was either good or evil. The author of this story encourages the reader to look impartially at the actions of Philip from the Great Sachem's point of view and then decide which view of him most closely captures his true character.

By studying the story of this great warrior, we perpetuate his memory and at the same time learn about one of the great struggles in American history.

Additional information about King Philip and his times can be obtained by reading the books noted in Appendix B.

PAUL REVERE

True Patriot

A hurry of hoofs in a village street.
A shape in the moonlight, a bulk in the dark,
And beneath, from the pebbles, in passing, a spark
Struck out by a steed flying fearless and fleet;
That was all! And yet, through the gloom and the light,
The fate of a nation was riding that night;
And the spark struck out by that steed, in his flight,
Kindled the land into flame with its heat.

So through the night rode Paul Revere;
And so through the night went his cry of alarm
To every Middlesex village and farm---
A cry of defiance, and not of fear,
A voice in the darkness, a knock at the door,
And a word that shall echo for evermore!
For, borne on the night-wind of the Past,
Through all our history, to the last,
In the hour of darkness and peril and need,
The people will waken and listen to hear
The hurrying hoofbeats of that steed,
And the midnight message of Paul Revere.

From *Paul Revere's Ride*
by
Henry Wadsworth Longfellow

PAUL REVERE

TRUE PATRIOT

Prologue

M ost readers throughout the Western world are familiar with the American patriot Paul Revere from Henry Wadsworth Longfellow's poem *Paul Revere's Ride*. Its lyrical words tell how before the start of the Revolutionary War this mounted hero alerted the sleeping inhabitants of the towns around Boston that the British soldiers were coming. Few people know, however, that Revere was also a printer who produced currency for Massachusetts; a proprietor of the foundry that cast the first large bell made in America; and an owner of the rolling mill that fabricated the copper for both the dome of the Statehouse in Boston and the hull of the warship, *Constitution*[16].

This fictional story tells in Paul Revere's words about his life and times—an era when brave men declared their independence from Britain, and a few self-governing states were molded into a nation that promised the never-before-realized "liberty and justice for all." The major events described in this story actually occurred. They are well documented by the writings of Revere, his contemporaries, and many historians.

*****

The famous patriot was born into a world that was in the midst of great upheaval. England and France had been at war with each other since 1689 both on the continent of Europe and in the outlying regions of settled America. In Europe, the two nations fought for dominance and prestige. In colonial America the fight was for control of a land that was rich in fish, furs, tobacco, and sugar—all items the two countries needed to import from the new settlements for a burgeoning population which increasingly desired such things. One of the wars fought in colonial America—the French and Indian War—was in progress as Revere was maturing. The recognized beginning of that war was in 1755.

Hostilities began when young George Washington, traveling on his way to build a defensive fort on the Ohio River, encountered French forces in Virginia. A minor battle ensued, and Washington, with his small ragtag army, won the skirmish. He went on to build Fort Necessity in what is now southwestern Pennsylvania. The shots fired in the encounter, however, resonated back in the home countries, and both England and France prepared to make bold stands in the colonies. They both understood then that the winner of the major conflicts sure to come would rule much of America.

This story begins on December 11, 1797. Paul Revere is sitting in his favorite chair in a corner of the Green Dragon Tavern on Union Street in Boston, Massachusetts. He is in the presence of a number of his Masonic friends who are happily recalling the events of the day. The smoke from their long-stemmed pipes clouds the room. The white-haired Revere, having just completed the maximum term of three years as their Grand Master, is soon to give his farewell address to the members of the Grand Lodge of Massachusetts assembling in the large chamber on the upper floor.

CHAPTER ONE

My name is Paul Revere. I am sitting here in the Green Dragon Tavern with a 63-year-old's tired bones but still active mind waiting to join my brothers gathering upstairs for a Masonic meeting at which I will offer my parting address. As I rest easily in this comfortable, brown leather chair, I would like to tell you how I have come to this wonderful time in my life. Before I start, however, let me take one more long puff on my favorite pipe. Ah...that tastes good....Let me see....Where do I begin?

I was born on December 21, 1734, and was baptized by Reverend Welsteed at the Second Congregational Church on Middle Street early the next day. The sturdy old building still stands here in town. Many call it the New Brick Church. You can identify it by the one hundred seventy-pound weathervane in the shape of a rooster that Deacon Shem Drowne had mounted on top of its tall steeple. In fact, that's how the church came to be known as the Cockerel Church by those who lived around it.

My father, a Protestant named Apollos de Rivoire, was born on November 13, 1702 in Riaucand, a town in the Bordeaux region of France. His parents were Isaac and Serenne. He was sent from his home when he was thirteen years old to stay with his father's brother, Simon de Rivoire, who had moved to the Island of Guernsey ten years earlier. Apollos was sent away to escape the religious persecution of the Protestants by the Catholic French after King Louis VIII revoked the Edict of Nantes[17] in 1685. After the king's revocation of the Edict, oppression of the minority Protestants became unbearable. Many children were taken away by the state because they were not Catholic. Others were killed. Some, like Apollos, were sent away by their parents to live in safety with relatives.

After a short stay in Guernsey, my father was sent by his Uncle Simon to America to become an apprentice of an established goldsmith named John Coney. There were about thirty-two goldsmiths in Boston at the time, but Coney commanded the greatest respect and was the most skilled of them all. Shortly after arriving here in 1715, Apollos de Rivoire changed his name to the more Anglicized "Paul Revere." He later told his large family that he took the new name so that his children could pronounce their name more easily. John Coney died in August of 1722, and my father paid his widow £40 to buy out the remainder of his apprenticeship. In 1729 he married my mother, Deborah Hitchborn, an attractive woman who was a neighbor of the Coneys. She was a descendent of seamen and tradesmen who plied their trade in New England for over a half century. My parents lived for a year in a house near the Town Dock, then moved to a North End house over against Colonel Hutchinson. They had eleven children, of whom I was the second born. The actual date of my birth was December 21, according to the Old Style calendar, but December 31, according to the New.[18] Our family lived for many years on the top floor of that small two-story house at the corner of Love Lane and Middle Street in North Boston. My father conducted his silver- and goldsmith business in a shop on the ground floor of the house.

As a youngster, I attended the two-story North Writing School, also on Love Lane. Like almost all of the structures in Boston, it was made of wood. Reading was taught on the first floor and writing on the second. Only boys attended because it was thought better at the time to teach girls at home. Our schoolmaster was Zachariah Hicks, and all of our teachers were women. Although few children were taught mathematics at the time I went to school, I showed a flair for arithmetic, and one schoolmistress spent extra time teaching me to add and perform other number functions.

As it did for most children, my formal schooling ended when I was thirteen. My writing then was poor, and I must say it has improved little since that time. The year before I finished school, I began a seven-year apprenticeship with my father, who by then was an accomplished and fairly well-known metal craftsman.

I enjoyed my work, and although it paid nothing other than my room and board at the time, it was an occupation that I have continued in, happily, for most of my life. To add additional funds to the family coffer when I was young, I also worked at Christ Episcopal Church on Salem Street. When I was fifteen, seven of my friends and I founded an association to ring the bells there. We signed a commitment to sound the bells three times a day on weekdays, holidays and anniversaries; when there was a fire or other emergency; when a member of the congregation died; or when special news, either good or bad, was about to be proclaimed. The eight bells we tended were known widely for their royal peal. That side job kept me quite busy on the days I was called upon to ring, but I enjoyed the activity and the excitement. My mother sensed my unbridled energy when I was young, and she often called me her "restless" or "unruly" son.

I have always been interested in family history, especially on my father's side. I corresponded quite a bit with members of the Rivoire family in France, and although most of my letters from Europe were written in French, my father was able to translate them.

From my mother, I learned much about her family, the Hitchborns. Her great-grandfather was David Hitchborn, who came to Massachusetts in 1641 from Boston, England. Thomas Hitchborn, my mother's father, married Frances Pattishall in 1703. She was the daughter of Captain Richard Pattishall, who was killed by Indians while he was aboard his ship off Pemaquid, Maine. Some of the fondest memories of my childhood were the visits to my great aunt, Anne Pattishall. She always thrilled me with stories about her family, especially the one telling how her father had been murdered.

My father died on July 22, 1754, and was buried with great solemnity near members of the Hitchborn family at the Granary burial ground. I was nineteen then and had not quite completed my apprenticeship. As the oldest son, however, I was called upon to help support our large family. The law at the time prohibited me from inheriting my father's business because of my age.[19] My mother, who by law could operate the shop as a widow, left the day-to-day operations to the experienced tradesmen that worked for her, but I did oversee some of the financial aspects of the enterprise with her assistance. Our varying income yielded enough for us to live acceptably, and I continued to learn many silversmith techniques from the skilled workers in our employ. In early 1756, my life of comfort radically changed.

CHAPTER TWO

Hostilities between our English military and that of France at mid-century were escalating in the Great Lakes region, in the Ohio River valley, and in other areas where the French and English confronted each other over ownership of land. France sent an army to Canada to back up her forces there. Our English government started to seize French ships bound for the colonies. General Braddock was sent to Virginia with a British army to bolster English defenses in America. George Washington was serving as one of his aides-de-camp. At one point, young Washington and some soldiers were moving toward the Ohio River under orders to build a fort to protect English forces threatened by the French military stationed at Fort Duquesne. On July 9, 1755, soldiers from that French fort intercepted Washington and his troops. Fierce fighting ensued. Our British soldiers and the colonial military men supporting them were forced to retreat.

When the news of the defeat arrived in Boston, there was a flurry of enlistment into the British armed forces. I was twenty-one and among those who felt an obligation to serve. I decided to offer my services to Henry Knox, a bookseller in Boston who was in command of an artillery company. I believed at the time that I could be of only limited assistance to my mother and the dependable silversmiths at our shop, and I longed to experience the thrill of battle and the brisk routine that I foolishly believed was the usual pace of army life. When I first met Mr. Knox, he was sorting heavy volumes in his book-packed establishment.

"Tell me about your abilities, son," he asked after I introduced myself and explained the reason for my visit.

"I am trained in mechanics and metalworking," I replied. "And I am familiar with mathematics and writing, sir. My father, who recently died, owned a busy silversmith shop in Boston. I was his apprentice for almost seven years. My mother is running the business now."

We talked at length about my family history and my apprenticeship as a silversmith. After two hours of discussing my qualifications and the requirements of a soldier in the British army, Mr. Knox said he would suggest to the local military officials that I receive a commission in an artillery company. I've always felt that my mathematical background allowed me to be considered for assignment to an artillery branch rather than to the infantry. I thanked Mr. Knox for his decision, then ran home to tell my family about his offer. I saw a look of disappointment in my mother's eyes when I shared my news, but my siblings congratulated me and began to march around the house in formation loudly singing martial songs and mimicking soldiers.

Later in the week I was notified that Governor Shirley, commander of all English forces in North America, had signed my commission. Dated February 18, 1756, it specified that I was to report for duty as an officer—a second lieutenant—in the Train of Artillery commanded by Captain Richard Gridley.[20] The day after I received my commission, I traveled to a British fort in Boston Harbor where I was officially mustered into the army, issued uniforms and equipment, and introduced to the soldiers who were to serve under me. Later, I treated them all to a glass of ale at a local tavern where we all joked about my receiving a commission at the ripe old age of twenty-one. I spent the next six weeks learning military drill and army tactics, and practicing cannon firing techniques with the men under my command. When our training period was over, we were allowed a week's time to say goodbye to our families. Our whole detachment then left for our first assignment—I on a frisky steed, and the others in my unit tending horses and oxen that pulled wheeled cannon, and their accompanying supply wagons.

CHAPTER THREE

The objective of our campaign was to assist in the capture of the French fort at Crown Point, New York, about two hundred miles to the northwest. It was positioned some distance north of Fort Ticonderoga, another major French stronghold on Lake Champlain. General John Winslow was in charge of all the Massachusetts men in our expedition.

Our route passed through Natick, Framingham, Southbury, and Westbury in Massachusetts, then in New York through Albany to Fort Edward and finally to Fort William Henry on Lake George.

On the first few days of our march along the well-traveled roads, the spirit of the soldiers around me was high. Although moving the cannon and supplies was laborious, the men joked aloud and entertained themselves singing ditties that mostly cursed the French. As we advanced farther to the northwest, the roads deteriorated into paths, and the men struggled to move their bulky artillery pieces forward. Word came to us that some men had deserted due to the rigorous work, but my unit stayed together and increased its efforts to move the guns along the ever-thickening forest growth. Flying insects and snakes added to our duress, but I was able to keep all of my men advancing to the north with my encouragement and humorous chatter. Soon, even the narrow paths disappeared, and it became necessary to hack our way through the brush in order to move forward. Food supplies dwindled, and many of the soldiers hunted for game and fish along the way to add to our stocks. We were almost two months making the journey.

The soldiers in the expedition who completed the march finally joined up with other men under the command of Lieutenant General Phineas Lyman at Fort William Henry. We stayed cooped up at that fort from May to November without seeing any action. Our time was spent swatting flies, cleaning equipment and discussing the peculiarities of our leaders. When he heard of French General Montcalm's victory over our forces at Oswego, our commander, General Winslow, thought that the enemy's leaders would then be sending a large army into the Champlain Valley where we were positioned. He believed that we could offer no effective opposition against such a large French force, so he called off the assault on Crown Point. On November 26, after six months of inaction, although our troops were primed for combat, General Winslow ordered us to return to Boston. We left our artillery pieces at the fort and began the long trek home. The fruitless expedition from Boston cost the lives of about twenty soldiers who died from exhaustion, malnutrition, poisonous bites, or scurvy. Those who deserted our ranks didn't fare too well either—they were subjected to courts-martial or were forced into hiding.

Once back in Boston, I spent the remaining portion of my one-year enlistment period guarding prisoners at the Castle—the fort on Castle Island protecting the entrance to Boston Harbor where I had been inducted into the army. On the day I surrendered my commission, I promised myself I would never again join the military. I had little idea at the time that upcoming events would bring me back into the army, and that I would also play a significant part in our fight for freedom from English domination.

CHAPTER FOUR

After my minor military service, I returned to work at the Revere silver shop with a greater understanding of the ways of the world. My mother watched with pride as I quickly took over management of the craftsmen and the finances of the business. During the relatively short period of my absence, our sales had increased and our name "Paul Revere & Son" had become much more widely known. I was also extremely thankful that our reputation for superior work had remained untarnished.

Each day, as I sat at my workbench forming or engraving one of our many products, I could glance up and see the passersby through a small window at the front of the shop. One young lady who walked by often was about my age and seemed to possess a gentle manner. I had seen her at church but never inquired about her situation. One of my employees informed me that her name was Sarah Orne, and that she was unmarried and lived quite near our shop. One day in June, my male urges overcame me when I spotted the attractive girl walking by. I stepped out the front door with the sole purpose of meeting her. She stopped and smiled, a bit surprised. As I approached her, I stammered,

"Good day, Miss Orne, I've seen you at church and notice that you pass by here often. We make many silver products inside. May I show you some of the more unique ones?"

"Good day to you, sir," she replied. "I indeed pass by your shop frequently on my way to the local shopkeepers. I would certainly like very much to see the items you make in your shop. I've been wondering about the kinds of articles your workers seem to busy themselves with so diligently."

"Please come in then," I said. "We're making some wonderful items, and I'd be pleased to show you around."

In the weeks that followed, that simple introduction blossomed into a series of discussions about my family and hers. She told me that she belonged to an artisan family that had its roots in Salem and Boston. I told her that my forebears came from England and France. My newfound female companion—whom I called Sary because Sarah sounded too formal—and I began to see much of each other. Our relationship grew in its intimacy. On August 17, 1757, we were joined in marriage by Reverend Ebenezer Pemberton, the minister at our Congregational church. The ceremony, attended by my family and hers, was short and simple. I can state with complete honesty that my love for this wonderful woman never faltered during our relatively short period of marital bliss. Our blessed union, which lasted a mere thirteen years, brought to life eight children.

Our first child, a girl, was born on April 3, 1758. There was much talk about her untimely arrival, but when we encountered such gossip, Sary and I would wink at each other. We named our healthy newborn Deborah, after my mother. Two years later our son Paul was born. Six more daughters were to follow, but two died in infancy.

In 1760 I joined the Masonic order. My being a Mason propelled me into worlds I could only imagine. I loved the sense of belonging and worked for the fraternal organization with energy and dedication.

Almost every day I pursued additional business. I solicited new customers wherever I could. To accomplish the increased work, I hired a number of journeyman silversmiths who could not afford to set up a shop of their own. I even employed some of my relatives as apprentices. I firmly believed in diversification, and when a small printing press became available for purchase I bought it. I paid Isaac Greenwood £15, 15 shillings for it one day in December of 1761. Buying the press seemed like a logical thing to do since I had many talented engravers in my employ who could assist me in etching some of the copper plates I would require for printing.

In 1762, Sary and I—we had two children at the time—moved into a house on Fish Street that we rented from a Dr. John Clark for £60 a year.

Up to that time I had been too busy with my businesses to concern myself with politics. In that year, however, my focus changed.

CHAPTER FIVE

F or years before I was born, and as I was growing up, our Parliament in England was passing laws to control trade—most to favor Britain—based manufacturers. In 1651 and 1660, the Navigation Acts were passed. In 1699, the Woolen Act. In 1732, the Hat Act. And in 1733, the Molasses Act. All of these laws aided English industries and penalized the country's colonial counterparts. Because most of our people ignored the restrictions put on them by these unilateral regulations, the British government began to issue Writs of Assistance. These proclamations gave their military officers the right to search for goods in the colonies anywhere and at any time.

Although the many punitive laws affected other trades, they had little direct effect on my silversmith business. That changed in 1763. In February of that year the Treaty of Paris was signed, bringing an end to the French and Indian War. In the same year leaders in England began formulating policies coinciding with the beliefs of most of their countrymen—that since the colonies derived most of the benefit from the war fought in North America, the colonists there should bear much of its expense.

George Grenville, leader of the House of Commons, sought additional ways to obtain money from the American colonies. He advanced several new policies. One placed a 100,000-man army here, ostensibly to protect the colonists, the costs of which were to be borne by taxes on the colonies. He also proposed that the frontier west of the Appalachian Mountains be closed to further development. And his last proposal—the one most injurious to us—apportioned several new taxes directly on the colonies.

These new regulations began to affect my customers, and my sales began to plummet. I grew concerned about this loss of business and decided to change the output from my printing press. Up to that time, it was being used to make consumer items such as labels for clocks and hats, illustrations for books and magazines, and advertising literature. I then began to print more relevant items like political cartoons and anti-tax handbills.

Late in 1763 I became aware of a group that had been organized to influence public opinion and coordinate the patriotic actions of the various colonies against the British ministry. The movement originated in New York and Connecticut and soon came to Massachusetts. The individual associations in the group were called "Committees of Correspondence," and Samuel Adams headed the new Boston faction. My continued and vocal opposition to the punitive English rulings came to the attention of the Committee in Boston, and I was invited to become a member of that organization. When I attended my first meeting I was introduced formally to the outspoken Mr. Adams. He was a short man with a carefully groomed white wig. My first impression of him was favorable, for he seemed energetic and able to control every situation. I had often heard of his strong position against the Crown. At the meeting he spoke of the colonies' need to resist payment of the many taxes that Parliament had imposed on us—he considered them unjust and unlawful. It was at that meeting that I resolved to fully support the cause of the patriots who favored resisting all taxation by what was then our mother country.

In December of 1763 the smallpox epidemic that was spreading through the colonies struck us in Boston. By the following February, seven families had contracted the dread disease. My family and the Hitchborn's were two of them. The town selectmen wanted us to send our sick children to a pesthouse located away from the center of town, but we both refused. After many heated arguments we were allowed to keep our stricken children at home, provided we mounted a flag in front of our house and let a guard be stationed there to ensure the quarantine. With the hope that I could escape the dreaded malady, I went back to our old house at the wharf to stay, leaving the care of my family to Sary and my mother. Within a month of the outbreak in Boston, 1537 people had left town to save themselves.

On March 31, 1764, during the quarantine, our fourth child Mary was born. The little lamb lived for less than a year. By the end of June the epidemic was brought under control in Boston. Although my family had been spared, one hundred and seventy other souls had died from the disease.

The same year, Boston experienced another tremendous loss. Harvard College, including its well-stocked library, was devastated by fire. Also, in

1764, the Sugar Act, which levied taxes on exports of sugar, was enacted by Parliament. The Act also mandated an even more detestable measure—that customs officials be sent to America to enforce the collection and payments to England of the new taxes.

By the year 1765, Boston was in economic trouble. Most businessmen fell on hard times, and I was no exception. I was short of cash at one point, and one of my creditors, Thomas Fletcher, to whom I owed only £10, attempted to attach my property. Thankfully, we were able to settle out of court, but my other money problems continued. To weather the storm, I rented part of my shop to Thomas Berry as I had already been doing with Joseph Webb. I also began the engraving of copper printing plates to increase my income.

That year we shopkeepers were faced with yet another new tax. Parliament enacted the Stamp Act.[21] Compliance to it added costs to official transactions, paper purchases and many of the other materials I needed in my work. This ruling gave me the needed push to become more active in the growing rebellion. I gladly joined the shopkeepers, the legal community, and other vocal opponents of the tax. Patrick Henry, the well-known gentleman from Virginia, also opposed this new levy. He claimed that only Americans have the right to tax themselves, and he offered five resolutions to gain repeal of the new assessment. His inflammatory statements against this tax were printed in newspapers throughout the colonies, and I gladly printed many handouts for local distribution that quoted his critical pronouncements.

CHAPTER SIX

S oon after the Stamp Act was passed, I became aware of an organization in New York that was strongly against the new tax that Parliament had imposed. Its members were called the "Sons of Liberty." They were committed to fuel the agitation for freedom from taxation in the colonies. Sam Adams and I, with other members of our Committee of Correspondence, established a local chapter. Our primary purpose was to intimidate the Boston distributors of the new stamps and do everything possible to show our opposition to the enforcement of the Stamp Act. We invited other protesters to join us and were surprised at the number who embraced our cause. For a motto, we chose "Equality before the law." We held our meetings late at night in secret, under a large elm tree at the corner of Beach and Orange Streets. We ceremoniously named the tree the "Liberty Tree" on August 14, 1765. As part of our dedication, we hung on it many effigies including one of Andrew Oliver, the local Stamp Officer. We established a secret code for recognition of members, and I designed a medal that was worn around our necks. On one side, the medallion had the words "Sons of Liberty" inscribed above a muscular arm, which held in its hand a pole with a liberty cap on top. On the other side, there was a likeness of our Liberty Tree and the engraved initials of the wearer. I still have my medal at home. It's slightly tarnished, but it reminds me of our great struggle whenever I look at it.

The ministry's enforcement of the Stamp Act incited riots in many of the colonies. In Boston, after hearing a rousing sermon against the Act by Jonathan Mayhew, minister of the West Church in Boston, a group of outraged colonists attacked the house of the Registrar of the Admiralty and destroyed all of his papers. The angry crowd then plundered the house of the Controller of Customs. In the evening, a larger mob of merchants, shopkeepers, and ne'er-do-wells, maddened with liquor, completely destroyed the mansion and documents of Thomas Hutchinson, the Lieutenant Governor of Massachusetts. Among his valuable papers thrown into the gutter were the source material of his early Massachusetts' history and many of the priceless records of old Massachusetts Bay. After the destruction of his home, Hutchinson left Boston and retired to his large estate at Unkity Hill, near Milton. The general public was outraged at the treatment of the Lieutenant Governor, but many Whig leaders secretly saw the demonstrations as welcome acts of rebellion. On November 16, Stamp Officer Oliver, the symbol of unfair taxation, was forced by the Sons of Liberty to swear before Justice Dana under the Liberty Tree that he would never sell another stamp. To our knowledge, he never did.

Our fierce resistance to the Stamp taxes finally forced Parliament to rescind the Act.

On May 16, 1766, when we learned that the Stamp Act was repealed, I helped organize a great demonstration to be held on Boston Common. We scheduled it for May 19, and I designed a huge obelisk to commemorate the occasion. It was made of paper and was illuminated with two hundred eighty lamps inside. I covered its four sides with symbols of liberty and slogans of defiance. The structure was to be placed under the Liberty Tree when the celebrations were over. Unfortunately, on the evening of the demonstration, fireworks destroyed my work of art. The detailed engraving I made of my handiwork, however, still survives.[22]

With the revocation of the Stamp Act, other members of the Sons of Liberty and I felt that the purposes of the organization had been fully served, so we disbanded it. The desire to continue opposition to the other repressive measures that Parliament forced upon us, however, prodded champions of freedom to form new groups around Boston. These associations were called caucuses. In 1797 I was asked to join one called the North End Caucus. Sam Adam's father founded it for the purposes of exchanging views with the other caucuses and of recommending, at town meetings, slates of officers that supported our cause. Our group met initially at the Salutation Tavern on Salutation Alley at the corner of Ship Street. Many of its members were from the Sons of Liberty, and they included Sam Adams; John Adams; the publishers of *The Boston Gazette*, Benjamin Edes and John Gill; and Dr. Joseph Warren, a reformer only slightly less vocal than Sam Adams himself.

Unfortunately, the relief from Britain's taxes after the Stamp Act was repealed proved short-lived. In the same year that I joined the North End Caucus, Parliament passed the even more reviled Townshend Revenue Acts.

CHAPTER SEVEN

Charles Townshend was Chancellor of the Exchequer in London in 1767, the year he proposed to Parliament a new way to raise revenue from the colonies.[23] The new levies were no more acceptable than those decreed by the Stamp Act, and again riots by the tea drinkers and those who used the other items broke out in the colonies. Many of the customs officers' lives were threatened, and the angry crowds destroyed a number of their homes. Feeling my duty, I joined other members of the re-established Sons of Liberty. With blackened faces we went out on moonless nights to harass the custom commissioners. The Massachusetts legislature took supportive action, issuing a Circular Letter[24] to the other colonies urging them to uniformly resist the measure. When the King ordered the Circular Letter rescinded, the Legislature, by a vote of ninety to seventeen, refused. The Sons of Liberty men were ecstatic over the support shown by our government. In 1768, the organization commissioned me to make a silver punchbowl to celebrate the victory. I fashioned the "The Rescinders' Bowl," sometimes called the "Sons of Liberty Bowl," and emblazoned it with the names of the "Glorious 92" who voted with us to challenge the King's order.

Another event of that year is worth mentioning. The many engravings I had produced seemed to give me a high degree of manual dexterity, so I entered an entirely new field—dentistry. At my request, a Surgeon Dentist named John Baker, who was staying temporarily with my old friend Joshua Brackett at the Cromwell Head, instructed me in the latest techniques for cleaning and setting teeth. My response to his teaching must have been satisfactory, because before leaving Boston, Mr. Baker complemented me on my abilities to work with false teeth. At first I only replaced fore-teeth, but as my experience grew I was able to fashion and wire in all missing teeth. I used hippopotamus tusk imported from Africa or teeth from other animals, such as horses and cows, to make the replacements. I was dissuaded from using elephant ivory because it discolored quickly. I soon began to advertise the fact that I could produce and attach teeth. I added an illustrated sign to the front of my shop and handed out flyers promoting my dental abilities. One of my customers was my friend, the gentle, overweight agitator, Dr. Joseph Warren. He had lost two teeth, one a molar, and engaged my services to replace them. I fashioned the two new teeth from a piece of hippopotamus tusk and wired them to his remaining teeth. At the time I had no idea that the artificial teeth I fashioned for him would become the means of later identifying the good doctor's decaying remains.

I'll return to the political front after I take another puff…drat! My pipe is nigh out…

There, that's better.

Soon after the British government learned of our defiance of the King's order, it responded with the most inflammatory action thus far. It sent a large number of troops to Boston to combat the growing rebellion. On September 30, 1768, a British fleet entered Boston Harbor. The ships were positioned in an arc around the waterfront, their guns pointed toward the town. I dutifully recorded the name of every ship: *Beaver, Bonetta, Glasgow, Launceston, Martin, Mermaid, Romney* and *Senegal.*

The many commissioners of the Crown who had fled to Castle Island from fear of the unruly mobs in Boston were delighted that their saviors had finally arrived. To celebrate their rescue, they waved flags and shot off fireworks. I watched as two regiments of Redcoats landed at Long Wharf and marched with fife and drum to the center of Boston. I hurried home and made an engraving of the anchored ships that were threatening us. I distributed prints of my work, hoping to incite more people to action.

The result of the troop deployment was predictable. Wherever soldiers appeared, they were harassed and demeaned. Stones and other more vile objects were thrown at them, and they were spat upon. I made up many drawings depicting the soldiers as invaders and devils, and had them exhibited throughout the colonies.

On February 15, 1770, I bought my first house.[25] It was located on North Square, opposite Dr. Clark's home. My old accommodations near Clark's wharf were a bit too confining for my five children and my mother. I kept my shop where it was to keep my business at the site familiar to my steady customers.

With acts of resistance by rebels occurring everywhere, tensions grew, and I knew it was only a matter of time before the shedding of blood. That fateful circumstance occurred on March 5, 1770, and it marked the first time British soldiers willfully killed their kinsmen in the colonies.

Late in the evening on that date, in front of the Boston Customs House on a snow-covered King Street, a few British grenadiers from the 29th Regiment were surrounded and taunted by an angry mob of 50 or 60 men and boys. During the disorder, a sentry named Montgomery was struck down by the club of a mulatto who had just arrived on the scene with a number of seamen. The injured soldier stood up, and in response to the call 'fire,' leveled his musket, pulled the trigger, and killed the colored man. Then other frightened soldiers lowered their muskets and fired into the crowd, killing five colonists and wounding six.

When the news of that horrendous act spread, it inflamed the populace. As a result, opposition to all British laws grew even more intense. I did an engraving of the despicable event, copying from a drawing made by Henry Pelham. Later I had a well-known artist[26] colorize it.

In the foreground of my work, which I labeled *The Bloody Massacre Perpetrated in King Street*, I drew Crispus Attucks[27] lying dead. He was the colored man who had struck the sentry. My portrayal of him made him an instant martyr. I quickly printed and sold hundreds of prints with the hope that my depiction would popularize the tragic event and further inflame the people. It did, far beyond my expectations.

The moderates in town insisted on a fair trial for the eight British soldiers involved and also Captain Preston, their commanding officer. Attorney Josiah Quincy, 29 and in the late stage of a fatal disease, together with the respected John Adams, agreed to defend the accused. Attorney Sam Quincy, Josiah's older brother, was chosen to represent the prosecution. At the hearing, I supplied some of the evidence. The final verdict acquitted all of the soldiers on the charge of murder. Two of them were convicted of manslaughter, but were released after agreeing to have their thumbs burnt, a moderate punishment at the time.

Understandably, many other acts of violence followed the bloody incident. In the same year as the Massacre on King Street, a customs officer, frightened by a mob that had gathered in front of his house, fired his musket and killed a boy named Christopher Seider. As news of that incident and the growing number of violations of colonists' rights spread, more and more citizens called for retribution and absolute freedom from unjust taxation. The sparks of rebellion were being fanned with each publicized event, and I knew in my bones that a fire of immense proportion was soon to consume us.

CHAPTER EIGHT

It became evident to Parliament that refusal of the colonies to buy the imported goods that bore the tariffs, along with the excessive cost to implement the Townshend Act, made the measure unprofitable. On the same day as the massacre in Boston, the British Parliament voted to abolish all of the duties imposed by the Act, except the tax on tea. In addition, it called for the withdrawal of the British Regulars from Boston. We were happy with the removal of the Redcoats and felt that we could live with the single tax on tea, but when Parliament passed the infamous Tea Act, we were once again called to arms.

At that time, the East India Company in London was in financial difficulty and had its English warehouses full of tea. The new Act allowed the company to ship tea to us, then sell it directly to retailers, eliminating the wholesale merchants. This infuriated our businessmen, who felt that they would be put at a disadvantage since other wholesalers—those who imported tea from other places—could undersell them. Other merchants felt that if the ministry could so easily eliminate the middleman in tea trade, it could expand the practice to other goods, and their businesses would also be destroyed. At secret meetings the affected merchants pledged that none of the East India Company's tea then aboard ships traveling to Boston would be permitted to leave our docks for delivery to retailers.

On Sunday, November 28, 1773, the ship *Dartmouth* arrived in Boston Harbor with a hundred and fourteen chests of tea. Shortly thereafter, the ship *Eleanor* and the brig *Beaver* arrived with more tea. The three moored at Griffin's Wharf and waited there to be unloaded.

Sam Adams, seeing the British action of eliminating wholesalers as another legitimate basis for revolt, posted bills that invited the public to a general meeting at Faneuil Hall in Boston on November 29. When it became apparent that the hall would not accommodate the thousands of concerned people, we all walked to the Old South Meetinghouse on Marlborough Street. Dr. Joseph Warren, John Hancock and Dr. Thomas Young, all outspoken agitators, were among those who attended the raucous meeting. The contentious Sam Adams sponsored resolutions declaring that the tea should not be landed; that it should be returned to England; and that no duty should be paid on it. The group adopted his terms unanimously. Adams then called for the appointment of a guard of twenty-five men to ensure that the tea would not be off-loaded. I was one of the two who served as guards the first night. John Hancock, Sam Adams, and Henry Knox were among the other volunteers. All of our efforts were successful. Without the British Regulars, who had been recalled from Boston, we were able to continue our threats of retaliation against the ships' officers if they did allow any unloading. The fearful captains and crews remained in their cabins and no tea was taken from their ships during our watches.

Over the next few weeks I attended many meetings around Boston that concerned the disposition of the captive tea. I was pleased to join the members of the North End Caucus and the Sons of Liberty who called for its forceful destruction. Most other gatherings echoed our sentiments. Sam Adams, our chief agitator, uttered the final challenge at a meeting at the Old South Church on the evening of December 16.

"This meeting can do nothing more to save the country," he declared at the end of his provocative speech.

The crowd went wild. They began to stomp on the floor and yell. Above the din I could hear some of the shouts: "Boston Harbor a teapot tonight!" and "Hurrah for Griffin's Wharf!"

I made my way through the unruly crowd and left the church. Hundreds of men, all with determined looks, accompanied me into the clear, cold night. We all walked in silence to the wharf where the ships were docked. We boldly boarded the vessels as they rocked silently at anchor. The officers and crews watched helplessly as we broke open the containers and spilled the contents of three hundred and forty-two chests of tea into the dark water below. Many of us had dressed as Indians to conceal our identities. Hundreds of citizens stood on the dock and applauded our actions aboard the three vessels. We were careful not to harm anything else aboard ship—a few men in our party even repaired a broken lock. We wanted it known that our quarrel was not against property. One man who was caught stealing some of the tea for his own use was made to run the gauntlet where a line of men beat him with their whips and sticks. As further punishment, he had his coat nailed to a whipping post, an act of derision by judgmental citizens.

The impromptu operation immediately gained the name *The Boston Tea Party*. The tea we destroyed was valued at £18,000, and we knew that when the ministry back in England heard about the loss, it would react harshly.

The day after our "Tea Party," I volunteered to ride to the sympathetic Whigs in New York and Philadelphia to advise them of our act of rebellion. I carried letters from the Boston Committee of Correspondence calling for solidarity against the punishment sure to come. I also carried a large number of copies of the actual Tea Act. I had garnished the decree with a crown, and a skull with crossbones, then printed it on my press. I distributed the illustrated sheets in villages along the way as I hurried through them on horseback, handing the inflammatory papers to men anxious to hear about the progress of our defiant acts against the king.

When I got as far as Providence, I stopped at a spring near some sheltering trees. The location seemed suitable for watering the large gray horse that I was riding. While I rested, a friend of mine, John Ludlow, surprised me with his greeting. He was atop a large black horse and was carrying a message from New York to Boston. His communication assured our leaders that New York would stand by Massachusetts in our hour of destiny. John and I ate our lunches at the pleasant spot and filled each other in on local happenings. We then waved farewell, and continued on our separate ways. I stopped in New York for only a short time, then traveled south, ending my ride in Philadelphia. Our friends there gave me letters that also promised their support. Without delay, I returned to Boston with the favorable news of the endorsement of our actions. My associates here in Boston were overjoyed when they learned of the widespread support of our sister colonies.

The high spirits I felt weren't destined to last for long, though. On May 3, 1773, my dear wife died. Our last child, Hannah, had remained in ill health from the time of her birth the previous December. Sary's constant attention to the baby's condition wore heavily on her health and was probably the cause of her demise. I was much disheartened by her untimely death. She was the love of my life. Faced with caring for seven children—including Hannah, who was still sickly and required continued care—I felt the obligation to hastily find a new wife and mistress for my home. Dear young Hannah died on September 19, 1773, just a month before I took a new wife.

Rachel Walker, daughter of Richard and Rachel Walker, was a dear friend of the family. She was fair of face, and I considered her a charming woman.

Although she was eleven years my junior, I felt that she might be willing to marry me. After considerable soul searching, mostly about the relatively short time since Sary's death, I asked Rachel to become my wife. We spent weeks agonizing over the implications of such a hasty marriage. Thankfully, she accepted my proposal, and on October 10, 1773, Reverend Samuel Mather joined us in marriage at the New Brick Church. After the ceremony Rachel and I walked, with much concern for our future, to my home at North Square. Circumstances dictated that I not remain housebound for long.

CHAPTER NINE

As expected, Parliament responded to our destruction of the tea with many drastic measures. It quickly enacted a series of offensive regulations we called the "Coercive Acts." These edicts mandated that we do a number of things. One, close the Port of Boston from the first of June until the East India Tea Company was paid for its loss of tea, and move the location of the customs house from Boston to Marblehead. Also, change the Charter of Massachusetts to lessen the power of its citizens and increase the influence of the Crown. One particular mandate required that members of our Provincial Council be appointed by the Royal Governor, instead of being elected by the people. Also, limit the agendas of our town meetings by restricting the types of things we could discuss. Also, create a new court system whereby officers of the law were to be selected by the royal governors. Also, alter the method of appointing juries to assure favorable treatment of accused Tories. Also, allow British officials in the colonies to send Tory citizens accused of capital crimes to England for trial instead of having them tried in the colonies where they would likely be convicted. And lastly, give the English governors of the colonies the power to quarter British soldiers in our barns and uninhabited buildings without our consent, in order to minimize their building of barracks to house them. To enforce the new laws, King George sent General Gage back to Boston with British troops.

We learned about the passage of the laws early in 1774. Our local leaders were enraged at their severity. We also labeled them "The Intolerable Acts." Once again I offered to take the news about the new decrees to New York and Philadelphia. In addition, I carried letters appealing to the other colonies to join us in the plans for resistance that we in Boston had formulated at a town meeting on May 13, 1774. I left home the next day and arrived in Philadelphia on May 20, setting, I'm sure, some kind of speed record for the trip. I returned home with new written promises by officials of both colonies that they would support our cause, and that they would advise the other colonies of our plans for defiance. The Philadelphia letter I carried back also called for the convening of a General Congress made up of representatives from all of the colonies, a development that the defiant Sam Adams had desperately desired for some time.

Under the leadership of the indefatigable Adams, the Massachusetts assembly quickly issued an invitation to the other colonies to gather in Philadelphia in September to discuss the impasse that had arisen between our Mother Country and us. He suggested that the meeting be called a Continental Congress, and that it concern itself with deliberating and determining wise and proper measures for the recovery and establishment of our just rights and liberties. Over the next few months the rebels I supported engaged in bitter disputes with the loyalists who wanted to appease Britain. Despite the Tories loud objections, the assemblymen planned a Continental Congress to be held at Carpenter's Hall in Philadelphia on September 5, 1774.

I didn't attend because I was not anxious to involve myself in the unending discussions I knew would take place, nor did I want to leave the side of my Rachel who was six months pregnant with our first child. I spent much time in Boston rousing public support for our cause and fabricating the silver articles for which I had been increasingly getting orders. I also found time to make etchings that ridiculed the monarchy, and assuring that they were placed where they would have the most impact.

On September 10, I was again asked to go to Philadelphia, this time to carry letters to the Massachusetts delegates representing us at the Continental Congress. Dr. Joseph Warren had composed what were termed the *Suffolk Resolves*, a set of resolutions agreed to by representatives of our Suffolk County. The Resolves proclaimed that the Intolerable Acts were unconstitutional and recommended sanctions against England. They also urged the people of Massachusetts to form their own government and prepare to fight in its defense. I left Boston the next day and reached Philadelphia on September 16, covering the three hundred and fifty miles in five days. This bettered my previous record run by two full days. I was appreciative of the generosity of the many people who allowed me to use their horses, since that was the key to my rapid travel. I compensated many of them, but some were willing to donate their animals for the cause we so strongly believed in.

On September 17, the new Congress enthusiastically endorsed the Resolves, and I started home the following day with the encouraging news. Although I was saddle-sore for most of my trip, I completed it again in the remarkable five days. Shortly after my return, I learned that a convention had been held in Worcester, its members urging the various towns to organize companies of militia. They also recommended that groups of riders be selected throughout Massachusetts to observe British movements and to warn the scattered settlers of any perceived British aggression.

In October, the Massachusetts Legislature—officially abolished earlier by the Intolerable Acts—met in defiance of General Gage, British Commander-in-Chief in America, who had the duty to keep such an event from happening. The Legislature boldly declared itself to be the First Provincial Congress, and it created Committees of Safety and of Supplies to further its endeavors. We learned that General Gage was not able to invalidate our Congress, for he had only 3,000 Regulars capable of facing a militia that could potentially muster more than 30,000 men. Our spies in the general's inner circle also reported to us that he had earlier asked for 20,000 reinforcements—at a time when only 12,000 Regulars existed in all of Britain. We later found out that he was sent a battalion of only four hundred marines and told to get on with the job.

Meanwhile, I wanted to actively assist with the execution of the resolutions made at the Worcester convention concerning observations of British activity. To that end, I organized a voluntary association of about thirty mechanics and tradesmen to watch the movements of the British soldiers as well as those of the pro-monarchy Tories among us. I was to report our findings to the Whig leaders in Boston. I elected to be head of the clandestine organization, and we met regularly at the Green Dragon Tavern to schedule duties. For reasons of security, we reported our observations only to John Hancock, John Adams, Dr. Warren, Dr. Church, and one or two other trusted rebels. Our members took turns, traveling in pairs, to watch the soldiers by patrolling the streets at night. It was unfortunate that we didn't know at the time that our associate Dr. Benjamin Church was a traitor who was relaying information about all of our actions directly to General Gage.[28]

Up to the time of the Worcester convention, the majority of Englishmen in America would have been satisfied to remain a British colony if Parliament had been more just in its taxation and tariff laws. The Convention seemed to be the major turning point for the colonies. The initial call for fairer treatment by British Parliament began to be replaced by a more pronounced resolution to procure our complete independence from our Mother Country. Before long, the inevitable became known in all our hearts.

CHAPTER TEN

Early in December of 1774, Britain, learning of our actual goal and attendant military preparations, issued an Order of Council that prohibited the export of arms to America. It also ordered the Crown's officials to improve safeguards of their own munitions in the colonies. My network learned of this order, and also of the fact that there was a large cache of the King's arms, powder, and cannon at the lightly-guarded Fort William and Mary on the coast of New Hampshire some fifty miles north of Boston. When we also found out that a large British expedition had been ordered to secure the fort and that warships were probably already on their way, I decided to ride to New Hampshire to advise our associates there of that important information. I left Boston on the morning of December 13, braving the snow and biting cold common to New England winters. I traveled up the North Shore, across the Merrimack River to Hampton Falls. I arrived in Portsmouth late in the afternoon and went directly to the home of our correspondent there, a merchant named Samuel Cutts. He immediately called for a meeting of Portsmouth's Committee of Correspondence. When the members had gathered, I provided them with what I knew about the British expedition.

Early the next morning, a fife and drum corps marched down the streets of Portsmouth summoning militiamen to arms. By noon, four hundred men had answered the call, and they prepared for an attack on the fort. I later found out that a loyalist had spotted my arrival in Portsmouth and had reported it to John Wentworth, the Royal Governor there. I also learned that the governor alerted the small garrison at the fort and had sent a rider to General Gage and Admiral Graves back in Boston with requests for immediate assistance. The British Admiral dispatched the sloop *HMS Canceaux* with a detachment of marines to Portsmouth and ordered the larger frigate *HMS Scarborough* to sail there as soon afterward as possible. Before the colonists' attack on the fort, a few couriers and I raced around the countryside encouraging the citizens to join the fray. By mid-morning hundreds of armed men had gathered in Portsmouth and were marching toward Fort William and Mary.

By three o'clock in the afternoon the determined men approached the fort by land and sea. I watched in awe as Captain Cochran, leader of the small group of defenders, commanded the militiamen not to enter, but the attackers cried out in unison: "We will!" Before the outnumbered garrison was forced to surrender, they fired at us with three cannon and a few small arms. In less than an hour, however, hostilities subsided. I saw Captain Cochran came out of the fort and offer his sword. I was surprised when our leader would not take it. The captain, in defiance, then re-gripped his sword and lunged at the closest militiaman. Another New Hampshire man quickly raised his musket and shot the captain, who fell to the ground. It was not a fatal hit, but it convinced the wounded captain to concede defeat. The colonists then gave three cheers and hauled down the King's Colors as the soldiers in the fort watched in horror. The raiding party then broke open the magazine and loaded a hundred barrels of gunpowder onto boats for shipment to safety at our own quarters in nearby Durham. They also carried away many muskets and sixteen cannon, but had to leave about twenty artillery pieces behind because they were too heavy. I returned to Boston tired but elated. As I now look back at the encounter at the fort, I realize that the first shot we fired in our struggle for independence was not at Lexington, but four months earlier at Fort William and Mary in New Hampshire.

The *HMS Canceaux* did not start to sail from Boston until three days after the fighting was over. When she arrived at Portsmouth, a Yankee pilot who supported our cause, brought her into shallow water at high tide, a condition that left her helpless for days. The *HMS Scarborough* set sail two days after the *HMS Canceaux*. Storms delayed her arrival at Portsmouth until a week after the attack on the fort. By that time our militiamen had released their prisoners and had faded into the countryside.

When General Gage at his headquarters in Boston was informed of the results of the fight at Portsmouth, he must have considered it a great defeat. He also had to recognize that it was the first act of armed rebellion. I thought for a time that I would be seized and thrown in prison for my contribution to the affair, but the General, a staunch believer in the rule of law, allowed the Whig leaders and me to remain at liberty.

It was relatively quiet during the next month. Our leaders spent the time secretly organizing the substantial militia that would be necessary to respond quickly to acts of British aggression. We also secured large quantities of military supplies and stored them in Concord, Salem, and other places far from the prying eyes in Boston. British spies, however, were not unaware of our actions.

CHAPTER ELEVEN

Sometime in February, General Gage decided to capture the munitions that his informers told him we were accumulating in Salem. We were converting ship's cannon into field artillery there as well as receiving shipments of brass cannon from abroad. I learned about his mission despite the General's enforced secrecy. On Saturday, the day before the expedition was to depart from the British fort on Castle Island in Boston Harbor, some of my associates and I rowed across the harbor to observe the island fort and determine Gage's probable schedule for action. British soldiers, who appeared to know of our coming, captured us as we approached the fortified island. We were charged with trespass and held behind bars on the island until Monday to ensure that there was no leak of their Salem plans. I was unable to provide any relevant information to Salem, but later I learned that as the Regulars marched toward the town on February 26, news of their arrival by local residents spread rapidly. Many cannon were quickly taken away by our forces from the forge where they were being modified. Citizens and militiamen delayed the soldiers' advance by many improvised means. When the British troops finally got to the forge all traces of the weapons had been removed. Having thus failed in their mission, the King's army returned to Boston in disgrace. It was their second defeat. When the other colonies learned of our successes at Portsmouth and Salem they were emboldened by the success of both actions.

Throughout 1774, and during the early months of 1775, the citizens increasingly mocked and humiliated the British Regulars stationed in and around Boston. We learned that many in the military were stricken with diseases, short on rations, running out of potable water, and increasingly addicted to the cheap rum that was available everywhere. We heard of mass desertions, and the whipping of a soldier who had sold his musket for drink. I witnessed a young private who had attempted to desert three times face a firing squad on the Boston Common. Another soldier from the 10th Regiment was shot for attempted desertion on Christmas Eve. As we saw the growing inclination to desert by the desperate soldiers, we gradually began to support their decision and spread the word that anyone who left his unit would receive a new life and three hundred acres of prime land in New Hampshire. Most of the Regulars felt an overriding loyalty to the King and refused our offer. The despicable conditions under which the men lived even drove some to fight against each other. The officers of higher rank were apparently not free from conflict among themselves. I watched one parade where, in a rage, a Lieutenant Colonel drew a sword on one of his junior officers. I heard later that both were ordered court-martialed by General Gage.

Tension among the citizenry was also growing. On March 6, 1775, I attended the fifth anniversary celebration of the Boston Massacre held at the Old South Meetinghouse. John Hancock,[29] John and Sam Adams, and other notables were in attendance. Also in the audience were several British officers who sought to disrupt the meeting. After Dr. Warren, dressed humorously in a Roman toga, gave a stirring speech from the black-decked pulpit, Sam Adams moved that Dr. Warren be presented with the thanks of the town. The British officers hissed loudly at the suggestion. Then one officer shouted, "Oh! Fie! Oh! Fie!" The words apparently sounded like "Fire! Fire!" to the attendees, and panic ensued. As the screaming audience pushed toward the exits, a British regiment, beating drums, happened to march past the building. The frightened people believed that they were under attack and prepared to defend themselves with the canes and muskets they were carrying. Calmer heads prevailed and soothed the crowd, but the experience showed me how close we were to a deadly confrontation with the British army.

Three days later, I read where Thomas Ditson, a peddler, entered the quarters of a British regiment and offered to buy military uniforms and weapons. When the commander learned of this, he had his guards seize the peddler. He ordered his men to tar and feather the man and parade him through the streets to the Liberty Tree, all to the beat of fife and drum. My informers told me that General Gage was appalled by the act and chastised his men for performing it.

Many additional confrontations between the British military and the colonists followed. I took advantage of the liberties extended to the press by the local governors and printed many leaflets criticizing the British forces in America and the government in England. The Imperial officials made no secret of their rage with me, and other publishers who ridiculed the Crown even more than I did. I read papers that derided General Gage by falsely accusing him of being an alcoholic and a child molester. He was even charged with being a Papist who wanted to convert all America to Catholicism. Sam Adams said publicly that the General had no humanity and deliberately deprived us of our liberty. As displeasure and tensions grew all around us, so did the peoples' unified desire for absolute independence from the Crown.

CHAPTER TWELVE

Inside informers advised me that General Gage's letters to his superiors in Britain condemning the acts of resistance by the colonists were answered consistently with calls for him to take stronger action to repress them. Apparently the good general could not bring himself to act decisively. Our friends in London informed us that the Crown's ministers had lost patience with him and had demanded that he arrest the leaders of the colonial rebellion. We learned that formal instructions to accomplish that were sent to him on two ships. They arrived at Marblehead on April 2. When our Committee of Correspondence there learned about the orders to jail the top echelon of our rebel leaders, they sent a rider to Boston immediately to alert us. We were thereby informed in a timely fashion of the plan to jail our prominent rebels before General Gage received his orders. Our leaders thus had sufficient time to pack their bags and leave Boston for safer locales.

The dispatch ship *HMS Nautilus*, which carried the secret orders from the ministry, finally arrived in Boston from Marblehead on April 14. Our informers told us that the orders specifically commanded General Gage not only to seize the ringleaders of the rebellion, but also to disarm the population. The orders also contained a message to Gage that promised additional troops. These we found out were to be comprised of seven hundred marines, three regiments of foot, and a regiment of dragoons that were especially trained to suppress civil disturbances. Notwithstanding the commands to the General, we knew from letters to us from our friends in Britain that the King's ministers earnestly believed that our rebellion was of little consequence and that we would offer little, if any, resistance. But within the next week the whole world was destined to know of our willingness to die for freedom.

General Gage, despite Parliament's refusal to accept the degree of our resolve, knew, even before he received the instructions to act forcibly, that his only hope of success in crushing the growing rebellion lay in acting secretly and quickly before we could muster a formidable militia. Our side, however, was not idle. In many towns we were gathering arms, casting ball, accumulating supplies of powder, and training militia. Sam Adams traveled around warning our men that we must not be the first to fire in the upcoming confrontation or we would lose the moral advantage of our cause. The leaders in New England assured him that they would not become active until General Gage went on the offensive and dispatched his forces.

We learned from our informants that the general had sent two men dressed as colonials to Worcester where we had a large cache of weapons and powder. The apparent instruction to the two was to map the roads from Boston and designate the areas that would be safe from ambush. The subtly suspicious look of the British spies, however, along with their covert movements, caught the attention of the wary residents. Cautious citizens ascertained the identity and mission of the men and sent the details back to us in Boston.

Gage, after hearing his returned spies' report, apparently decided that Worcester was too far away and too risky a target. He then sent the two men with similar instructions to Concord where he knew another supply of our arms was stored. Once in Concord the spies asked a woman for directions to the home of Daniel Bliss, a loyalist lawyer. The woman alerted our friends in Concord about the query and the suspicious men who questioned her. Our associates there sent a message to lawyer Bliss telling him that if he didn't leave Concord at once, he would be killed. Frightened by the warning, he accompanied Gage's men back to Boston. The two spies reported to the General that the Lexington Road they had taken on their return to Boston was a better route than the one they had taken on their way to Concord. Our informers told us that General Gage was pleased to know about the route selected by his map makers.

On April 7, our observers on shore saw sailors on the British ships in the harbor launching their longboats and securing them under the sterns of their warships, apparently preparing them for rapid deployment. We were also informed that a group of British officers was sent to Concord by way of Lexington to re-map the roads. We put the pieces together and formulated our plans, based on the Regulars traveling to Concord to capture the arms stored there. I was asked to ride to alert our people in Concord of the British plan. On the afternoon of April 8, I left Boston and headed for Concord. I arrived in the evening carrying a letter from Dr. Warren informing the leaders in Concord that the Regulars would be coming the next day to confiscate their munitions. As it turned out, Dr. Warren and I erred on the date, but my message was well received. The citizens of Concord began immediately to move their military supplies to other locations. The members of the Provincial Congress who were meeting in Concord at the time quickly packed up and left town, as did many other well-known revolutionaries.

Early on April 15, we learned that General Gage had issued the command that all of his elite companies of infantry be relieved of unnecessary duty until further notice. We believed that his action was another sign he was preparing for an offensive move. On the 16th, although a Sabbath, I rode to Lexington to alert Sam Adams and John Hancock about Gage's latest order. On the way back I stopped at Cambridge and Charleston to tell the Whig leaders there about the recent developments. At both towns we discussed how to establish a system throughout the colonies to warn of British troop movements out of Boston. I joined the leaders in making plans to provide a means of alerting the nearby towns if the Regulars were to move stealthily at night and British guards were stationed at exits from Boston to prevent our messengers from leaving to alert the nearby towns. We agreed to a three-way approach. First, we would try our usual deployment of fast riders. If that were not possible, we would send messengers by routes not normally traveled or patrolled. If these methods failed, we would alert our friends across the Charles River with a system of lantern signals that would provide notice that the Regulars were on their way.

Our spies in the Tory establishment alerted us that Gage was aware of the trips I was making to speak with the officials of surrounding towns. Our informants also made us aware that the General knew that some munitions had been removed from Concord but that a large stock of weapons still remained there.

On April 18, mounted British officers along the roads to Concord were stopping and questioning all riders whom they believed might be messengers sent to alert the towns of the upcoming march of the Regulars. These patrols, according to witnesses, were making no secret of their presence or their mission, nor did they seem to hide their interest in the locations of John Hancock and Sam Adams.

Concerned citizens brought reports of this patrol activity to Dr. Warren and me in Boston since all of our other leaders had long since left town.

Weeks earlier, John Hancock and Sam Adams had gone to attend the Provincial Congress in Concord. After the Congress was disbanded they decided that it would be safer for them and their families to settle in Lexington. Other leaders relocated to Cambridge, Charlestown, or Watertown. Dr. Warren and I used his office in Boston as a command post.

As the afternoon hours of April 18 passed, the number of messengers bringing news of British preparations grew rapidly. Our people reported seeing longboats being readied in the harbor. Others advised us that the activity aboard the warships had increased considerably. We were told that there was more than the usual movement around the British fort. One boy told me that he had heard at the livery stable a soldier remark that there would be "hell to pay" the next day.

Dr. Warren and I suspected from the volume of information we received that the Regulars were now preparing to march on April 19. The doctor, however, felt that he needed positive confirmation. He told me that he had a secret informant close to the British command. After secretly meeting with his contact later in the day, he was confident that our suspicions were correct. His informer[30] had told him that there indeed were orders issued to seize Sam Adams and John Hancock and to destroy the military stores at Concord. When the sun went down, I went home for dinner, aware that the next day would probably bring the confrontation with the King's armed forces that we had long been anticipating.

CHAPTER THIRTEEN

By ten o'clock that same evening Rachel and I had finally got the last of our seven children safely to bed. We were discussing the events of the day when there was a sharp rap at the door. Thinking that there might be soldiers outside waiting to take me into custody, I got my pistol and opened the door cautiously. It was a relief to see that it was a messenger sent by Dr. Warren.

"Sorry to trouble you at this late hour, Mr. Revere," he said, "but Dr. Warren wants you to come with great haste to see him."

I kissed my wife and hurried to my friend's office. He was alone, pacing the floor nervously when I arrived.

"Paul," he said, "I have just received notice that British soldiers are now gathering at the bottom of the Common where there are boats to receive them. It means they're preparing to march. I want you to set off at once for Lexington to advise our friends, Hancock and Adams, that they must depart for safety at once. I assume you'll be taking a boat across the Charles as you've planned. I dispatched William Dawes, the tanner, about an hour ago to carry the same warning. He's traveling the land route down through Boston Neck. May God grant that at least one of you succeed with our mission to save our two great patriots."

"My plans are to cross the river as you say," I said. "I have a boat waiting, and I will leave Boston immediately. But first I would like to notify Charlestown by lantern as we planned to do in case neither of us is successful in getting by the British sentinels."

"Of course, do that before you go," he responded, "and from the activity we're hearing about in the Harbor and on the Common, the troops must be planning to travel to the mainland by crossing the Charles. My instincts tell me they'll be leaving for Lexington this very night."

I agreed with the doctor. and assured him I'd lose no time trying to get the message to Hancock and Adams. Once outside, I hurried to the house on the corner of Salem and Sheafe Streets where church sexton Robert Newman lived. I knew and trusted him—his two older brothers had been my schoolmates. He and Captain John Pulling, a member of the North End Caucus, had agreed in the afternoon to make themselves available to send the signal to our comrades in Charlestown. When I arrived at the Newman house, I approached carefully and peered into the front windows. I was shocked to see a number of British officers playing cards at a parlor table. I went around to the rear of the house to a small garden. As I was pondering my next move in near darkness, my friend Newman jumped from the shadows.

"What's going on?" I asked. "Why are the Redcoats inside? Is this a trap?"

"No," Newman replied. "The soldiers take board with my mother. When they sat down to play cards earlier, I said I was going to bed. I went upstairs and quietly climbed out the window and down to the ground. I have been watching for you. Captain Pulling and Tom Bernard are standing guard round the side of the house. Tom agreed to help with the mission."

"Good," I said. "Let's get them and hurry to the church."

Christ Church, on Salem Street, was only a few streets away. It was an Anglican Church, and the congregation closed it when its rector, Dr. Mather Byles, a staunch Loyalist, began giving sermons praising the King. As we walked, Newman fumbled for his sexton's key, and I reviewed our plans.

"Remember to show the light of two lanterns," I cautioned. "That's the way we are supposed to indicate the troops are crossing the Charles and not taking the time to march to South Boston where the land connection is. Our friends across the river already know that if the Regulars plan to take that route, only one light will be shown."

As I watched the trio cross the street and head for the large stone church with its belfry and one hundred ninety-seven-foot steeple towering over all the other buildings in Boston, I felt a tinge of nostalgia. I remembered that they were going to the same church where I had so often during my childhood climbed the one hundred and fifty-four steps to the belfry to ring the bells. I wasted no time reminiscing. I hurried home to get my boots and riding coat. I was going to take my pistol, but I thought better of it. I left home without it to meet Tom Richardson and a boat builder named Josh Bentley. They had earlier agreed to row me across the Charles.

I couldn't take a public ferryboat across because General Gage, for security, had ordered that all of them to be brought next to one of his warships at nine o'clock every night. In the bright moonlight of that cool April night, the three of us hurried toward the wharf where I had hidden my boat. When we realized that we had nothing to wrap around our oarlocks to muffle the sound of rowing. Josh led us to the Ochterlony—Adana house at the corner of North and North Center Streets. While we hid in the shadows, Josh quietly whistled. A woman appeared in an upper window. We heard him speak to her in a low whisper. We saw the woman retreat and then drop something out the window. Josh scooped up what looked like several woolen undergarments, and we continued on our way to the Charles. To cross the river, we had to pass near the large bowsprit of the 64-gun, man-of-war *Somerset.* It was positioned there to prevent rebels from leaving Boston. Thankfully, the darkness and our sound-damped oars allowed us to pass near the ship without being detected by the armed sentries standing watch fore and aft.

After we landed on the other side of the river, and the others had set off back to Boston, I made my way in the semidarkness to where I knew Colonel Conant and several Sons of Liberty would be waiting. They told me that they'd seen the two lights across the water, and I felt pride at our success with the signal system we'd devised.

Deacon John Larkin had brought a sturdy horse named Brown Beauty. He said when he had asked to borrow it for me to ride, his father, Samuel, was pleased. As I was preparing the reins, Richard Devens, a member of the Committee of Safety, told me that while he was riding to Charlestown from Menotomy[31] in his chaise after sunset he had passed nine mounted and armed British officers headed back toward Charlestown. He warned me to use great caution, for many British guards were about. I left the group at about eleven o'clock. The night remained clear and cool, and it felt good to once again undertake a mission with a strong mount under me.

As I was traveling past the outskirts of Charlestown, I spied two mounted men hiding in the shadows at a narrow part of the road. Though the moonlight spread over the road, I could barely make them out under the trees. As I approached I could see they were British officers. One immediately advanced on his horse toward me. I reined my horse sharply and veered past them, galloping toward Mystic. One rider sped after me but got mired in a clay pond. I rode hard to Medford, where I sought out the home of the captain of the local militia. It was maybe 11:30 when I banged on his door and awakened him. He rose up immediately and set about gathering his men. I continued on through Menotomy to Lexington, slowing at each house only long enough to make the occupants aware that the Regulars were on the march toward Concord.

CHAPTER FOURTEEN

In the town of Lexington, I sought out the home of a loyal Whig I knew. He answered my knock in his nightshirt and recognized me immediately. I asked him if he knew the location of Colonel Hancock and Mr. Adams. He directed me to the home of the Rev. Jonas Clarke. At the entrance to the Clarke house, eight guards confronted me and I was ordered to stop. One, a Sergeant Monroe, cautioned me not to make noise.

"Noise!" I shouted, "You'll soon have a noise that will disturb you all. The Regulars are on the way and will soon be among you!"

I then heard a shout from within the house. I recognized the voice. It belonged to John Hancock.

"Come in, Revere," he laughed, "We're not afraid of *you*."

A clock in the parlor showed midnight as I entered. I warned the two revolutionaries that General Gage had issued orders to arrest them and destroy our military stores in Concord. I added that British soldiers would soon arrive in Lexington and that this time the information was irrefutable. They seemed grateful for the warning and we talked over the situation in Boston. William Dawes, the first messenger sent by Dr. Warren, arrived as we spoke. He had ridden by way of Roxbury, Brookline and Cambridge and had warned many outlying towns about the coming of the British troops. I greeted Dawes warmly. We refreshed ourselves and our horses then made plans to continue on to Concord, although that was not part of our original directive from Dr. Warren. We wanted to stress to our fellow Whigs there to relocate any military stores not already hidden.

We remounted in the cool night air and raced along the Concord road side by side. Soon a rider came up from behind us at full gallop. By the light of the moon I could tell that the horseman was a young gentleman, elegantly dressed. He called to us that he was Samuel Prescott, a doctor from Concord. He said he was returning home from Lexington after visiting Lydia Millikan, the girl he was engaged to. We told the friendly doctor about our mission, and he offered to help us spread the alarm. He said that he knew many families who lived along the road and his familiarity would surely add to our credibility. We decided to stop at every house along the way and alert the men to ready themselves for a call to fight. The three of us agreed to take turns going from one farmhouse to the next.

When we arrived at Lincoln, about two miles past Lexington, I reckoned we had covered about half our planned route. We approached the cluster of Nelson family homesteads there. My two partners left the road to alarm the Nelsons while I took off for the next farm.

When I had advanced about two hundred yards, I could see two men hiding behind a tree not far ahead. I slowed my horse's gait. Their bright red uniforms identified them in the early morning hours. I called out for the doctor and Dawes. They approached rapidly, and we moved toward the riders slowly. Dr. Prescott turned the butt of his riding whip toward the officers, hoping they'd see it as a pistol. Suddenly two more Regulars appeared from an adjacent pasture with swords and pistols. They forced us at gunpoint into the fenced grassland.

As we slowly advanced into the field, Dr. Prescott gave me a subtle signal to run, and we spurred our horses mercilessly. Prescott escaped after jumping over a low stone wall and heading into the woods. I sped off toward the woods in another direction, only to be intercepted by six more mounted and armed officers. One of the guards pointed his pistol at me. Another grabbed the reins of Brown Beauty, forcing me to dismount. The tallest rider, who appeared to be in charge, looked me over carefully.

"Where are you coming from?" he commanded.

"Lexington," I said nonchalantly.

"What's your name?" He peered at me closely in the dim light.

"Revere," I said, just as simply.

"What? Paul Revere?"

"Yes." Once more, I feigned indifference.

"Are you one of the express riders?"

"Yes."

"What time did you leave Boston?"

"About ten o'clock," I responded, then continued, "and before I left, I saw your troops starting to land at Lechmere Point. You can expect five hundred American militiamen here long before your men come because we've alarmed the country all the way up."

My questioner abruptly turned from me and joined the others in his company waiting just off the road. He spoke to one, then five of them approached me at a gallop. One dismounted and introduced himself as Major Edward Mitchell of the 5th Foot. He ordered that I be searched for weapons. Finding that I had none, he leveled a pistol at my head and said, "Revere, I am going to ask you some questions, and if you don't give me true answers, I'll blow your brains out."

I gave him more or less the same answers to his line of questioning. The officer remounted and indicated for me to do the same. He ordered one of his men to take the reins of my horse and ride in front of me. He called to four casually clothed men hidden in the bushes to come out and mount their horses. When one of them rode up beside me, he quietly told me his name was Elijah Sanderson. He said and that he and his friend, Jonathan Loring, were sent from Lexington to observe the British. He said they were captured by the British patrol they were following, but didn't reveal their intent when questioned. He said that a third man named Soloman Brown, who was a messenger heading for Concord, was also a prisoner, as well as a one-armed peddler named Allen. Our conversation was interrupted by the major, who commanded his Regulars to surround us. Once the Regulars were in place, we all proceeded to the highway. The major then directed everyone to set off back toward Lexington.

After covering about a mile, he rode up alongside the soldier in front of me. He told him to turn me over to a sergeant. The noncommissioned officer approached, and the rider in front of me fell back. I heard the major say to the sergeant: "If he attempts to run, or anybody insults you, blow out the brains of Revere here." I never tried to run.

CHAPTER FIFTEEN

We rode at a gentle pace to the outskirts of Lexington. There the silence of the night was broken by a blast of gunfire from the center of town. Major Mitchell called for us to halt. He approached me and asked if I knew what was going on. I confidently said that the gunfire was to alarm the countryside. The officer became visibly annoyed. He ordered the other captives to dismount, and they obeyed. One of his men cut off the bridles and saddles of their horses and drove the animals away. The major turned and faced the civilians and told them that they were free to go home. The released men hurried over a fence into a ploughed field and disappeared into the night. I asked to be let go also but was refused. We were then ordered to continue into Lexington.

When we were within sight of the meetinghouse there, we heard another burst of gunfire. The major ordered everyone to stop. He approached me again.

"How far is it to Cambridge?" he asked.

"About ten miles," I answered. By then, I was hungry and tired, my patience running thin.

"Is there any way to get there without using the main highway?"

I said I knew of none. He turned his horse and rode back to the sergeant.

"Is your horse tired?" he asked him.

"Yes," the sergeant answered.

"Then take Revere's horse," said the major.

The sergeant rode up beside me and motioned for me to dismount. I got down quickly. He got off his horse—a small one compared to mine—and swung up on Brown Beauty. I took the reins of his small horse, but he jerked them away. Without speaking, and with the two horses, he moved to the rear.

The whole party of red-coated riders then set off for Lexington, leaving me on the road alone without a horse, bewildered, and drained of energy.

I made my way cautiously in the semidarkness for a few miles, passing through a burying ground and a number of rutted pastures. When I finally came to my destination, the Rev. Clarke's house, I knocked loudly. The heavy door swung open and there before me were John Hancock and Sam Adams. They encouraged me to sit, have a drink, and recount what had happened on my way to Concord. I emphasized the urgency of their leaving Lexington, and after much discussion they decided to travel to the widow Jones' house in the second precinct of Woburn[32], which, they believed, was a safe distance from the path of the British troops.

As dawn approached, Hancock and Adams left the Clarke house in Hancock's stately coach and traveled over the dirt roads toward Woburn.[33] I followed them on a frisky mount, and we made the five-mile trip in less than an hour. When I was certain that they were safe, I returned to Lexington. Near the Clarke house, John Lowell, a confidential clerk to Hancock, approached me. He said that Colonel Hancock had a heavy trunk full of important papers at the Buckman Tavern on Lexington Common. He told me the colonel had asked him to retrieve it and move it in a more secure place. I agreed to assist him with the relocation. On our way to the tavern we encountered a rider who hollered to us that the Regulars were coming. Lowell and I hurried to the tavern to spread the news about the approaching British soldiers. Once inside, we were told that there was no cause for alarm, that my message was a mistake. As I was about to assure the noisy group that my information was correct, another messenger hurried in to alert us that the Regulars were indeed less than a half-hour away.

John Parker, captain of the Lexington militia, rose from his table and immediately called his men to action. I could soon hear muskets firing and alarm bells ringing outside. I turned and saw Lowell motioning to me to get on with our work. As we hurried upstairs to retrieve the trunk, we heard shouts, commands, and the pounding of hoofs. From the upper chamber window, in the early morning light, I could see a British column in the distance marching towards us. Lowell and I struggled down the stairs with the heavy leather-bound trunk and got it outside. Our plan was to hide it back at the Clarke parsonage. As we crossed the Common, lugging the heavy weight through the gathering group of Captain Parker's excited militiamen, I heard him shouting: "If the Regulars come upon us, let them pass by. Take no action unless they start something."

CHAPTER SIXTEEN

owell and I carried our load across the Common. We passed over a road and headed for a likely spot among the trees where we could rest. When we got to the tree line, we hesitated and looked back to the Common where the militia was forming up. Approaching the disorganized men was a line of British soldiers marching shoulder to shoulder. I could readily see the glint of their shiny bayonets by the light of the rising sun. We resumed our mission. When I heard a shot ring out, I turned to see a plume of smoke rising from between our militia and the British formation. Lowell insisted vigorously that we hurry. We hobbled with the trunk to a stand of trees, then lowered it to catch our breath. We anxiously looked back toward the confrontation. I saw puffs of smoke appear and heard the irregular bursts of musket fire. Suddenly and horribly, there were full volleys of musketry. The battle had erupted in continuous white puffs bursting forth from the British infantry.

Soon the area where the men were lined up facing each other was enveloped in a thick haze. I could smell the acrid odor of burned gunpowder. The wounded fell, some dying on the spot. Our men were hit hard, and many tried to run from the Common. The Redcoats fanned out, advancing toward private houses. Through the thinning smoke I could see some British soldiers heading for the Buckman Tavern. Lowell and I looked at each other with a mixture of deep panic and sadness. Charged with our mission, we were helpless to even consider joining the fight.

Suddenly, we heard the sound of a drum roll. As if by magic, all firing ceased. The Regulars slowly came together and crowded around an officer who seemed to be giving instructions. Our militiamen all appeared to be running away from the area. Then there was a thundering blast as the soldiers fired together into the air, followed by what sounded like a wild cheer for victory. The British troops left the area en masse and marched along the Concord road close by where we were hiding. Their triumphant voices nearly drowned out the harsh commands being barked by their stiff-backed sergeants. After they all passed our spot, Lowell and I recovered our senses, gripped the trunk, and headed for the Clarke house. The brightening morning sun lifted our spirits as we struggled with our valuable load.

The Reverend held the door wide for us as we entered the safety of his parsonage. Lowell and I deposited John Hancock's chest in a secure hiding place on the second floor. Sleepless for the last two days, I collapsed next to the trunk[34], relieved to have fulfilled our mission. Lowell found a bed, but I slept soundly on the wide-planked floor until about eleven o'clock that night.

Later I learned that during the Lexington battle eight of our militiamen were killed and ten wounded. The only British casualties were two wounded privates. We had yet to kill one British soldier. Although this confrontation had been relatively minor, it was the first of many bloody encounters in what would come to be called the American Revolution—a nearly universal call by the colonies for complete freedom from Britain.

CHAPTER SEVENTEEN

I left the Clarke house in the early morning after a fine breakfast and headed for Cambridge. I was surprised when, along the way, I encountered red-coated bodies and dead horses strewn everywhere. Both farmers and militia were gathering the dead for burial, and moving the wounded to houses where doctors could attend them.

I arrived in Cambridge as the sun shown full on the town. I immediately went to the house where I knew Dr. Warren was staying. The doctor was aware of the Lexington fight that I had partially observed from the woods. He showed me where a clump of his blonde hair had been shot away by a British ball when he was with the men harassing the Redcoats as they retreated past Cambridge toward Boston. The good doctor had joined the other militiamen firing at the Redcoats who were hurrying back to where they had started early in the morning. He knew that on the previous day, Major Percy had arrived at Lexington from Boston with fresh men and two cannon and had escorted the surviving British troops back to Charlestown. He speculated that the Redcoats would have suffered even greater losses during their retreat if Major Percy had not joined them and led them to safety. As I rested in a chair, I could see Dr. Warren pacing the floor as he anxiously waited for news about what had actually happened earlier at Concord.

At one point, he suggested that I accompany him to a meeting of the local Committee of Safety that was to be held on Friday, two days hence. After eating, as we were puffing on our pipes and talking about the momentous events of the day, there was a knock on the front door. My host took his musket from the wall and opened the door cautiously. I stood close behind him, wondering who would call so late in the evening.

A short, rustically-clad visitor stood in the doorway. He blurted, "Ev'nin', Dr. Warren. I'm Reuben Brown, a saddler from Concord. Some British officers took my horse and chaise from the stable to carry their wounded men back ta Boston when they was in Concord, so's I joined the militia who was harrass'n the retreat'n Redcoats. We was shootin' at them from behind the trees and stone fences. When we got near Charlestown, Cap'n. Parker got me a horse 'n' said to come and tell you what happened today at Concord."

The doctor and I asked the young messenger to tell us what did happen. He appeared eager to recite his story. He told us that when the British soldiers arrived at Concord, they searched for our military supplies. He said most had been hidden so the soldiers couldn't find them. He added that the Regulars did find some wooden tools and they burned them. Also, a Liberty Pole. When they did locate three large cannon, they burned their gun carriages. When the burning carriages set fire to a town house, Reuben said with a smile, the British soldiers helped put it out. He said they never found any of our hidden supplies.

"What about the fight?" I asked.

The messenger answered that all of our militia had left the center of Concord before the British troops arrived so they wouldn't be tempted to start a fight. He said when the Redcoats found all of our men gone, lots of them went to Wright's Tavern to eat and drink, and the townspeople even brought out chairs to the lawn for the officers to sit down. He continued, saying the Colonel in charge stayed in town and sent out small groups of men to destroy the North and South bridges that led to Concord, and that about nine o'clock in the morning one captain with a number of men went to the North Bridge, They found none of our men there. He added, our militia had gathered up at Punkatasset Hill, about a half mile from the bridge so they could see everything that was going on in town.

Reuben stopped talking and began staring at the wall. He appeared to be reliving the action in which he had participated.

"Continue, man," Dr. Warren urged. "Then what happened?"

Reuben shook his head and continued telling us how a British captain ordered a number of his companies to continue over the bridge to Colonel Barrett's house to look for guns. Meanwhile, he said, the number of our militiamen kept growing on the hill and were appearing from all directions. He added, when the British soldiers saw the militia gathering, they moved back in front of the bridge. He said when smoke was seen coming from the center of Concord, our men believed that the British soldiers had set the town on fire. He described the next events in detail: Captain Parker ordered his men to move toward the bridge. Most of the British soldiers moved back over the bridge, leaving some to rip up its planks. Major Butt'rick yelled to leave the bridge alone. The soldiers stopped their destruction and joined the other Redcoats who were forming a line on the other side of the bridge. They all stood there, facing the colonists who were approaching the bridge. "And what happened then," asked the doctor, impatiently.

"One of the British soldiers fired a shot," Reuben continued, "but our militia kept advancin'. The soldiers then fired a complete volley at us and a lot of our men was hit. Major Butt'rick yelled, 'Fire, fellow soldiers, for God's sake fire.' Then all hell broke loose. There was smoke everywhere, but I could see that men on both sides was hit. Finally, the Redcoats broke ranks and started to run back toward Concord. Our men hurried alongside in the woods and kept pickin' off the retreating soldiers. When the Redcoats got back to Concord center, their captain musta held them there until the men who had gone to Colonel Barrett's house rejoined them. Then the whole British force regrouped and headed back toward Lexington. We ran alongside them in the woods. No shots was fired until we all come to the corner where the Meriam house is. There, the firing began again, and it continued all the way to Lexington. Mostly from our men hidden along the road. I saw a lot of Redcoats fall. At Lexington a group of Redcoats from Boston with a cannon met the British soldiers there, and they stopped us from firin'."

Reuben then told us that he stayed with our militia, and when the British left Lexington, our men began firing again, and it continued all the way back to Charleston. He said that's where Captain Parker told him to find Dr. Warren and tell him what went on in Concord.

Dr. Warren, satisfied with the report from Reuben, thanked him and offered him some libation. The messenger, after finishing off a large mug of rum, left with unsteady steps and a satisfied look to find his horse and return to his home in Concord.

CHAPTER EIGHTEEN

S oon after Reuben left, it began to storm. The flashes of lightning and crashes of thunder that accompanied the rain seemed to foreshadow the violence to come. I went upstairs to a bed provided by my host. My weariness brought sleep quickly. I slept soundly until about four o'clock in the afternoon. When I awoke, the weather had cleared.

I could not stop thinking about Rachel and the children, so as night came on I made a plan to see her. I searched for and found a boat that I could use to row across the Charles River to Boston. There had been no sign of Gage's men since they were ferried to Boston the night before, so I confidently pushed off from shore. In the darkness of the cool April night I rowed across the river and stealthily walked to my house on North Square. I knew that General Gage had restricted all civilian entry to and exit from Boston so I kept in the shadows and avoided areas that were occupied by soldiers. Rachel was sitting at her sewing when I came through the door. Overwhelmed with relief, she jumped up and threw her arms around me. I visited with her, my mother and my seven children until a little after midnight. Rachel gave me the money she had on hand, and I told her to collect what money she could from my customers and send it to me. When I finally departed for my return to Cambridge I felt better in some ways but unsettled as well.

In the early morning hours, I returned to where Dr. Warren was staying and after a large sampling of spirits, I returned to bed. At noon the doctor finally awakened me. He said we were to attend the meeting of the Committee of Safety that evening at the Hastings house. He told me that he'd already arranged to move the seat of the Massachusetts government to Cambridge until the British army was driven out of Boston.

We arrived at our destination about six o'clock. Many of the members of the Committee of Safety were there as well as some of the leaders of the Massachusetts government. We greeted each other and waited for others to join us before beginning our session. At seven o'clock Dr. Warren called us to order. He spoke eloquently about our new and now hostile relationship with Britain, and the events that had brought it about. His description of the fighting, he said, was an early, true and authentic account of an inhuman proceeding. He insisted that for our survival we must form our own standing army, and he felt it should consist of about 8,000 men. He also stated that our first objective should be the clearing of British troops from Boston. It was his belief that an organized siege would be the only way to attain that objective.

The Committee spent long hours in debate, for there were many among us who opposed open hostilities with Britain. In the end, Dr. Warren's terms were agreed to by most in attendance. Before I left, the doctor asked me if I would perform the "out-of-doors" business of the Committee. I gladly agreed to do as he requested without even knowing what I was being asked to do.

Early the next day, Dr. Warren gave me a horse and handed me many copies of a Circular Letter that solicited support for our own continental army. I was instructed to deliver copies to committee leaders throughout New England. On April 21 I promptly set off and for seventeen days I rode from town to town to deliver the plea for concerted action. As I traveled I often thought about Rachel and our children who were being held hostage with most Bostonians by General Gage's men. I found out much later that Rachel had sent me a letter after our night meeting. With it she included £125 for my ongoing expenses. She had given the package to Dr. Church for delivery. She selected him for he seemed to have the ability to pass through British lines freely. I never received the letter nor did we ever see any part of the money. That appeared to be additional proof of Dr. Church's complicity with the British cause. As you well remember, this same man was later tried as a British spy. At one point during my many travels to distribute the letter, I was called upon by the Provincial Congress to give testimony regarding the events I had witnessed on Lexington Green.[35]

General Gage must have realized that the Lexington and Concord encounters were only the beginning of armed resistance so he organized his forces in Boston to withstand the siege he felt would be coming. We were informed that he was jailing his known adversaries and demanding that all weapons be turned over to selectmen before their owners could leave town. Passes were required to leave Boston, and although they were easily obtainable, the Whigs and other rebels that got them were forbidden to return home. Many Tories who lived outside Boston, fearing harm from the liberty-seeking revolutionaries, traveled into Boston for safety. Soon, in town, food and all kinds of fuel became almost impossible to obtain.

I stayed in Cambridge for a while, waiting for the money I had asked Rachel to send to me, but I soon realized it would not be forthcoming. Her infrequent messages smuggled to me showed her increasing isolation and hardships. In May I moved to Watertown, a farming community about seven miles from Boston, where the center of the Massachusetts government had been re-established. I began staying at the Cooks house with Henry Knox and his wife, Lucy. Once settled in, I quickly made arrangements to have Rachel and the rest of my extended family join me. On May 3 she and all but one in our family came by wagon, traveling across Boston Neck. My 15-year-old son, Paul, stayed in Boston to look after our property. He shared my shop with a Tory engraver named Isaac Clemens, thereby saving it from the destruction that most other Whig properties in Boston were experiencing. Rachel also arranged to have my printing press brought to me by young Billy Dawes, the rider whom Dr. Warren had also dispatched to Lexington on April 18. Dawes was somehow successfully making weekly visits to Boston. He also brought me a number of copper sheets, and I began producing leaflets and posters advancing our cause with the assistance of young John Cook, a member of the family graciously housing my family and me.

When the Provincial Congress was informed that I had the facility for printing, it engaged my services to print money for Massachusetts. Since copper for the required printing plates was virtually impossible to obtain, I engraved the backs of previously used plates. One of these bore my illustration of Boston and a scene of the Boston Massacre. My currency printing included every denomination—from six-shilling to four-pound notes. I printed the bills on any paper I could find, and some of it carried little resemblance to official money. As bad as the bills appeared, they were accepted as payment for army payroll and the purchase of much-needed military supplies. To maintain security, the local Congress authorized a military guard to stand a twenty-four-hour watch around the building that housed my printing operation.

At that time, the Continental Congress in Philadelphia also felt the need for paper currency. A committee, including John Adams and Benjamin Franklin[36], was established to secure a source for their money. When members of the currency committee became aware of my printing money for

Massachusetts, they engaged me to print money for the other colonies. This work kept me busy until the end of the year. The irony of the situation became apparent to me when I was paid with the money of dubious value that I had just printed.

On May 15, 1775 the Provincial Congress in Watertown received notice that Ethan Allen, a Vermont patriot, had brought about the surrender of Fort Ticonderoga, a British outpost on Lake Champlain, without firing a shot. The news spread quickly, and men throughout the colonies became eager to join the fight.

On June 14 the Continental Congress, meeting in Philadelphia, authorized a military establishment and commissioned the best-qualified men in the colonies to staff it. By unanimous vote the representatives appointed George Washington as commander-in-chief of the new American army.[37] He quickly left that thriving Pennsylvania town to come to Cambridge so he could assume command of the militiamen scattered around Boston, where fighting had already occurred.

As I was working at my press late on June 17, a young Whig I had met only once entered the room. He greeted me with an enthusiastic, "Allo, Mr. Revere," then blurted, "Do ya know what's happenin' over in Charlestown?"

I told him I had heard some shooting over the river, but I thought it was the militia practicing. He told me that it was the Redcoats that were shooting at our men on Breed's Hill. He said that General Gates' army attacked there because he thought we must have been a threat looking down at him in Boston from the high ground next to Bunker Hill. He added that our boys took a heavy toll of his men, but our militia had to stop fighting and retreated when their ammunition got low.[38]

I learned later that my close friend, Dr. Warren, was fatally shot during the Breed's Hill encounter. He was president of the Massachusetts Provincial Congress and had just been made a general of Massachusetts' troops. He was waiting for his appointment to become effective when Gates' army stormed the encampment at Breed's Hill. Not wanting to be left out of the action, he joined our men as a private. Dressed in his best clothes, and with a musket taken from a retreating sergeant, he faced the enemy. A few minutes after he joined the fray on that hot June day, he was fatally hit in the head by a British ball. He was ordered buried unceremoniously at the site by Captain Walter Laurie, who had been commander of British troops at the North Bridge fight in Concord.

About two months after the doctor's death, two of his brothers and I went to Charlestown to reclaim his body. I identified his remains by inspecting his jaw. I recognized them as my friend's when I saw the set of artificial teeth I had made for him. We brought his body back to Boston for a proper funeral. I was proud to give my next-born son the name Joseph Warren Revere.

CHAPTER NINETEEN

General George Washington arrived in Cambridge on July 3 after a two-week trip from Philadelphia. Soon after his arrival we heard about the Declaration of Independence that had been issued there.[39] Release of the document meant that the die had been cast for complete freedom of the colonies from all British rule. Although most Bostonians welcomed the news, there were Tories living here who believed the act to be a foolish one. I personally was elated, for it was the culmination of all we had worked so hard to achieve. It did mean full-scale war, however, and that we colonists then were to live in danger of our lives. Washington, coming when he did, was a Godsend. He immediately began turning our ragtag militia into a respectable fighting force. With the hundred and twenty cannon that patriot Ethan Allen had seized earlier from Fort Ticonderoga—and General Henry Knox had masterminded the way to bring through the wilderness to Massachusetts—Washington laid siege to Boston to free it from British occupation. He took over the heights in Dorchester, about a mile from Boston, and was able to prevent ships from supplying the British garrison. He also prevented all food from coming into the city through Boston Neck, the only land approach to town. As the siege progressed, about 14,000 Bostonians left their homes and went to live in surrounding towns in order to escape the lack of food and fuel.

In August, our new Commander-in-Chief recognized the need for gunpowder for the military. Our defense of Breed's Hill had been hindered by the lack of it, and there were few manufacturers of it in the colonies. The colonial government in Massachusetts decided to set up a mill for making powder in Canton, but soon found out that there was no up-to-date information available on the technique for its manufacture. In November I was contacted by the Provisional Congress at Watertown and asked to travel to Philadelphia where a man named Oswell Eve had a modern working gunpowder mill. I was instructed to learn from him about mill design and the process he was using to make the much-needed material. I traveled to Philadelphia and received from Robert Morris a letter of introduction to Mr. Eve with a request that he provide me with all relevant information. The cautious Mr. Eve allowed me to only take a quick walk through his factory, withholding any details on the manufacturing procedure. No doubt he was fearful of the competition if we set up our own process.

With the information I gleaned from my rapid walk through his plant, and the plans Sam Adams was able to get from a Mr. Wisner, a patriotic powder mill employee, I was able to oversee the rebuilding of a mill at Canton and the installation of the necessary machinery. I started work in January and was in full production in May. The product made in Canton was not of the highest quality, but it served the army well throughout the war. In 1779, fortunately after sufficient supplies of powder were stockpiled to supply the troops until the war ended, the plant blew up, as powder mills often do.

Before the siege General Gage had returned to Britain, and General William Howe had taken over command of the British army in America. For eleven months the British occupied Boston, but General Howe refused to attack the American gun positions around the town probably for fear of another defeat like the one at Breed's Hill. Instead, to our amazement, he evacuated Boston on Sunday, March 17. His ships—with all of his troops and 1,100 civilians who supported the King and wanted to leave Boston—remained in the harbor for several weeks. Before sailing away, General Howe landed some soldiers on Castle Island to dismantle the military installation and spike the cannon there. He then moved the entire British force and the fleeing Tories to Halifax, Nova Scotia, leaving Boston clear of a British presence. I suppose the general felt that with the success of the blockade he had little to gain from staying in Boston, and much to lose.

On March 20, Washington and his triumphant army entered Boston where he was greeted with cheering crowds, banners, fireworks and the discharge of a thousand muskets. The siege of Boston—more blockade than bombardment—had lasted for almost a year and had ended without a great number of casualties. More people actually succumbed to starvation than to armed confrontation. The returning Whigs were, however, shocked to find the degree of destruction to their homes and belongings. The British had destroyed many houses and a good deal of furniture to supply heat through the winter. A number of trees, including our beloved Liberty Tree, had been chopped down for firewood. The presence of my son Paul and the Tory, Isaac Clemens, in our house and shop prevented the British military from harming my belongings.

Soon after the British evacuation, General Washington requested that I go to Castle Island to see if I could repair the cannon that the British had attempted to disable. At the abandoned fort I found that many guns could be salvaged, and with some mechanics' help I was able to repair many of them. I also designed and had built a new type of gun carriage, which went into manufacture at that time and proved to be eminently useful throughout the war.

By early 1776, it was abundantly clear to all households in the colonies that the resistance to taxation movement had turned into an all-out war for independence. Thomas Paine had just published his pamphlet "Common Sense," and his stirring words influenced many to join our cause. Although some colonials still supported the King, increasing numbers were joining us in our resolve for complete freedom from Britain.

When General Washington left Boston, he took most of the Massachusetts troops with him to fight the more threatening British forces in New York and Philadelphia. We were left to defend ourselves in case of a British attack. I felt pressed to participate more fully in our fight for freedom, and after much soul-searching I decided to rejoin the Massachusetts military. On April 10, I was made a Major in the First Regiment of Militia. Our mission was to defend Boston, and I was paid £15 per month for my services. When my experience with leading an artillery unit was recognized, I was transferred the following month to an artillery regiment. On November 27, I was promoted to Lieutenant Colonel and put in charge of the regiment. My new monthly pay was £18 per month. In addition to my new duties, I was subject to an unwelcome regulation—I had to powder my hair. General Ward was my immediate commander. I was indeed a proud father when shortly after receiving my new rank, my son Paul was commissioned a Lieutenant in the 4th Company of my regiment.

Although headquartered in Boston, I was stationed most of the time at Castle William in Boston Harbor, the British fort on Castle Island that had been abandoned when the King's troops evacuated Boston. It was also where, the year before, I had been confined behind bars during General Gates' ill-fated Salem Expedition. As commander of the island fort—named Fort

Independence after the British left—it was my job to prevent the return of the British military to Boston. That was not a difficult thing to accomplish, since the King's troops never again tried to recapture the town. I spent most of my time keeping my bored soldiers from deserting, and presiding over the courts-martial of men who tried to. Others whom I disciplined were men who got caught stealing, got drunk or played cards on the Sabbath.

On April 17, I attended a town meeting where I learned that Danbury, Connecticut had recently been sacked by British forces. I felt the deep concern of the Boston leaders that our town might be in a similar danger. There was much talk about a preemptive strike against the British in Connecticut in order to prevent a like attack on us. At the time I would have welcomed any activity that would have allowed me an escape from the helplessness I was feeling.

On April 19, 1777, the second anniversary of the Lexington fight, the Whigs in Boston, who'd been living among the many Tories that refused to leave in General Gates' flotilla, were encouraged to rid the town of some of the more strident monarchists. Late in the day a Whig, dressed in clothes that made him unrecognizable, forced five Tories into a cart and on his white horse escorted them to Roxbury. There, the rider, identifying himself as Joyce Jr. dumped the five and warned them under penalty of death not to return to Boston. Other Tories were similarly treated in the days that followed.

Sadly, my mother, Deborah, at age seventy-three, who had lived with me ever since my father died, joined him in death on May 23, 1777, after a short illness. She was sorely missed by all that knew her. Every day I think of her and remember the many blessings she brought to my life and others in our family. Rachel was unable to join me at the funeral, for in addition to the five older children she cared for at home, she was attending to our son, Joseph Warren, who was just one month old. My dear mother was buried in the Old Granary, next to my beloved father.

On June 14, Congress declared that the flag of the new United States would consist of thirteen alternating red and white stripes, and a blue field with thirteen white stars. Flags of this design immediately began to fly throughout Boston.

I was called upon a number of times to leave my post at Fort Independence in order to conduct military missions. On August 28, 1777, I led an artillery detachment of a hundred and thirty men to Worcester to collect the six hundred to seven hundred British soldiers commanded by Colonel Baum, who had been captured by General Stark and his New Hampshire militia at the Battle of Bennington in Vermont. On the way to our destination, we spent the first night in Watertown and the next in Marlborough. After arriving in Worcester, we waited four days for the prisoners to arrive, then brought them back to Fort Independence for internment.

In September of the same year, I joined the State's Train of Artillery as part of a detachment ordered to Rhode Island to dislodge the British forces there. They had taken possession of part of New York and of Newport, Rhode Island. Our leaders had anticipated that an attack might be launched against Boston from Newport and were determined to thwart it. Our mission to eliminate the British presence there was unsuccessful, however, mostly due to the insufficient time allotted to gather our needed war materiel, the inexperience of the officer in charge of the mission, and the unusually bad weather at the time. Upon my return to Boston, I again took command of our fort on Castle Island.

Boston at the time was a gloomy place. Food was scarce, winter was coming, many husbands and young sons were in the army away from home, and the threat of a return of the British army brought despair. In the fall of 1777 the people finally received some encouraging news.

Up until that time, General Burgoyne and his superior forces had been winning territory for Britain as he moved from the Lake Champlain area to the Hudson Valley. He was headed for Albany where he hoped to join another large army led by Sir Henry Clinton. Together they planned to split the colonies in two and crush the rebellion. When Burgoyne arrived in Saratoga, New York on his way to combine forces with Clinton, however, he was confronted on October 7 by an American army led by General Horatio Gates and my friend, Benedict Arnold. After a long, bloody battle, Burgoyne's forces were surrounded and overcome. The 5,700 British soldiers who survived the fighting surrendered to General Gates. We did not know at the time, but that extended battle saved New York and New England, and was the turning point of the American Revolution.

France and Spain had been supplying us with guns and other war implements for they feared the military aspirations of England, but they had been hesitant to engage in direct combat with that island nation because of its superior forces. They hoped our resistance would weaken England's ability to threaten their countries. They needed some indication that we would be successful in our rebellion before they committed their navy to fight on our behalf. Our substantial victory at Saratoga finally persuaded both France and Spain to actively join us in our fight against England.

On March 13, 1778 The French warship *Nymphile* entered Boston Harbor. I was ordered to salute its arrival with cannon fire, and I did with alacrity. The newly arrived Frenchmen helped me to add fortifications to Castle Island, then established the town of Hull as their center of war activity. In September a fleet of 12 more warships and 15 frigates under the command of the notorious Count d'Estang joined the *Nymphile*. Up to that time my command had seen little active service. With the powerful French command positioned in Hull, Fort Independence seemingly became even less relevant.

In the summer of 1778, I got involved in a second, more coordinated attempt to break the British hold on Newport. General Washington sent men from Connecticut and Rhode Island to support our troops. John Hancock was Major General of the 3,000-man Massachusetts militia, and I led, and supplied men from the fort for, the artillery train. The French Fleet was brought in to assist us with ships and men. Unfortunately, a great storm at sea disabled or destroyed large parts of both the French and British fleets. The loss of the French ability to support the ground troops with bombardment from the sea rendered us incapable of resisting the British forces when they launched an unexpected land offensive. General Hancock, recognizing our position as futile, and considering a drawn out campaign tiresome, ordered us home. Disheartened by the failed mission, my men and I returned to our boring duties at Fort Independence.

During the first week of November another violent storm brought disaster to more of the British fleet. On November 5, 1778, the British man-of-war *Somerset*—the ship I had so diligently avoided as I crossed the Charles on the night before the Lexington fight—was one of the vessels destroyed off Cape Cod by strong winds. It was blown onto Peaked Hill Bar, then onto the clay pounds of the beach. Four hundred and eighty seamen and naval officers from the ship surrendered to the surprised inhabitants of the local town. Sixty or seventy sailors on the vessel died in the disaster and were buried by local fishermen.[40]

Although we remained on heightened alert for a few months after the Newport debacle, it was a futile exercise, for the British never attacked Boston.

My next and last military venture from the fort was an absolute disaster. Let me tell you about it in detail.

First, another long puff...

CHAPTER TWENTY

O n June 26, 1779, I was ordered to prepare one hundred of my matrosses[41] to join a Massachusetts expedition sent to capture a British fort being built on the coast of Maine at Maja-Bagaduce,[42] near the mouth of the Penobscot River. The outpost was being established by the British to provide a suitable jumping-off point to counter the increasing number of privateers who were taking over their ships along the coast and to prepare a permanent home for the many loyalists who fled under British protection to Nova Scotia. Our Massachusetts leaders grew alarmed because it was also an ideal place for the British to mount an offensive against Boston. In July, the Massachusetts General Court ordered a force to take over the unfinished installation—named Fort George after the reigning English King. Brigadier General Soloman Lovell was in charge of 1200 Massachusetts' militia, and again I led the accompanying artillery train. On July 19, with a fleet of forty ships, nineteen of which were armed vessels carrying a total of three hundred guns, all commanded by Commodore Dudley Saltonstall[43] of the Continental navy, we sailed for Maine.

On July 24, after a stop at Townsend[44] to pick up additional men, a landing which turned out to be fruitless, we arrived at Penobscot Bay. We came upon a force of only three British warships, and assumed that the rest of the enemy fleet was at Halifax. Our first forays were eminently successful. Our men captured the lightly defended Nautilus Island in the outer bay that contained a British battery. Next, our Yankee marines scaled the heights of the mainland and, with the guns from the ordnance brig that I unloaded and had hoisted up, we began to fire on the fort from a distance. That action forced all of the British soldiers located outside the main compound into the partially built, dirt-walled installation. General Lovell then called upon the Commodore to destroy the few British gun ships nearby in order to protect our men that were ready to attack. Saltonstall insisted that the ground troops first capture the enemy fortress and its single long-range cannon. Believing that we'd be destroyed if we advanced under British naval fire, General Lovell pleaded with the Commodore to fire on and destroy the inferior British fleet. Again the naval commander resisted. At a council of war on board the brig *Hazard* on August 7, Commodore Saltonstall, General Lovell and I voted against continuing the siege, but we were outvoted by the other leaders who felt that we were capable of capturing the fort. General Lovell believed additional troops would be necessary to defeat the enemy without naval support, as did six of our ship captains who thought their sailors would desert within days, so averse were they to the whole endeavor. The pointless stalemate continued for two weeks, a delay that allowed the makeshift fortifications at Fort George to be substantially reinforced, and the alerted British fleet at Halifax to return to Penobscot Bay.

On August 13, when Saltonstall saw the enemy warships appear on the horizon, he ordered his armed vessels to retreat up the Penobscot River. He overtook and passed our slow unarmed transports and barges, leaving them with no defense. The British men-of-war began firing at our unprotected support vessels as they chased our warships up the river. The enemy allowed us no escape. The frantic, trapped sailors of both armed and unarmed vessels hastily beached and burned their ships, then raced into the nearby woods. I was in one of the last vessels to be beached, and I watched the frightened men leave the flaming boats and dash for the safety of the forest. In the engagement, thirty-eight of our ships were destroyed and two were captured.

I searched for and gathered most of my men on shore, but when I stopped and took a boat to get other sailors from a schooner that had lost its own boat, many of my men left for the protection of the inland forest. After searching guardedly along the river and in the near woods for my men for two days without success, I made my way to Fort Western[45]. There, on August 19, I found most of my officers and men. I supplied them with all the money I could spare and told them to return to Boston on their own by the quickest route.

Leaving the wrecks of their ships smoldering on the banks of the river, most soldiers and sailors found their way with the help of the Penobscot Indians through the wilderness and back to Boston. Many were sick and half-starved when they got home. Others, with insufficient food and scant clothing, died along the way.

When I arrived home after the long trek, mosquito-bitten and with sore feet, I was besieged with harsh criticism about our failure. Nevertheless, on August 27, 1779, the Massachusetts Council ordered me to resume command of Fort Independence. My stay at the fort, however, didn't last long.

Within ten days of my return to Boston, a formal complaint was issued against me concerning my actions in Maine. The Captain of Marines, Thomas Carnes, who was aboard the warship *General Putnam* during the expedition, claimed that I had disobeyed the orders of General Lovell, was negligent in my duties in caring for my men, behaved unmilitary-like, and was a coward, all charges that were patently untrue. I was arrested on September 6, 1779, the same day that the charges were filed, ordered to resign my command at Fort Independence, and confined to my home. Thankfully, after three days the confinement warrant was removed, and I was freed of restrictions while awaiting investigation of the complaints against me. I believed that Carnes' accusations were inspired by the confrontations I had earlier when I requested an order from the General Council that the ship's officers that accepted my men who had deserted from Fort Independence return the men to the fort. Pressing for a full investigation of the trumped-up charges, I wrote many letters to the Council detailing my version of the events in Maine, but I received no answer. I was sure that the Council members were inclined to wish away the whole Penobscot debacle.

On October 10, I wrote once again to the Council urging it to convene a full court-martial to hear all the facts. On November 11, a Committee of Judgement met to review the charges against me. On November 16, the committee reported to the Council that my conduct at Penobscot, which even General Lovell found meritorious, deserved condemnation. I was shocked by the finding, and on January 17, I once more demanded a full court-martial to hear all of the facts, stating that that was my right.

On April 13, 1780, the Council finally voted for a military court-martial to sit at the county courthouse in Boston beginning April 18. For some reason not made known to me, that trial was cancelled.

Throughout the next year, as I waited impatiently for information about the status of my trial, I heard and read about the war news. How the British took Charleston, South Carolina; how Benedict Arnold betrayed our cause[46] and was made a brigadier general in the British Army; how Spain had asked Britain for Gibraltar as a reward for joining the war on the British side, and when Britain refused, joined France in its war against Britain; and how Connecticut soldiers mutinied because of the shortage of food. But all during that time I never heard from the Council about my requested court-martial.

In 1781 I wrote to the Council again, insisting to be heard and have my name cleared. The Court ordered that consideration of my petition be delayed until the next session, to be held the following year. While I waited anxiously, our revolutionary army fought a series of bloody battles under the command of George Washington in Pennsylvania, New York and New Jersey. In the fall of 1781, the ingenious Washington feigned an attack on New York causing the British to reinforce their garrisons there. Instead of attacking New York, however, the general moved his troops south.

On September 2, 1781, with the assistance of the French fleet, his army attacked British fortifications at Yorktown. General Cornwallis, unable to escape, and knowing his 7,000-man force was no match for the continental army, surrendered to Washington. That decisive defeat brought about the end of the war.[47]

As the news spread throughout the colonies, the people went wild, celebrating with parades, fireworks, cannon firings, and huge bonfires. I enjoyed the victory, but could not rest easy with the alleged dishonor of Penobscot on my name. With a heavy heart I yearned for a fair hearing and continued my silversmith business.

On February 19, 1782, almost three years after the original charges were made against me, my requested court-martial was finally convened. The jury consisted of twelve captains, with Brigadier-General Wareham Parks as president and Joshua Thomas as judge-advocate. After reviewing all of the events that led to our failure to capture Fort George and my part in them, the court acquitted me of all the charges made by my detractors. The court also acquitted all of the other army officers in the expedition of all wrongdoing. Massachusetts Governor John Hancock studied the final report and officially noted his approval of the court's long-delayed opinion. I had suffered humiliation and chagrin in the intervening years, but in 1782 I felt great relief with the favorable outcome of the official court-martial I had so steadfastly petitioned to be held. At last I could fully savor our victory over Britain and appreciate the glorious victory I had so often labored to help bring about.

CHAPTER TWENTY~ONE

In 1783 I opened a hardware store on Essex Street, near where the original Liberty Tree once stood. I hoped that by having more than one business I could increase my worth faster. In my new shop I stocked items made by my silversmiths as well as other locally made and foreign goods. I sold many silver pieces, including tankards, spectacle frames, tureens, shoe buckles, and candlesticks. I also carried utilitarian products such as sandpaper, sealing wax, pumice stones, door locks, hinges, and sleigh bells, as well as men's and ladies' hosiery, specialty cloth, wallpaper and merchandise imported from Europe. Although hardware made up most of the business, I had felt that I would easily sell other strictly English products to my customers, so I ordered £500 of various goods from England. I notified a friend, Frederick William Geyer, who'd left Boston with other Tories fearing for their lives when General Gates sailed away, to begin making arrangements in England to ship me goods as soon as a peace treaty was signed. They were finally brought to Boston by the British ship, *Rosemond*. Everything arrived in good condition.

Although, in general, my business prospered, at times I overextended myself. Occasionally, my income was so sparse that I paid part of my bills with scraps and filings of precious metals scavenged from the floor of my silver shop. The years directly after the war were good for most businesses, but after a few years of prosperity, the British and other foreign merchants deluged Boston with cheap goods, causing many local businesses to fail. In 1789, when orders from my customers declined because of the faltering economy in Boston, I rented my hardware store property to Ebenezer Larkin, the nephew of Deacon John, the gentlemen who had given me his horse to ride when I spread the alarm back in 1775.

Previously, in February of 1786, when business was still good, I had moved into a two-story house at 50 Cornhill Street, near Dock Square with my eight children, five of whom were under twelve. My previous home had become too small for my growing family. Rachel was overjoyed with the move, and I took great pleasure in the new, expanded living space.

In 1787 a Constitutional Convention[48] was held at Carpenters Hall in Philadelphia. People throughout the colonies showed great interest in the events that led up to final approval of a federal constitution. I looked upon the new document as a consummation of all of our efforts to be free.

In 1788 I was called to attend a special meeting at the Green Dragon. The Constitution, prepared the previous year, had to be ratified by a number of states before it could become official. When it got to Massachusetts most of our leaders were anxious to sign the document, but weren't sure whether Sam Adams would, since he hadn't expressed an opinion. The special meeting I attended was held in order to show our solidarity to the old rebel so he would be influenced to sign, for his name on the document would add much to its importance. When he became aware of the huge number of his countrymen who approved of the Constitution, he agreed to add his name. I thought it odd at the time that members of the meeting believed a man so committed to freedom and unity might hesitate to endorse that unity. Anyway, all of us breathed a sigh of relief when Sam penned his signature on the first official document of the United States of America.

CHAPTER TWENTY-TWO

I was knowledgeable in the metalworking field, so in the same year that Sam gave his approval to the Constitution I opened a small foundry at 13 Lynn Street near the corner of Foster Street. I planned to smelt brass and iron there and cast the metals into useful articles. I wrote to Mr. Brown and Mr. Benson who owned a furnace in Providence that made the pigs, or raw iron blocks, that I had to have for my operation. I asked for immediate shipment of ten tons of their pigs, offering to sell to the gentlemen one quarter or one third of my business as prepayment for that and some future orders. They did not accept my offer, but I was able to obtain sufficient raw materials anyway, some of it from abroad.

Early in 1789 I began to actually cast the pieces for which I had orders. At first I fashioned small items such as ship fittings, anvil hammers, stoves and hearths. Later, I cast some small brass cannon and larger ironware. In 1792 I cast my first bell. That fine bell was recast from a smaller five hundred-pound one that had been located at the Second Church on Middle Street. The bell was originally taken from the demolished Old North Church when it was dismantled for firewood. When that took place, the congregation of Old North combined with the one at the New Brick Church[49]. Together, they named the combined congregations the "Second Church." The New Brick Church bell cracked in 1792 after it had been moved from the Old North Church. The damage was such that it could only be used to announce fires. When recast, using the metal from the old bell and some of my own, the new bell weighed nine hundred and twelve pounds. I was paid £74, 7 shillings for my work. The bell has my name inscribed on it, and it still hangs and rings out there in the steeple of the New Brick Church.

Bells have always fascinated me, and they remain a big part of my business. To date my foundry has produced about three hundred bells, most weighing over five hundred pounds.[50] In 1794 my foundry cast some twelve-pounder cannon for Massachusetts, and ten brass, 8¼-inch howitzers for the new federal government. My foundry business still flourishes, and I am currently making bolts, spikes, sheaves, pumps and other parts for the frigate *Constitution*, which can now be seen under construction at Edmund Hartt's Shipyard.

Seeking additional ways to benefit fellow mechanics, I, with other artisans, organized an association in 1795 to assist the local merchants who were having trouble with their apprentices. We wanted to have the General Court revise the law covering these workers, some of whom were leaving their employers before their terms were complete. We wanted to strengthen the existing law regarding apprenticeship and provide benefits to the boys who served out their terms. One of our first accomplishments was the formation of an agreement to not hire boys who had run out on their employer. We also instituted the awarding of prizes to qualified workers and offered the boys financial help, trade periodicals, and personal advice. We call ourselves the Massachusetts Mechanics Association, and I am a charter member. I am also the President, and have been for a few years.

CHAPTER TWENTY-THREE

I find it hard to believe now that with all my revolutionary and business activity, I still had time to pursue my most enjoyable diversion—my fraternal Masonic duties. When I was initiated in Saint Andrews Lodge on September 4, 1760, I was twenty-five years old. I wasn't a stonemason then, nor am I now, but I believed in the things the organization stood for. At the time I was just pleased to be accepted into a group in which individual worth and personal merit were the only requirements for membership and advancement. I had no way of knowing at the time what Freemasonry would mean to me in my lifetime.

Saint Andrews was a relatively new lodge, and many of its meetings were held near my home in the north end of Boston, at the Green Dragon Tavern. I was the first candidate received after their charter was obtained in 1756 from the Grand Lodge of Scotland. I became a Royal Arch Mason and Knight Templar on December 11, 1769. I served as Junior Deacon, Junior Warden, and Secretary during the following year. On November 30, 1770, I was installed as Worshipful Master of the Grand Lodge of Scotland. At that time, the Massachusetts Grand Lodge was forming, and I was also serving there as Senior Grand Deacon. Except during the war years, I served from 1769 through 1797 as some officer in a Grand Lodge. Three years ago I was chosen as Grand Master of this Grand Lodge of Massachusetts. I was not the Lodge's first choice. That was John Warren, brother of my departed friend, Dr. Joseph Warren, who died at the Battle at Breed's Hill. John, who was already serving as Grand Master, declined to continue in the office and the assembled brethren proceeded to appoint me as his successor.

During my term, I introduced the Grand Master's tricorn hat and originated the position of Grand Chaplain. I understood that one of the major functions of our Grand Lodge was to charter new lodges and oversee the conduct of the lodges within our jurisdiction. Accordingly, in the three years I served as Grand Master, we chartered twenty-three new lodges within Massachusetts and Maine. I encouraged the distribution of the book titled *The Constitutions of the Ancient and Honorable Fraternity of Free and Accepted Masons*. This volume included history, addresses, laws, and songs of Masonic importance. It also stated the rules and regulations that are designed to ensure the smooth running of Masonic Lodges, as well as the charges used in the installation of new officers. As Grand Master, I composed the ceremony currently used when constituting a new lodge and chaired a committee to draft a resolve against the admission of unsuitable candidates for membership.

My more pleasant fraternal memories include the correspondence I had with George Washington; and my participation, as the highest lodge representative, in the laying of the cornerstone of the new State House near Boston Common. Governor Samuel Adams asked our lodge to share in the dedication because of our longstanding tradition as ancient stonemasons and master builders. The event took place on the twentieth anniversary of our country's independence. The stone was brought to the site on a wagon decorated with ribbons. It was drawn by fifteen white horses, each with a splendidly dressed leader. I placed an inscribed silver plate and a few copper, silver and gold coins beneath the cornerstone to commemorate the celebration. Before the official ceremony, I addressed a group of participants at the Old South meetinghouse, and after the ceremony I reveled in the cheering of an enthusiastic crowd and the roar of the customary cannon fire.

CHAPTER TWENTY~FOUR

I t seems they are now calling for me upstairs. Getting out of this comfortable chair takes longer as I get older, but I suppose I should be thankful that I am still able to do it. I'd better put out my pipe now, for I'll need all my faculties to negotiate the narrow steps that lead up to our great hall. We always intended to widen those steps but never got around to it.

*****

I suppose I don't deserve the applause I'm getting. Then again, maybe I do. The pleasant clamor is dying down. Well, for better or worse, here goes my address:

Right Worshipful Brethren,

The time is now arrived when it is the incumbent duty of this G^d. Lodge according to its Constitution, to proceed to the choice of a G^d. Master. This Constitution directs 'that no person shall be eligible for that office more than three years successively.' I have served that period and am not eligible for re-election.

Ever since I have had the honor to preside in the G^d Lodge, I can truly say I have endeavored to pay every attention to what I esteemed my duty. I have never omitted to do one act that appeared to be for the good of the Crafts. If I have done what I ought not to have done, you must impute it to my head and not to my heart.

There are now under this jurisdiction upwards of forty Lodges who pay their dues and are nearly all represented. There is one at Nantucket who received their Charter from G^d. Master Rowe. This Lodge has never sent their *charters to be endorsed. I have no doubt they will comply with the requisitions, provided a little attention is paid them by the Brother who shall fill this chair. St. Andrews Lodge I am told, have it in contemplation to form another G^d. Lodge in Boston, but I think Masonry has little to fear from it, provided the Lodges under our jurisdiction pay a strict attention to the resolves of our G^d Lodge. Besides, the G^d. Lodges in the Union will never countenance two G^d. Lodges in one state. I have no doubt the members of that lodge will ere long see the necessity of subordination among Masons.*

Free Masonry is now in a more flourishing situation than it has been for ages; there is no quarter of the Globe but acknowledges its Philanthropy. There are Grand Lodges in every state in our Union, they have pledged themselves to communicate freely with each other, and the resolves of many of them show their determination to pursue a regular system. The G^d. Lodge of England has shown their liberality and candor in acknowledging the G^d. Lodges in America, in offering to hold a free correspondence with us, and in engaging to receive our brethren as children of the same household. The G^d. Lodge of Nova Scotia has done the same. I have no doubt that if a little attention is paid to correspondence, that we shall soon have the pleasure to communicate with every G^d. Lodge through the Globe. I would recommend that a correspondence be immediately opened with the G^d Lodge of Quebec; it will be a means of securing the friendship of that body of Masons against those persons who may wish to make innovations in Masonry.

Every free and accepted Mason ought to be sensible that subordination among Masons is as essential as in any government whatever, and that without it no society will flourish. You will permit me to recommend a careful attention to our Constitution; that you never suffer the ancient landmarks to be removed, that a strict attention be paid to every Lodge under this jurisdiction, that they be treated with candor, and leniency; but at the same time they be not suffered to break through, or treat with neglect any of the regulations of the G^d Lodge.

The finances of the G^d. Lodge will soon be respectable. I would therefore recommend that a committee be raised to form regulations for the disposal of charity, or any other thing that will add to the happiness of Masons. I would likewise recommend that a plate be procured for the purpose of granting certificates by the G^d. Secretary, similar to the one received from the G^d. Lodge of England.

It is the greatest happiness of my life to have presided in the G^d. Lodge at a time when Free Masonry has attained so great a height that its benign *influence has spread itself to every part of the globe and shines with more resplendent rays, than it hath since the days when King Soloman employed our immortal G^d. Master to build the temple.*

Brethren, you will be so kind as to accept my most sincere and hearty thanks for your candor, and assistance while I have had the honor to preside in the G^d Lodge. It is owing to your kind attention and assistance that I have been enabled to do the little good which has been done. Continue the same kindness to all my successors in office, remembering the cause we are engaged in is the cause of humanity, of Masons and of man.

That the best of heaven's blessings may rest upon this G^d Lodge, will be the last prayer and wish of your affectionate brother.

EPILOGUE

The stepping down from the position of Grand Master in 1797 in no way lessened Paul Revere's desire to face challenges, or to contribute to his country's good. Although no longer holding a Masonic office, he was active with the Masons for many more years.

On January 11, 1800, in Boston, Revere participated in a Masonic commemoration of the funeral of George Washington. The respected ex-president had died the month before at Mount Vernon. A colorful procession that included Masons from all over Massachusetts marched from the State House through the streets of Boston. Hundreds of spectators lined the flag-draped thoroughfares to see the white horses, uniformed veterans, colorfully dressed Masons, civil dignitaries, and the trailing huge, symbolic urn deftly carved by a Mr. Reynolds. The white, artificial marble urn bore the inscription: "Sacred to the Memory of Brother GEORGE WASHINGTON; raised to the ALL PERFECT LODGE Dec. 14, 5799[51]—Ripe in years and full of glory."

At the funeral service, Timothy Bigelow and Reverend William Bentley preached funeral orations to the crowd. Afterwards, Revere hosted a supper in the upper chamber of an inn close by on King Street for the Rev. Bentley, Isaiah Thomas, Jacob Perkins and Mr. Reynolds. It was the Reverend's father who had rowed Revere across the Charles on the night before the Lexington fight. Thomas was the largest book publisher in America. Perkins was a highly decorated veteran and the inventor of a nail-heading machine that revolutionized construction. Reynolds was the sculptor who had fashioned George Washington's symbolic urn, as well as busts of many famous men, all out of a type of artificial stone. Revere was, no doubt, in his element, and the supper must have been one he would always remember.

259

Later, the gray-haired silversmith was appointed with other Masons to a committee, which had the responsibility to write a letter of condolence to Mrs. Washington. The letter contained a request for a lock of her husband's hair. The request was granted, and the Massachusetts Grand Lodge commissioned Revere to fashion a small golden urn with a wooden pedestal to hold it. The three-and-seven-eighths-inch-high cast relic, with jewels and the regalia of the Grand Lodge emblazoned on the outside, and Washington's lock of hair on the inside, remains to this day in the possession of the elected Grand Master of the Massachusetts Grand Lodge.

Revere was equally active in civic affairs. He contributed money to the Boston Library and the Boston Humane Society. He was the first of over eight hundred subscribers to sign the charter for the Massachusetts Mutual Fire Insurance Company.

Also in the civic area, he became the Suffolk County coroner, commissioned by Governor Samuel Adams. When an outbreak of yellow fever hit Boston in early 1799, Revere involved himself in the creation of the town's first Board of Health. In the years 1799 and 1800, he served as its President. During the same two years he acted as a ward representative in Boston.

Throughout the years Revere maintained his silversmith business. His first work was the making of buckles, pins, and other simple objects, but as time passed he made more fashionable things. When traveling or in the military service, his apprentices and hired silversmiths produced items that allowed his shop to continue in business. He belonged to many organizations and regularly solicited business from other members. During the years prior to the war, his shop produced 1,145 objects, the majority of which were personal items and flatware.

After the war, he made over 4,000 items, mostly flatware and harness fittings. He received a large contract for the fittings, and it represented a major part of his earnings.[52]

When Revere was sixty-six years old, an age when most men look forward to the joys of retirement, he began his most ambitious project. It was eminently successful and brought him great wealth. Thoughts about the venture in all likelihood began early in his career.

In the 1770s, when he was active in the preparation of engraved copper plates, and later when he was busy with his foundry, Revere was extremely aware of the shortage of copper available for commercial use. Many of his most famous illustrations had to be cut on the back of copper sheets that he had been previously engraved, for copper sheeting was extremely difficult to obtain.

In the spring of 1800, Revere was thrown from his chaise and suffered a painful dislocation of his shoulder. As he nursed himself back to health, he thought seriously about the copper shortage and determined to build a mill for rolling copper sheets since there was no such factory in America. He recognized that the enterprise would be costly, so with $25,000 of his own money and a loan of $10,000 from the United States government, he embarked on his endeavor. On March 14, 1801, for $6,000, he purchased property on the Neponset River in Canton that included the remains of an unused government gunpowder mill—it had blown up years earlier—a two-story frame house, a trip-hammer shop and a coal house. The government also lent him 19,000 tons of copper. Using rollers procured from Maidstone, England—he didn't think rollers made in America were precise enough—he constructed a suitable facility and began operation before the year was out. The next year he made his first major sale. He sold 6,000 feet of sheet copper to recover the dome of the State House on Beacon Hill. In 1803 the hull of the frigate *Constitution* was re-coppered with sheets from his mill. In 1809 the copper for fabricating boilers for Robert Fulton's ferry steamboats was supplied by Paul Revere.

Soon after his purchase of the Canton property, he converted the existing frame house next to the mill into a summer home. He called it Canton Dale and spent many happy years there socializing with friends and hunting in the nearby woods. His copper mill brought him great riches, and the copper business continues to this day under the name "Revere Copper and Brass Company." This corporation is an industrial giant, and some operations are still carried on in Canton, Massachusetts.

On October 9, 1804, a great gale blew the roof off and demolished his old foundry in Boston. The building was never rebuilt, and the foundry work, which hadn't already been transferred during the previous year, was moved to his rolling mill facility in Canton.

In 1811 Revere gave up ownership of all of his companies and properties. His son Joseph Warren Revere and two of his grandsons took over the businesses. Although no longer formal owner of the properties, Revere stayed actively involved with them until just before his death. The great patriot and businessman died at his home on Charter Street in Boston on Sunday, May 10, 1818. He was eighty-eight years old. That day, his bells tolled in many foreign countries, in most States, and on ships at sea, some marking the Sabbath or the time of day, but many in and around Boston announcing the passing of the man who had made them. Rachel, his devoted second wife and mother of eight of his children, had died five years earlier on June 26, 1813, of "a short, but distressing illness." His son Paul died the same year as his mother, at age fifty-three. Only five of his sixteen children survived him. He was buried in the family tomb at the Granary Burial Ground located off Tremont Street in Boston, where his wife, his friend Joseph Warren, John Hancock, Samuel Adams, six Massachusetts governors, and the victims of the Boston Massacre were also laid to rest.

Paul Revere's estate at the time of his death amounted to some $30,000. His will, like his life, was simple and straightforward. He left $4,000 to each of his five surviving children, and about $500 to each of his deceased children's children. To a favorite grandchild, young Joseph Eayres, he left an additional $250. To his maiden daughter, Harriet, the only living child of his first wife, Sarah, he also left all of his household furniture.

Although he had his detractors, most of his contemporaries and historians recognized his abilities and his dedication to the cause of liberty. Some critics accused him of failing to complete the ride he was famous for[53], or stealing the glory from the other riders[54], Dawes and Prescott. Richard Bissell, the dramatist, in his book *New Light on 1776 and All That* characterizes Revere as a coward and a traitor who sang like a canary to his British captors and betrayed his friends to save his own skin.[55]

Elbridge Henry Goss, on the other hand, in his excellent two-volume biography of the famous patriot *The Life of Colonel Paul Revere* sums up his personality as:

Cool in thought, ardent in action, he was well adapted to form plans, and to carry them into successful execution, both for the benefit of himself and the service of others.

Perhaps the best way to evaluate the man is to read a section of one of his poems in which he describes his day, a day near the end of his illustrious career:

> *At early morn I take my round,*
> *Invited first by hammer's sound;*
> *The Furnace next; then Roleing-Mill;*
> *'Til Breakfast's call, my time doth fill;*
> *Then round my Acres (few) I trot,*
> *To see what's done and what is not.*

Give orders what ought to be done.
Then sometimes take my Dog and Gun.
Under an aged spreading Oak,
At noon I take my favorite Book
To shun the heat and feed the Mind,
In elbow chair I sit reclined.
At eve' within my peacefull Cot,
Sometimes I meet, and sometimes not,
The Parson, Docter, or some Friend,
Or neighbor kind, one hour to spend;
In social chat, our time we pass;
Drink all our Friends, in parting Glass
The Parson, Docter; neighbour gone,
We prepare for Bed, and so trudge on.

Revere was an ordinary man who became extraordinary in an extraordinary time. His continuous dedication to the independence of the colonies, in small matters and large, shines like a beacon in the fight for America's freedom from Britain. Not of the elite class, he performed many secondary duties necessary for the Revolution to be successful. After his important midnight ride, he was unfairly condemned for not continuing on to Concord, and in the Penobscot affair he was unjustly accused of heinous crimes, but in both actions as well as many others, he acted with a patriotic fervor unsurpassed by most of his contemporaries. One must wonder what America would be like if he had never been born.

Additional information about Paul Revere and his times may be obtained by reading the books noted in Appendix C.

APPENDIX A

References for additional information on John Alden and his times:

*Ames, Azel, M.D.- with new material by Jeffry A. Linscott. *The May-Flower & Her Log.* Bowie, MD: Heritage Books, 1998.

Baker, James W. (Introduction). *Mayflower II.* Little Compton, RI: Fort Church Publishers, Inc. 1993.

Bradford, William. *Of Plymouth Plantation 1620–1647.* New York: Random House, 1981.

Heath, Dwight B. (Editor, from 1622 text). *Mourt's Relation.* Bedford, MA: Applewood Books, 1963.

* This reference has a detailed bibliography, and the reader is encouraged to refer to it for additional information.

APPENDIX B

References for additional information on King Philip and his times:

Averill, Esther. *King Philip, The Indian Chief.* New York: Harper & Row, 1950.

Bonfanti, Leo. *Biographies and Legends of the New England Indians* (Vols. I–V). Wakefield, MA: Pride Publications, 1968.

* Church, Colonel Benjamin. *Diary of King Philip's War.* Little Compton, RI: Lockwood Publishing, 4th printing, 1996.

Ellis, George W. and John E. Morris. *King Philip's War.* New York: The Grafton Press, 1906.

* Hakim, Joy. *The First Americans.* New York: Oxford University Press, 1993.

* Leach, Douglas Edward. *Flintlock and Tomohawk.* New York: W.W. Norton & Co., Inc. (The Norton Library). 1966.

* Roman, Joseph. *King Philip, Wampanoag Rebel.* Philadelphia: Chelsea House Publishers, 1992.

* Schultz, Eric B. and Michael J. Tougias. *King Philip's War.* Woodstock, VT: The Countryman Press, 1999.

* These references have detailed bibliographies, and the reader is encouraged to refer to them for additional information.

APPENDIX C

References for additional information on Paul Revere and his times:

* Egger-Bovet, Howard and Marlene Smith-Baranzini. *US Kids History: Book of the American Revolution*. New York: Little, Brown and Company, 1994.

* Fischer, David Hacket. *Paul Revere's Ride*. New York: Oxford University Press, 1994.

Forbes, Esther. *America's Paul Revere*. Boston: Houghton Mifflin Company, 1946.

* Forbes, Esther. *Paul Revere & the World He Lived In*. Boston: Houghton Mifflin Company, 1943.

Fritz, Jean. *And Then What Happened, Paul Revere?* New York: G.P. Putnam's Sons, 1973.

* Gipson, Lawrence Henry. *The Coming of the Revolution*. New York: Harper & Row, 1954

Goss, Elbridge H. *The Life of Colonel Paul Revere* (2 vols.- 3rd Edition). Boston: Howard W. Spurr, 1898.

* Leehey, Patrick M. and Janine E. Skerry and Deborah A. Federhen and Edgard Moreno and Edith J. Steblecki. *Paul Revere-Artisan, Businessman, and Patriot*. Boston: Paul Revere Memorial Association, 1988.

* Leehey, Patrick M. *What Was the Name of Paul Revere's Horse?* Boston: Paul Revere Memorial Association, 1997.

*Wirth, Fremont P. *The Development of America.* New York: American Book Company, 1937.

* These references have detailed bibliographies, and the reader is encouraged to refer to them for additional information.

ENDNOTES

1   Patents were land grants provided by the government of England to parties that agreed to settle in America and remain as subjects of the king.
2   Equal to 300 English miles
3   A small open boat fitted with oars or sails, or both, and used primarily in shallow waters.
4   Indian, meaning smoke.
5   Known to his followers as Yellow Feather.
6   The first was that of Edward Winslow to Susanna White, widow of William White.
7   The peninsular is now part of the state of Rhode Island.
8   Small beads that were the Indians' means of exchange.
9   Now, Taunton.
10 John Sassamon, the interpreter who composed Philip's message was one of the Indians educated by the missionary John Eliot. Mr. Eliot's school was at Natick, one of the Praying Indian villages where English was taught as a means to more easily convert the natives to English beliefs. Sassamon had attended Harvard College and was later a schoolmaster at Natick. In time, he longed to return to his Indian homeland. Alexander and Philip took him on as interpreter, for more and more it had become necessary to communicate with the English in ways both parties could comprehend.
11 This gruesome way of displaying fallen soldiers had been taught to the Indians by the English.
12 Located close to the English settlement of New Braintree.
13 The English settlement of Northfield.

14 A Nashaway Nipmuck stronghold near Princeton.

15 Alderman, a subject of Awashonks, was not the traitor whose brother was killed by Philip.

16 Also known as *Old Ironsides.*

17 The Edict of Nantes, originally proclaimed by King Louis IV's grandfather, granted many political rights and religious freedom to the French Protestants, known as Hugenots.

18 The Old Style, or Caesar's Julian calendar, did not accurately account for 365.2425 days in a year, and in 1582 Pope Gregory XIII decreed that his New Style corrected calendar be used in Italy. To account for the long-term error accumulated in the old calendar up to 1582, 11 days had to be added at some time during the year. The mainly Protestant American colonies did not change to the Gregorian calendar until 1752, when 12 days had to be added. September 2, 1752 was then followed by September 14, 1752, and the days in between were eliminated.

19 To operate a trade shop the law at the time specified that one had to be at least 21 years old, and have completed a suitable apprenticeship.

20 Captain Gridley was an experienced fortification expert who later became commander of the Artillery Corps and Chief Engineer of the Army under General George Washington.

21 The Stamp Act, another way Britain proposed to increase revenue from the colonies, provided that stamped paper must be used for all legal documents, pamphlets, newspapers, almanacs, and many other articles. Income from the use of the stamped paper was to be expended in the colonies for the purpose of defending and protecting them.

22 At about the same time, John Singleton Copley, probably the most capable portrait painter in Boston, owed money to Revere for gold and silver frames and cases he had made for him. To reduce his debt to Revere, the silversmith commissioned him to paint his portrait sitting at a workbench with his tools lying in front of him, and a typical silver pot in his hand. The revealing portrait is one of the most copied pictures of Revere and appears in most of his biographies.

23 Townshend's solution was to levy external taxes to be collected at the ports where the goods were received. Until then the colonies were being assessed only internal taxes, those imposed within the colonies. The new duties covered imports of glass, paper, printers' inks, lead, and tea.

24 Circular letters were official notices of intentions or actions by leaders of the Colonial governments sent by messengers to allied constituencies that

were too far away to receive the information on a timely basis through other channels.

25   The house still stands, and it is the only seventeenth-century house standing in a large American city. Today, it is one of the most popular National Landmarks in Boston.

26   Christian Remick

27   Crispus Attucks was an enormous black man, part Indian, part African-American, and part white. He was born about 1723 and lived in Framingham, Massachusetts with his mother, Phoebe, a Natick Indian, and his father, Prince, who was a slave of Colonel Buckminster. (In the 1700's there were many slaves in Massachusetts and the other colonies.) When Crispus was about 16, he was sold to Deacon William Brown of Framingham because he too frequently wandered from his duties. When he was 27, Deacon Brown sent him to Boston on a business trip, but instead of returning to Framingham, he took a job on a whaling vessel that was leaving port for a considerable time. In the fall of 1769, after many whaling trips, he stopped again in Boston and found the colonists demanding more freedom from British tyranny. The next year on his return to Boston, he became enraged at the way the Crown was increasingly violating the rights of the people, so he encouraged a group of seamen to walk with him to King Street where trouble was brewing. He confronted the sentries on duty in front of the courthouse, and the tragedy that is called The Boston Massacre began.

28   Dr. Benjamin Church was a physician trained at Harvard College. He was a member of the Sons of Liberty and had access to most of the colonists' secret plans and movements. When it was found that he was revealing them to General Gage, he was charged with holding a "criminal correspondence with the enemy" by a court presided over by George Washington. After a finding of guilty, he was sentenced to prison for life. He fell sick in prison and after a year of confinement was released and permitted to sail for the West Indies. The ship he left on was never heard from again after it sailed.

29   Hancock, the wealthiest man in New England, had inherited over £70,000 when his uncle, Thomas Hancock, Esq., died from apoplexy at age 62. The young heir was handsome, thin, and nervous. With his great fortune he openly supported the Whigs and their fight against British taxation.

30   Dr. Warren's source of information was suspected to be the American wife of General Gage. To date there has been no confirmation of the true identity of Warren's collaborator.

[31] Now, Arlington, Massachusetts.

[32] Now, Burlington, Massachusetts.

[33] Dorothy Quincy, known to her friends as Miss Dolly, and known throughout New England for her spirit and independence, wanted to leave with her intended husband, Hancock, but he insisted on traveling only with Sam Adams. Once safely in Woburn, Hancock sent his heavy coach back to get Miss Dolly, his wealthy aunt, and a fresh-caught salmon they had been preparing to eat.

[34] The famous trunk still exists. It is presently on display at the Worcester (Mass.) Historical Society.

[35] Revere's thoughts and those of many who had participated in the battles at Lexington and Concord were later edited and published so that a first-hand declaration could be made available about the causes and events that occurred on April 19.

[36] Benjamin Franklin was born on Milk Street, a short street near the center of Boston. Revere never met him. Franklin moved to Philadelphia in 1723, 13 years before Revere was born.

[37] Washington was a quiet, reserved surveyor who, when he joined the Colonial army, inspired confidence in his troops who were fighting in the French and Indian War. His many successful engagements, including the skirmish in Virginia, which led to the establishment of Fort Necessity in Pennsylvania, and his political savvy, well prepared him for the position of Commander-in-Chief. He was considered an expert on warfare by the men in Congress, and he eagerly accepted their nomination.

[38] The British soldiers under Sir William Howe killed 138 of our militiamen and wounded 276 in the battle at Breed's Hill, better known as Bunker Hill. Howe had 226 killed and 828 wounded. The British considered it a victory in spite of the numbers because they were able to overcome the Americans, who had fled when their powder ran out.

[39] In the spring of 1776, many colonial assemblies voted in favor of independence from Britain. The Continental Congress, after considerable debate, selected a committee composed of Thomas Jefferson, Benjamin Franklin, John Adams, Roger Sherman, and Robert Livingston to draw up a declaration for independence. After three weeks, the document, mostly the work of Jefferson, was complete. The Congress formally adopted it on July 4, and copies were sent throughout the colonies to be read publicly.

[40] In March of 1779, Revere led a party to the plundered wreck of the *Somerset* and salvaged 21 of the 64 cannon aboard. He was able to secure

them because they were too heavy for the earlier scavengers to haul away from the doomed ship. He set the guns up on Castle Island to aid in the anticipated, but never required, defense of Boston.

[41] Soldiers in the artillery unit, who load and assist with the firing of the cannon.

[42] Now, Castine, Maine.

[43] Dudley Saltonstall, son of Gurdon, was born in 1738 and always had a yearning to go to sea. He was appointed captain of the continental frigate *Alfred* on December 22, 1775, and participated in the successful capture of British military supplies at New Providence, an island in the Bahamas. He was promoted to commodore for the Penobscot Expedition, and the 32-gun *Warren* was his flagship. After the disastrous failure of the superior continental force in Maine, he was court-martialed aboard the frigate *Deane* and found guilty for "want of proper spirit and energy." He was dismissed from the naval service and became a privateer. He died in the West Indies about 1796

[44] Now, Boothbay Harbor, Maine

[45] Now, Augusta, Maine.

[46] Arnold's plot to surrender West Point to the British was uncovered when British spy John Andre was captured in 1780 with papers revealing Arnold's treasonous act. Andre was executed, but Arnold escaped to Britain. He returned with British forces and fought against his former friends. At the conclusion of the war, he returned to Britain. He died in London on June 14, 1801.

[47] A final treaty of peace with Britain was signed on September 3, 1783. In Paris, our representatives Benjamin Franklin, John Jay and John Adams concluded an agreement that not only officially ended the war, but, in addition, awarded the victorious colonies all territory between the Atlantic Ocean and the Mississippi River. It also required the British to evacuate their troops from all of the ceded territory.

[48] The convention was convened on May 25, 1787 for the purpose of revising the preliminary Articles of Confederation, which were used as a basis for central government from 1781 until a new constitution could be provided. The meetings were attended by many of the outstanding men in America, including George Washington, Benjamin Franklin, James Madison, and Alexander Hamilton. Washington was the presiding officer, and Madison, a government scholar, was the most influential member. Samuel Adams and John Hancock did not attend, nor did

Thomas Jefferson, who was in France, or John Adams, who was in England. The boisterous meetings led to a true federal constitution that was completed on September 17, 1787. It was agreed that when nine states ratified the document, it would go into effect. That process took less than one year, however, the thirteenth and final state, Rhode Island, did not ratify it until May 29, 1790.

49 Also called the Cockerel Church.

50 For a list of bells Revere made, and their disposition, see *HISTORICAL COLLECTIONS OF THE ESSEX INSTITUTE*, Vol. 47 & 48, printed for the Essex Institute by Newcomb & Gauss of Salem, Mass. in 1932.

51 The Masonic method of dating charters, warrants, and certificates varies from that adopted in general civil matters. Among the Masons of England, Scotland, Ireland, France, Germany, and America, the date is from the creation of the world, 4000 B.C., technically called "Anno Lucas" (in the year of light) or A.L. Thus 1799 + 4000 becomes 5799.

52 Among the silver pieces he produced-some of which are the best examples of his work are: The Sons of Liberty Bowl mentioned earlier; a double-bellied cream pot and sugar dish with elaborate heraldic engravings fashioned for Lucretia Chandler; a tankard that the students of Harvard professor Stephan Scales presented to him in gratitude for his tutelage; a three-piece tea set made for Edmund Hartt, builder of the *Constitution*; and a 45-piece service made for Dr. William Paine of Worcester, Mass. that he wanted for a commemoration of his marriage to Lois Orne, a distant cousin of Revere's first wife, Sarah. Many of his items are on display or in use every day throughout the United States.

53 Although Revere's intention was to ride only to Lexington, once there, he decided to continue his alarming to Concord. On the Concord road, he was captured by the British. Some critics believed wrongly that he was amiss in not continuing to Concord, an obviously impossible task.

54 Revere's enduring fame primarily stems from Longfellow's poem *The Midnight Ride of Paul Revere*. Many writers feel that Dawes and Prescott were shortchanged. But for the famous poem, Revere would likely be as unheralded as they were.

55 Bissell's analysis appears to be in variance to the facts. Revere was deemed by a military court-martial to not be at fault for the debacle at Penobscot, and his contemporaries judged him as a man of honor and a symbol of valor for his efforts before and during the War for Independence.

CPSIA information can be obtained at www.ICGtesting.com
Printed in the USA
BVOW070553251012

303871BV00002B/4/P